Casey Dorman

I0547571

# Chasing Tales

A Nyles Monahan Mystery

*Avignon Press*
*Newport Beach*

## Books by Casey Dorman

*Pink Carnation*
*I, Carlos*
*Unquity*
*The Prisoner's Dilemma* (Kindle ebook)
*Where Have All the Young Men Gone?*
(Kindle ebook)

Dorman, Casey, 1943-
Chasing Tales/Casey Dorman – 1st U.S. ed
Mystery – Detective - Boston


Avignon Press
Newport Beach, California, USA

ISBN-13: 978-0615623061
ISBN-10: 0615623069

To Lai, my wife and inspiration

# Chapter 1

Nyles Monahan tensed his muscles, trying to keep the tentacles of cold air from reaching to his very bones. The icy wind slid through the cracks between the sections of the walls of the airport gangway like arctic fingers grasping at his body and the only coat that he had brought was ineffectually draped over his arm because he hadn't thought he'd need it until he left the airport; but he'd been wrong.

Winter in Boston - it had been more than ten years since he'd been back. He remembered when he was a kid, more than fifty years ago, walking to school in the snow, sliding like an unsteady skier down the steep, icy sidewalk on Dorchester Ave. Those memories of an innocent childhood reminded him that not every child's life was as carefree as his had been. That was why he was in Boston. He was here to help a friend in trouble – a priest accused of using his position in the church to molest innocent children some thirty years ago.

He stepped into the terminal and scanned the sea of faces. When he spied his brother, Sean, his face broke into a wide grin. It had been almost six years since Sean and Millie had visited Cloris and him... back in the days when Cloris was barely able to speak, after her stroke. Sean was big as a house then. He hadn't changed.

A giant of a man, in his late fifties, puffed up like the Pillsbury doughboy in a massive quilted blue parka and wearing a red cap with white fur-lined ear flaps folded over the top so that he looked like an oversized comic book character, came striding out of the crowd. Sean Monahan threw two massive arms around his shorter, skinny older brother, almost suffocating him in a bear hug. "It's been too long, you old fart," Sean said, his broad, ruddy face beaming with a smile. His fleshy red cheeks puffed up, narrowing his eyes into slits when he smiled, giving him the face of a happy Buddha.

"You're still growing," Nyles said, pulling away and taking a long look at his younger brother by six years. Nyles' smile was, in keeping with his personality, more restrained than his brothers' although his joy was no less. "Millie stayed home?" he asked, looking around for his brother's wife.

"It's too fucking cold to come out unless you have to. Great weather for the heating oil business," his brother answered. Sean owned a heating oil company. It had made him rich, although having money hadn't changed his personality. He was still the affable, voluble, and concerned brother he'd always been. "Millie's fixing a big meal for us back at the house. She's invited Kaylee over with her daughter and her new husband." His expression became worried. "Hope that's OK. You know Millie, she likes to get the family together." His eyebrows knitted in concern. Sean's face had always been like that of an overgrown child, expressing his feelings with the exaggerated transparency of a silent film character. "I was sorry that Cloris couldn't come with you. How's she doing?" Sean had known his brother's wife since high school, almost as long as Nyles had, and she and he were close.

"Cloris is doing fine," Nyles answered in a serious voice. His wife, a veteran TV actress, had had a massive stroke several years earlier. She had been in a coma for weeks. She had gotten better, but she was still recovering. "Her speech is back to normal... or pretty much so. She still gets stuck on finding the right word now and then. She's not as steady on her feet as I'd like and I was afraid that, if she came here, she'd have trouble in the snow. She wanted to come, but it seemed like a bad idea."

"You're probably right. Anyway, we'll get everyone else together, now that you're back."

Nyles nodded. He wasn't here for a reunion, but it would feel good to be with family. He looked forward to seeing Kaylee, his brother's daughter. She'd been in some trouble when she was younger – drugs and alcohol as a teenager, hanging out with the wrong crowd when she was a young adult, an unplanned pregnancy - but now, in her early thirties, she had settled down. "Kaylee's still doing OK?" he asked.

They had begun walking toward the baggage area, Sean taking long, rolling strides and Nyles having to move his shorter legs rapidly to keep up with him. They looked like a comedy team from an old movie. No one would have said they were brothers, except if they looked at their eyes. Both had their mother's pale blue eyes – the icy blue of a mountain lake.

"Kaylee's fine." Sean turned to his brother. His face was serious. "Five years." he said.

"Five years?"

"Since I've had a drink. For Kaylee it's been about the same. We're both on the wagon. She calls it being in recovery. I call it purgatory." Though his eyes were serious, he smiled, clapping his smaller brother on the back, a habit Nyles remembered from years of being together. Sean's backslapping warmth was part of his personality. He got it from their father, which was where his alcoholism had come from, also.

"Congratulations… to both of you. Maybe I'd better stop and have a beer before we leave the airport." Nyles hadn't counted on staying in a dry house. Nyles didn't consider himself an alcoholic, but he looked forward to one or two beers each day. That had always been enough for him, even at the worst times in the middle of Cloris' sickness. Cloris wasn't allowed to drink any more, but Nyles still kept alcohol in the house.

"You're lucky you were always able to keep it under control. You weren't a party guy like me or dad," Sean said. "Anyway, I bought you a couple of six-packs of Sam Adams."

They'd reached the luggage area and Nyles grabbed his suitcase as it rounded the carousel. Sean reached one of his giant mitts over and took the suitcase out of his brother's hand. "You're my guest big brother. Besides, you're too damn skinny to carry that."

"I'm too damned smart. It's got wheels."

Sean turned the suitcase over and studied it until he found the handle and pulled it out. "So it does," he said, heading for the door to the parking garage, and pulling the suitcase along behind him as if it were a reluctant dog on a leash.

Once they'd left the airport, Sean driving him in his half-ton pickup with the name "Monahan's Heating Oil" on the side, Nyles became absorbed in his own thoughts. His brother was used to his silences, even though Sean had always found them hard to tolerate. Years of experience had taught Nyles' younger brother that it was better to let his brother think than to risk his irritation by striking up idle conversation.

Nyles' thoughts were on the reasons he had returned home. He had come to Boston after an urgent request from Father Tom O'Flannery, Cloris' priest, who was also Nyles' closest friend. Father Tom's parish was in Torrance, California, near Nyles' house, but he'd started out as a priest in Boston's Dorchester neighborhood nearly thirty years ago. He'd been summoned back to Boston by no less than Archbishop O'Malley. There had been an allegation of sexual misconduct on Father Tom's part, dating back to his earliest days as a priest at St. Aloysius Church in Dorchester. The Archdiocese was investigating, but the alleged victim had filed a criminal complaint against Father Tom and the priest had asked for Nyles' help.

Looking out the truck's window at the dark, overcast sky and bleak landscape of gray clapboard tenement buildings that lined the highway leading back from the airport, he was reminded of a scene from an old faded black and white movie. He realized he had gotten used to the blue skies, green palm trees, and white beaches of California. Here in Boston he felt out of place, even though this was where he had grown up. He didn't belong here anymore and he didn't know what he could do here other than give his friend moral support.

They'd turned south on the 405 freeway and were headed for Milton, the venerable, upscale suburb where Sean and Millie lived. "It's been in the papers here, you know," Sean said, unable to keep from breaking the silence between them.

"What has?"

"Father Tom's case."

Nyles felt a momentary wave of anguish for the priest. Father Tom didn't deserve to have his name dragged into the media.

"Yep," Sean continued, hunching himself over the steering wheel, his giant hands tightening his grip. Nyles recognized the signs of his brother's anger. "The Herald always tells all the intimate details of these priest abuse cases – hoping to get another victim to come forward is what they say. If you ask me, the paper's got a vendetta going against the church." There was a caustic edge to

Sean's voice. He was a Catholic and, like most Boston Catholics, he felt betrayed by the revelations of sexual abuse but was still staunchly supportive of the church that had been the central pillar of his life for as long as he could remember.

Nyles recognized the conflict in his brother's voice. "This kind of thing is hard to fight," he said. He was staring out the window at the run-down triple-deckers lining the highway, trying to see Dorchester Hill. His parents' house had been on the other side of the hill. The white snow gave the area an unspoiled quality, like an idyllic painting, covering the ugliness of poverty that still inhabited the old neighborhood.

Sean nodded, threading the pickup truck through a series of intersections then taking the road that led onto Milton Hill, the oldest section of the town. He wished his brother was more forthcoming, but he knew better than to expect that. "Why did they ask you to help, if you don't mind me asking?" he said, doggedly determined to get his brother to talk, although as soon as he said it, he glanced quickly, almost sheepishly, at the figure on the seat next to him and added, "I know you're his friend and you're an ex-cop, and now you're like a private detective or something, but what can you do here?"

Nyles paused before answering. Sean's question was the very one he had been asking himself. "I don't know. I know nothing about these kinds of cases. I was a homicide detective. I decided to become a private investigator just to keep busy during my retirement, but all I've done is consult to the LAPD on some unsolved murder cases." He sat looking out the window. The houses on either side of the snow-covered street here on Milton Hill were massive, bigger than those in Beverly Hills, reminding him of European country houses. Some of them

6

were over two hundred years old. "Father Tom hasn't got any money. He's got a cheap lawyer that he knew from the old days and the lawyer hasn't got anyone to help him. The lawyer said he needed to hire a private investigator and Father Tom asked me to lend a hand."

"Are you getting paid?"

"Father Tom is Cloris' and my best friend. I wouldn't ask him for money."

"What about the church. Don't they defend their priests?"

"They won't lift a finger. Except Archbishop O'Malley requested the Archbishop of Los Angeles to stop Father Tom from saying Mass or wearing his clericals."

"The Church can be hard." Sean was maneuvering the pickup down a narrow street with four houses on it, three of them massive colonials with broad, circular driveways, none of them younger than a hundred and twenty years. "That's how the Church got into trouble in the first place, protecting itself by covering up so much Goddamn abuse. That's why Cardinal Law, the hypocrite, is out on his ass." Sean's face reddened, and he pursed his lips in a frown, as if he was embarrassed to have said so much. He looked like an overgrown kid who had talked out of turn in class. He pulled the truck into a broad driveway in front of the last house, an immense, four-story Victorian "Welcome to my home," Sean said, giving a beep on the horn to let his wife know that they'd arrived.

Chasing Tales

Chapter 2

Detective Sergeant Nate Hilton heaved a weary sigh and put his head down on his arms. *Jesus Christ I hate these cases.* He'd been transferred out of the Boston Police Department's Mattapan-Dorchester division to the central precinct four years before. Banished, he told himself. It had been his own fault – the price of success. He'd been overzealous trying to show his superiors what a great detective he was. The Father Geoghan case had been the most notorious instance of clerical sexual abuse on record and Nate had located nearly a third of the victims. Geoghan had molested over a hundred young boys and it was some of Nate's detective work that had gotten him convicted. Instead of getting promoted and put on the homicide detail, as he'd hoped, Nate had been assigned to the special task force that followed up all the cases of sexual abuse related to the church.

He raised his head and looked across the desk at his partner, Randy Colton. "We both know the drill. Let's go down our list again and see how many of O'Flannery's altar boys we can still locate - besides those we've already interviewed." The Special Sexual Abuse Task Force was housed in a tiny office and Nate and his partner were packed into the small room along with the records of the hundreds of cases that had been unearthed so far. The task force was "special" because it only dealt with cases of sexual abuse involving priests, although that fact was never stated publicly. Tracking down cases of priest sexual abuse was different than a lot of other police work, mainly because the majority of the crimes they investigated were from the distant past and the paperwork such investigations generated was voluminous.

# Chasing Tales

The office, which had been a storage room before it was taken over by Nate's Task Force, was jammed with file cabinets containing the records of previous cases, so that it still retained the appearance of a storage room more than it did an office. At least the desktop computer, which had held their files on the cases on which they were working, had been replaced. It had sat on a small desk on wheels so that it could be turned to face either Nate or Randy, but which mostly made it difficult to walk through the office without bumping into it. Now they each had new laptops, giving them more walking space, which they'd quickly filled up with more boxes of material related to the ongoing O'Flannery case. Unlike most of the other offices in their building, there was no window, either to the outside or to the larger room where the other officers worked. Randy Colton referred to their small space as "the confessional." Nate said he and his partner had been relegated to "cold storage."

"Y'know this whole Goddamn scandal has put my faith in the church to the test," Randy said. He was in his thirties and wiry, with sandy blonde hair that he kept cut short, almost in a crew, which made him look even younger than he was. He spoke with a strong Boston accent and had a habit of leaning forward and squinting his eyes when he talked, as if he was trying to obtain a closer look at whomever he was speaking to. He always talked as if he was making an important new pronouncement, even when what he was saying was something he'd said several times before. Randy was less dissatisfied with his assignment than was his partner. He was also less ambitious. If his investigations involved mostly tracking down old cases and scouring old records, he didn't mind. One job was as good as another to Randy and at least this one didn't force him to work overtime or get shot at. He had a wife and three kids at home. He worried less about getting promoted and more about job security.

"Why? No priest ever tried to fuck you did he?" Hilton asked.

Colton shook his head. "No, but I wasn't an altar boy or anything. Nuns ran our school. There were a couple of young sisters who I wouldn't have minded if they'd fucked me." Colton chewed gum and when he squinted his eyes and chewed, he looked as if he was thinking hard about a topic. Nate had learned that Colton's facial expression was a poor gauge of the depth of his thought, which mostly ran to puerile jokes.

"Shit, Randy, you only went to Catholic school so you wouldn't have to go to public school with me and my friends." Nate was a large, well-muscled Black man in his forties who had begun to shave his head when his hair had begun to thin on top, giving him the appearance of an aging wrestler or prizefighter. He spoke in a bitter tone. His family had moved into Dorchester when he was a toddler, occupying a house that had been sold by an Irish family taking flight to the suburbs to avoid having Black neighbors. The public school he had attended had been populated by mostly black kids. The white families that had remained in the neighborhood had sent their children to Catholic schools to avoid racial integration. Most of the time Nate's expression was set in an angry scowl and mostly he complained about the prejudice in the city and in the police department, which he felt had held him back in his movement up the ladder of promotion.

"Only two or three of these guys are still in Dorchester," Colton said, thumbing through the papers with the names and addresses of the former altar boys. They had been able to get locations on nearly a dozen men who had served as altar boys while Father O'Flannery was priest at St. Aloysius. "There's a few in Southie, then the rest are scattered around in the suburbs; Randolph, Canton, even a couple in Newton and one in wealthy fucking Weston – I guess that's one guy who did all right for himself - here's one in Salem and one in Fall River."

"What about Tim Russell? He's the one who made the accusations against Father Tom. We need to get more out of him before we turn anything over to Reilly." James Reilly was the assistant district attorney who would be prosecuting the case if it came to trial. Reilly handled all the church-related abuse cases.

"Russell is pretty flaky," Colton offered, leaning toward his partner and squinting his eyes. "He's angry as hell at Father O'Flannery, but can't give us much details about what the Father actually did to him. The truth is, our case is pretty weak with only some guy who barely remembers anything."

"Shit," Hilton growled in his low voice. "Russell gives me the willies. He's already tried to kill himself once, and he looks like he's ready to do it again. I'm afraid to question anything he says for fear of pushing the dumbfuck over the edge."

"No offense, Nate," Colton said, squinting at his partner, "but I don't think you're – how should I say it – able to relate to Russell."

"You mean he doesn't like Blacks?" Nate asked, his tone demanding.

"Well, yeah, when you get right down to it. Also you're not Catholic. Let's face it, the guy probably likes to talk to one of his own." Colton's expression was bland, as if he was stating an obvious fact.

Detective Hilton's face showed his anger. "He doesn't like Blacks? I'm not a Catholic? For Christ's sake, it was a Goddamn white Catholic priest who diddled around with him when he was a kid – not some Black Baptist minister, for crap sake."

"Hey buddy, don't get your ass in a sling. You're the one who always says 'let me talk to 'em' when we've got a Black witness."

"Black people are suspicious of Boston cops, especially Irish ones. They have reason to be." He glared at his partner across the desk.

"So sometimes it goes both ways, that's all I'm saying." Colton heaved a sigh. "Anyway, let's get back to the case, OK? You and I, we need to talk to the priest again – or at least one of us does."

Nate glared across the desk at his partner. " You mean you. I suppose I'm not capable of interviewing O'Flannery because I'm not an Irish Catholic."

Colton shook his head. "Jesus, Nate, give it a rest will you. O'Flannery hit it off fine with you. Believe it or not, all Irishmen don't hate Blacks. Why don't you take O'Flannery – he's staying with his sister over in Southie - and I'll talk to Russell again, OK?"

Nate nodded. "I'm sure I'll be warmly welcomed in South Boston… a damn fucking Irish ghetto."

"Christ, Nate," Randy said, shaking his head in disgust, "try to give it a break."

# Chasing Tales

## Chapter 3

Sean and Millie's house was old by California standards, although one hundred and twenty-five years was not greatly aged in New England, where two hundred year old houses were not uncommon and three hundred year old cottages could still be found in Plymouth and Cape Cod. But their stately Queen Anne style Victorian, with its gingerbread gables, its scalloped cedar shingles, and the beautifully curved turret on one corner of the house, made no secret of the fact that the house belonged to another era, not unlike many of the houses on Milton Hill, home to the preserved estates of some of Boston's wealthiest residents of previous centuries.

In keeping with the age of the house, Nyles' brother and his wife had furnished it with antique furniture and Persian rugs. The original woods and the fireplaces, with their polished marble hearths, had been restored to their historical specifications. Even the fixtures – ornate Victorian parlor lamps and two gigantic crystal chandeliers in the living room and dining room - were immaculate reproductions. The only exceptions to this rule were the kitchen appliances and the electronic devices – computer, flat screen TV, Danish wall stereo – that occupied Sean's "den," which served both as his home office and the family entertainment center.

Millie had greeted Nyles effusively, as if he were a prodigal son returned home, and her enthusiasm was equaled by their dog, Ranger, a large black Labrador, who'd almost knocked him over when he came in the door. Nyles had been shown to his room on the third floor. The bedroom, with its slanted, high ceiling, was as large as his and Cloris' living room in Los Angeles and enjoyed a view across the tops of the trees down Milton Hill to the center of the small town. At the base of the next rolling, snow-covered hill he could just make out the towers of Milton Academy, the exclusive private school, which had educated such luminaries as T.S. Eliot and Edward Kennedy.

As he came out of the bathroom, which was across the hall from his bedroom, he could hear voices from downstairs. The dog was making a racket and Nyles guessed that Sean's daughter, Kaylee, and her family must have arrived.

When he arrived downstairs he braced himself in the expectation that Kaylee would rush up and hug him, as she'd always done, even when she'd been at her most angry and difficult periods with her parents, but when he entered the living room and she turned and saw him, she uttered the same delighted, "Uncle Nyles!" that he remembered from the past, but stayed where she was, standing near the marble fireplace, like a mannequin frozen in place. Her enthusiastic expression lasted only moments before it was replaced by a melancholy, almost tearful look that caused Nyles to speculate that she was coping with some kind of major problem in her life, although he'd been told by his brother that his niece was doing well.

He crossed the room and gave Kaylee a hug, kissing her cheek in a fatherly way, then he stood back to look at her. She had aged more than he'd thought possible for someone still in her early thirties. Her hair, which had always been long and straight, had been done in a short bob, and its dark brown natural coloring had been highlighted with not unattractive, blond streaks; she also wore more makeup than he had seen her wear before, but it wasn't enough to cover the lines at the corners of her eyes or around her mouth, lines that aged her face another

14

five years. But mostly, her eyes looked frightened. She was dressed in a long, blue, wool skirt and matching figured, crew-necked sweater, giving her the appearance of a model in a stylish fashion magazine. Nyles was used to seeing her in jeans.

"You never change, Uncle Nyles," she said, managing to broaden her smile for his benefit, although her tone was subdued and her gaze darted away as if she was embarrassed, almost as soon as he caught her eye.

"The virtue of having aged prematurely," Nyles remarked, hoping to provoke a smile in his niece. He was still feeling unsettled by being confronted by a weary and frightened young woman, rather than the impish, bubbling young adult he had remembered and he worried that his concern was noticeable.

"Do you remember, Katherine?" His niece asked, and for the first time Nyles was aware of a child standing close, almost hiding, behind Kaylee. "She was just a baby when you met her, now she's eleven years old."

A tiny blond head peeked out from behind her mother's dress. Kaylee moved to the side and gently pulled the child into the open. She had an exquisite face, like a pixie, Nyles thought. Her hair was tied behind her head in a pink ribbon and hung down in a ten-inch ponytail. Her eyes were large and pale blue, just like her mother's and her uncle's and her grandfather's and she had high cheekbones set in a narrow face and a tall, slim body. In contrast to her delicate features, she wore an almost garish amount of bright red lipstick and eyeshadow, making her look older, despite her diminutive size. She was dressed in low-slung jeans and a sleeveless pink sweater that matched the ribbon in her hair and left her flat, child's midriff exposed. Her wide eyes looked up at her uncle as if she was in awe.

Nyles smiled and fell into his usual reserved manner, sensing that, despite her almost brazen appearance, his niece's daughter could be easily frightened.

"Give Uncle Nyles a hug," Kaylee urged. Her voice was soft, as if she recognized that her daughter might be intimidated by this older man for whom she probably had no recollection.

Katherine stepped forward, like a timid puppet, holding her arms woodenly to her sides. Nyles gingerly put his arms around her, as if he were encircling a fragile piece of china. He could feel her body trembling. He stepped back and patted her gently on the shoulder. "You look like your mother when she was that age - except for your beautiful blonde hair." The young girl's eyes were glued to the floor.

"Her father's only legacy," Kaylee said, a frown on her face. She had never married Katherine's father, a drifting guitarist with an unsuccessful rock band, and a drug addict whose life style had attracted Kaylee at the time, but who had wanted no part of her when he'd found that she was pregnant.

"She's going to grow up to be beautiful," Nyles said, attempting to sound positive, though he was still troubled by the fear he saw in the eyes of both his niece and her daughter.

"That's what I always tell her," a voice came from behind him.

Nyles turned and saw a distinguished looking man dressed in slacks, a baby-blue crew-necked sweater with a button-down shirt underneath and a camel's hair sportcoat over the sweater. He was graying at the temples but otherwise had jet-black hair and was well-tanned, though how he managed a tan in the middle of a New England winter was a mystery to Nyles. He gave the impression he had patterned his attire on that of the same    fashion magazine as had Kaylee.

The man approached him with his hand outstretched. Nyles had turned toward the stranger and from behind him he heard his niece telling him that this was her new husband, Alan.

"The uncle who's the famous police detective from Los Angeles." Alan said, shaking Nyles' hand and smiling broadly. "It's a real pleasure to meet you, Nyles." Behind his smile there was a hard, cold quality to his eyes, as if his face was animated but the eyes were set in stone.

Nyles stared, unblinking, at the man before him, his calm, blue eyes causing his niece's husband to drop his gaze as his smile became uncertain. Something about his niece's new husband's manner provoked a feeling of unease in Nyles that he was unable to conceal. But his hope of getting to know the younger man better was dashed when his sister-in-law entered the room. Millie was carrying a glass of beer in one hand and a glass of what looked to be whiskey in the other. She handed the beer to Nyles and the other drink to Alan. "We drinkers are a fading breed in this family," she said to Nyles. She picked up a half-full glass of wine from the coffee table. "I can't say I'm not glad of that though." Millie had retained her youthful figure although her face had filled out, giving her a warm and friendly appearance that was in keeping with her generous personality. Like her husband, she was in her late fifties, but somehow she had avoided gaining many of the signs of age —wrinkles, age-spots, gray hair, although the latter was no doubt because of artificial coloring – that marked her husband and his brother. Sean, having been good-looking, popular, and an athlete, had married the most beautiful girl in his high school class and Millie still

17

looked the part. She had always adored both Nyles and Cloris and she treated Nyles as if she were his sister.

Alan raised his glass toward Nyles' "Amen to that, Millie, but we can't let it stop us, eh?" He laughed, a little too loudly, then took a long sip of his drink.

Nyles looked around for Kaylee and her daughter, but they both had stayed across the room near the opposite wall - shrinking against it, was the phrase that came to his mind when he saw them standing there. He wanted to ask his brother what was going on with Kaylee, but Sean had been cutting a roast in the kitchen and just then he stepped into the living room and announced that dinner was ready.

# Chasing Tales

## Chapter 4

The line of narrow, three-story gray clapboard houses on Dwyer Street in South Boston stood old and proud like a row of aging soldiers, but the fact that her house was almost indistinguishable from its neighbors did nothing to lessen Molly O'Flannery's pride in her home. After thirty-five years working first as a waitress, then as a grocery store clerk, and, for the last fifteen years as a bank teller, she had, eight years earlier, at age fifty-three, finally been able to buy her own home.

Molly was especially proud to be able to offer her younger brother, Tom, a place to stay while he was in town, although the reasons necessitating his visit dismayed her and terrified her beyond her normal state of pervasive fear. She had lived a life filled with anxiety, which was the reason that, despite being a reasonably attractive woman, she had remained single all of her 61 years. With the exception of two friends from high school, Molly shunned relationships. She wasn't antisocial; she was just frightened – frightened to leave her home and to venture out in public. Like a frightened kindergarten child leaving the safety of home for the first time, she had to struggle each morning to leave her house for work and every minute while she as at the bank having to face the public, was a moment of agony. She returned to her house each evening drained of energy.

"You must be Nyles," Molly said, opening the doorway for her brother's friend to enter. She was a tall, thin woman, with sharp elbows and shoulders, who on this Saturday morning was dressed in a long gray skirt and a white blouse which showed her angular collar bones, as if she were a young girl in parochial school, but with her gray hair pulled back tightly into an old maid's bun. She wore wire rimmed glasses and no makeup, which added to her plain appearance, but her smile, although uncertain, was sweet and ingenuous and her face, with its symmetrical features and prominent cheekbones, might have been pretty, in a Katherine Hepburn or Julia Roberts sort of way, if she'd at all tried to make it so.

Father Tom and another man were sitting in the living room and both men stood when Nyles entered the room. Father Tom was dressed in a pair of khaki pants and a wool shirt, looking like an actor in a retirement commercial. He strode across the room and put his arms around Nyles. "I knew I could count on you," he said. Father Tom's usually jovial, round face looked strained and the sunken quality to his eyes made Nyles think the priest must have lost weight, but he did his best to conceal his concern for the other man's health.

The other man in the room was introduced as Bill Phelan, Father Tom's attorney. Phelan was a short man, of medium build, in his mid-fifties, with thinning hair and watery eyes behind black-rimmed glasses. He reminded Nyles of a washed out high school biology teacher. He glanced briefly at Nyles then shifted his gaze to the floor, like an embarrassed child. He had the ruddy face of a drinker with splotchy patches of red veins on his cheeks. He was dressed in a wrinkled suit that was thin with wear at the elbows and cuffs and he greeted Nyles with a limp handshake.

"Bill and I go back to high school days and he's doing me a favor by taking my case," Father Tom said to Nyles. "He's doing it for almost nothing and he doesn't really have a staff – which is why I asked you to help."

Nyles' first impression of Phelan wasn't positive – the man looked like an habitual drinker whose clothes gave him the appearance of being down on his luck and he could barely conceal an underlying agitation that was disconcerting to watch - but Nyles was willing to suspend judgment until he heard what the lawyer had to say. "I'm not sure what I can do in this kind of situation, but I'll do whatever you think will help," he said.

"I'm not sure if I'm the man for this, myself" Phelan began, looking sheepishly at both of them. He had a nervous habit of rubbing the arms of the chair with both of his hands, as if he was trying to remove something stuck to his palms. "Tom and I are old friends, but I haven't been involved in a criminal case in awhile. I do mostly automobile accidents - arranging medical depositions, checking coverages - that sort of thing."

"Bill was the brightest guy in my high school class at St. Michael's. He graduated first in his class at BC and was on the law review at Harvard," Father Tom said to Nyles. "He's selling himself short. He used to do a lot of criminal law."

Nyles listened in silence. He wondered what had happened to turn the lawyer into an ambulance chaser. Was it his drinking or was his drinking a response to something else?

The attorney was still rubbing the arms of his chair, although he seemed to be unaware he was doing it.

"Have you started working on a defense for Father Tom?" Nyles finally asked. Even though Phelan had referred to his old friend as simply Tom, Nyles couldn't bring himself to do so. He didn't even call him Father O'Flannery as his parishioners did. Throughout their nearly twenty years friendship, he'd always called him Father Tom and that was how he thought of him.

Phelan nodded. "His accuser has mental problems, but he has no history of filing grievances against the church or against anyone for that matter. In one of the

21

cases that was successfully defended, the plaintiff was an obvious fortune hunter with a history of suing people. That doesn't seem to be the case with Tim Russell, the man who's made the accusations against Tom."

"If he wanted money wouldn't he sue the church?" Nyles asked.

"Of course. But a civil suit is much easier to win following a criminal conviction."

"What about mistaken identity?"

Phelan looked over at the priest. "There's no question that Russell was an altar boy for Tom. You remember him, isn't that right?"

"He was an altar boy at St. Aloysius. I remember him vaguely. He was quiet, followed me around like a lost puppy."

Nyles was about to ask more about the priest's relationship with his accuser, when they were interrupted by Molly bringing in coffee on a tray. Her face was drawn and anxious and she smiled briefly and shyly at Nyles and then raised her eyes to give her brother a worried look. Father Tom smiled back, encouragingly, and thanked her for bringing the coffee before she retreated back to her kitchen, like a housemaid having completed her task.

It felt painful for Nyles to watch Father Tom and his sister struggling with such monstrous accusations. Neither of them looked as though he or she was doing well. "What kind of evidence gets presented in a case like this?" he asked. He'd occasionally collected rape evidence on murder cases with the LAPD, but it was mostly physical evidence and never from thirty years earlier.

"The Boston PD has a task force for these cases, Phelan answered. "They're pretty skilled at building a case and it's pretty much the same each time. The first thing they look for is other victims. Almost every conviction so far has involved multiple witnesses. When priests go in for this sort of thing, they don't just focus on one child – it's a repetitive pattern of behavior. That's why transferring a priest to another parish – which has been the Church's solution – doesn't work."

"If the police found some of those other altar boys and they had nothing negative to report about Father Tom, it seems like that might be something you could use in his defense," Nyles said. "And if this is a case of mistaken identity, then maybe one of those boys could identify the real priest who molested Russell." He knew he was sounding more like a policeman looking for evidence than someone investigating for the defense, but he was used to thinking like a cop - used to building a case.

Phelan sipped on his coffee. He had a tremor and had to hold the cup in both hands to keep from spilling. "That's a good thought, Nyles." He shook his head, as if he was angry at himself. "I should have thought of that. Maybe you can work on that. The police will probably share their list of former altar boys with you, at least they're supposed to. If not, you can get it from the Church –Monsignor Hurley's office." He looked bewildered, as if his mind had wandered off and he couldn't call it back.

Nyles continued to be alarmed by the signs of the lawyer's infirmity, but he held his tongue. "I'll start with the police then, and try to track down those altar boys," he said. "Maybe I can talk to this Monsignor Hurley."

Phelan's face relaxed in relief.

"God is going to lead us along the right path," Father Tom said. He had a placid smile on his face. It was a look Nyles remembered from the time when he, himself, had been struggling with Cloris' illness and Father Tom had been his greatest source of comfort. He wasn't comforted now. He said nothing. He knew he wasn't going to leave anything up to God - or anyone else for that matter - not if he felt that he could do something himself.

# Chasing Tales

## Chapter 5

Monsignor Andrew Hurley was both a priest and a lawyer but it was his training in canon law that had gotten him placed in charge of orchestrating the Boston Archdiocese's response to the sexual misconduct allegations that had tarnished the Church's reputation and almost bankrupted the Archdiocese over the last several years. The need for a well-thought out Church response to such allegations was made abundantly clear after reports in the local and national media had told the story of how former Archbishop, Cardinal Bernard Law had swept the evidence of priestly sexual misconduct under the carpet for decades.

Although the Archdiocese's response to the epidemic of allegations of priestly sexual misconduct was political, the Monsignor's mission was personal. His ordination vows represented a pact between him and God and in his mind it was this pact that was the rock upon which the Church was built. The Monsignor regarded it as his personal mission to seek out those corrupted priests and see that they were punished and driven from the Church.

Today, the Monsignor was making a visit to see Father Thomas O'Flannery at the accused priest's sister's house in South Boston, to gain additional first hand information from Father O'Flannery with regard to the allegations, which had been made not just to the police, but to the Archbishop's office. The Monsignor, a tall, ascetically slim man in his mid-fifties, dressed in a priest's black suit and collar, waited with the grim visage of an inquisitor while Molly O'Flannery roused her brother from his afternoon nap. Monsignor Hurley had not called to announce his visit.

# Chasing Tales

Waiting for Father O'Flannery to make his appearance, the Monsignor finished the slice of carrot cake Molly O'Flannery had served to him and, for the sake of decorum, he had accepted, and walked to the kitchen. He prided himself on living a simple life and he was used to cleaning up after himself. He ran his plate and fork under the faucet until all the remains of the cake had been washed off, then set them down in the bottom of the sink. He looked around the old, but comfortable kitchen, with its Formica drainboard, the cakeplate sitting invitingly on top it, a neat array of three matching flowered jars labeled flower, sugar, and coffee, a basket with a loaf of French bread still in its wrapper next to half-full bottles of Cabernet Sauvignon and Bushmills, a wooden block with kitchen and steak knives sticking from it and the chipped, porcelain sink containing his dishes. He had grown up in a house much like this – one of two children in a modest, working class Irish family in Billerica. The childhood memories touched by the sight of Molly O'Flannery's kitchen caused him to feel a pang of regret that his life had become so isolated and lonely. He shook himself free of such thoughts. The fight for what was right demanded much from him and he had no room in his life for regrets.

Back in the living room the Monsignor sat stiff-backed, like a judge, his face set in a stern frown until Father Tom finally came down the stairs, apologizing for keeping him waiting. They shook hands cordially, although their last visit, in the Archdiocese offices, had been an unpleasant one for Father Tom since it had been Monsignor Hurley who had given him the news that he had asked Archbishop Gomez in Los Angeles to forbid the priest from wearing his clerical vestments or to say Mass until his case in Boston was resolved.

# Chasing Tales

"I've got nothing new to report," Father Tom answered the Monsignor's inquiry. "I've got a lawyer and I've brought a friend out from California – a private detective – to help do some investigating, but I guess it's going to come down to my word against young Russell's. I wish I could talk to the man to find out why he's saying these things."

Monsignor Hurley's eyes widened in alarm. "It's not a good idea for you to talk to Russell. Any judge would look very negatively on such a thing. What is your friend, the detective, doing?"

Father Tom was surprised at his own reticence to discuss his case with the Monsignor. He had the feeling that he had not only been abandoned by the church, but that the Archdiocese, at least in the presence of Monsignor Hurley, who reminded Father Tom of a vengeful inquisitor, was more on the side of the accuser than on his. "That's really between him and my lawyer," he answered. ""Don't I have a right to face my accuser?"

"You will have, in court. Not before." The Monsignor's tone was clipped.

"Would I be breaking any laws by doing it?"

The Monsignor hesitated before answering. His expression was drawn and serious. "It's not against the law, it's just unwise. These allegations are something that must be faced in a court of law; they're not something the victim can be talked out of. Not only would the court disapprove of that, but so would the Church." There was no doubt that when the Monsignor mentioned the Church, he was referring to his own position.

Father Tom's face showed his annoyance. "My intention isn't to talk Mr. Russell out of anything. I only want to find out why he's making these claims, which are completely untrue. I've never known when two men talking to each other in order to try to straighten out a misunderstanding between themselves isn't the right thing to do. I don't want the law or my fear of the law to get in the way of a normal human relationship."

"The court and the Church are charged with determining the truth, Father. Taking it upon yourself to talk to the witness against you would not be in your best interest," the Monsignor answered. Any traces of friendliness that had been in his manner were gone and his tone carried a hint of threat.

"Thank you," Father Tom answered, standing and sticking out his hand. He didn't like the Monsignor's attitude and he didn't feel any obligation to entertain the man any further.

The Monsignor's face showed his shock at being dismissed, but he nevertheless rose and extended his hand. "Thank your sister for the coffee – and the cake." He looked at Father Tom with a glinty stare. "Heed my words. It's in your best interest."

\*\*\*

Tim Russell heard the knock on his front door. He was watching television in his stocking feet and counting the hours until his wife dropped off his two children who were living with their mother in the couple's house in Braintree. Saturday evening, his wife allowed him to take the two boys, who were eleven and seven years of age, overnight at his apartment in Dorchester although he had to restore them to her custody by dinner time on Sunday. She acted as if he was a criminal, in danger of corrupting his boys. He'd actually felt as if he *were* a criminal when he'd discovered that his secret homosexual liaisons had resulted in infecting him with HIV, as if a divine hand had inflicted a deserved punishment on him. He reminded himself, that he was, as his therapist constantly told him, just bisexual – and that was no crime. He slipped on his loafers and walked across the room to open the door, hoping that his wife had brought his two sons early.

He was taken aback by the man who faced him on the porch. "Father?" he said.

"Can I come in? I'd like to talk to you."

Tim had been warned by his own lawyer about talking to anyone from the Church about his case. They were likely to try to get him to recant his testimony, or settle the case for a small sum and withdraw his criminal complaint. Despite the cautionary thoughts crowding into his mind, Tim's lack of confidence got the best of him. Who was he to forbid a priest from entering his house?

The man entered, but instead of taking the seat offered to him, stood tentatively in the middle of the living room of the small house, not making any move to remove his coat or his gloves, his right hand remaining ominously in his pocket. "So you remember me?"

Tim stared at the man. He'd automatically addressed him as Father when he'd opened the door, even though, in his overcoat, he couldn't tell if he was wearing clericals or not. "You were at St. Aloysius." He felt his anxiety returning... the same feeling he had every time he entered a confessional or when his therapist, Robert Gilbert, dimmed the lights in his office, flooding him with buried memories. "It *was* you, wasn't it?" he said in wonder. He hadn't been sure up to now that the vague memories he had retrieved during therapy weren't figments of his imagination. Now he was confronted with their reality.

"You've answered my question," the man said, sighing, as though he was shouldering an immense burden. "I'd hoped you wouldn't remember."

Tim's emotions were a jumble of fear and anger. He knew his fear was from those childhood days when the man in front of him had kept him under his absolute control – a victim of his own longing and his fear of the man's volatile temper. The anger was of more recent origin. This was the man who had ruined his life. "You're going to pay for what you did to me," he threatened through clenched teeth.

"I'm already paying" the man answered sadly, his mouth trembling at the corners as if he might begin to cry. "I'll keep on paying, but not to you, Tim. I will pay God what I owe him for my sins – which I can't seem to help committing." The man's sadness seemed to deepen and from his pocket he withdrew a long kitchen knife, its menacing blade shiny in the light from the window and it's handle, which he grasped firmly in his right hand, black, heavy plastic.

Tim watched in horror as the man moved threateningly toward him, drawing the knife back to gain momentum then thrusting it forward, like a medieval sabre, into Tim's stomach. Then, withdrawing the blood-dripping blade, he raised it high in the air and, with a savage stroke, brought it down again, this time into Tim's chest. The young man's expression changed from shock to fear and finally pain, then nothing. The man withdrew the knife before his victim collapsed, lifeless, to the floor in a widening pool of his own blood. Standing over the body, he looked down and closed his eyes, then let the knife clatter to the floor while he remained transfixed for more than a minute, until, crossing himself, he turned and let himself out the door.

# Chasing Tales

## Chapter 6

Less than thirty minutes drive southwest of the Boston city limits the town center of Stoughton still looked much as it had for most of the previous century, a lackluster, blue-collar manufacturing town. After the Second World War, when the factory jobs moved further south to the immigrant-filled cities of Brockton, Fall River and New Bedford, the town had become a bedroom community for mostly lower middle class workers who commuted to Boston or Providence, Rhode Island. With increasing land prices, the financial status of the residents had become more upscale and by the end of the millennium, Stoughton was mostly a middle-class suburban community for people who worked in Boston, although it retained its telltale factory-town flavor, particularly in the modest city center.

Kaylee Demme, formerly Kaylee Monahan, lived in a prosperous neighborhood in one of the new developments that had sprung up during the 1990's on the outskirts of town. In contrast to the historical Victorian home in which she had grown up, everything in her house was glitteringly new. Her husband, Alan, had insisted on refurbishing the fifteen-year-old house with upgraded appliances, carpets and drapes – anything to make the house look more expensive than its surrounding neighbors.

On this Saturday afternoon Kaylee had dropped Katherine off at a friend's for the afternoon and was waiting anxiously at the Stoughton Diner, just off the main town square, for the appearance of her uncle Nyles. With Alan at home watching a Celtics game on television, she wouldn't have been able to talk to her uncle with any assurance of privacy if she had invited him to her house and what she wanted to confer about was very private.

# Chasing Tales

Stirring her light brown coffee, Kaylee swept her gaze around the café, seeing, with relief, no one she recognized. She had not grown up in Stoughton and few of her neighbors, whom she barely knew anyway, came to the downtown area. The more popular stores - Nordstrom and Macy's for the housewives, The Gap and Old Navy for the teens - were in either of the two malls, which sat like oases on the eastern and northern borders of town- one of them only a mile from her home. The café was nearly empty, save for two older men who sat, like two solitary hermits, oblivious to each other and to her, drinking coffee and completely absorbed with staring into the spaces in front of each of them.

When Nyles walked in, he felt the familiar rush of pleasure he always felt when he saw his niece. He was hoping that she would explain why she had insisted in meeting him at this odd rendezvous spot instead of at her home. He slid in across from her in the old wooden booth and ordered a cup of coffee.

"Alan is at home and I wanted to talk to you alone." Kaylee's manner was subdued, like a worried child, rather than the usual exuberant young woman Nyles remembered. He noticed again the lines creasing her face and the heavy makeup she wore to cover them. In her wool knit pants suit and heels she was dressed more for an expensive restaurant than this ordinary diner. Nyles noticed an expensive looking fur parka next to her on the seat.

"To talk about what?"

She lifted her face toward his but avoided his eyes. Her expression was strained.

"I hope it's nothing... just my overactive imagination."

Nyles sipped his coffee, peering at his niece over the rim of his cup. "You hope what is nothing?" He'd learned a long time ago that when someone wanted to tell you something, it was best just to listen.

Kaylee heaved a helpless sigh. "This is so hard to talk about, Uncle Nyles. I've always been so strong, so sure of myself. Now I'm confused. I don't even want to think about this, but I'm terrified it won't go away." She sounded like the youngster he remembered – the youngster who had always been in trouble and for whom the only adult in which she could confide was her uncle.

Nyles reached across the table and put his hand on top of hers. "What?" His voice was soft.

Her gaze flitted across his face, then around the perimeter of the room, as if she was looking for an escape. She blinked, as if fighting tears. "I think…" she hesitated while Nyles continued to rest his hand on hers. "I think," she continued, "that Alan may be too interested in Katherine."

Nyles' impulse was to pull away, feeling a self-protective need to distance himself in order to absorb what his niece had said, but he knew that he could not let his horror at her words be so starkly evident, so he left his hand resting on hers. "Tell me exactly what you mean," he said.

"I don't think he's done anything. Not molest her, I mean." Red splotches were spreading across her face, like accusing fingers of embarrassment. "He's just too touchy-feely with her, if you know what I mean. He puts his hands on her, rubs her leg when he sits next to her, puts his hand on her shoulder. And he's walked in on her when she's bathing several times." She looked away, as if she was ashamed.

"How has Katherine reacted?"

His niece looked stricken. "She used to complain. A year ago she told me about him walking in on her. She said he stared at her and it creeped her out."

"Did you talk to Alan about it?"

"I tried to, but he got mad. He said I was accusing him of being a pedophile. I was afraid I would make him so mad he would leave us, but he calmed down and for awhile I thought everything was alright."

"Did Katherine stop complaining?"

"Yes. But over the last several months, I've noticed him doing it again. Now she doesn't move away when he touches her. She just looks afraid. When I asked her if he was still coming into the bathroom when she was in the tub, she said no, but I'm not sure if I believe her."

"Have you talked to Alan again?"

"I can't." She looked helpless, ready to cry. "I've got no proof of anything and I'm afraid he'll leave me if I accuse him of something he's not doing."

Nyles wondered what had happened to the strong, independent young woman he had known only a few years earlier. He remembered a similar case in Los Angeles. He had heard the story only after the wife had shot her husband. A jury had ruled the homicide justifiable after the daughter testified as to the years of molestation she had endured.

"And Katherine won't tell you anything?" He remembered that the daughter in the LA homicide case, because of her father's threats, had been afraid to tell her mother anything. It was only when she walked in on him with her daughter that the wife had realized what had been happening... and killed her husband.

"She barely talks to me about anything anymore. Even at school, her teachers are worried that she's withdrawing into herself."

"I thought she dressed a little grown-up for someone her age," Nyles said cautiously, not wanting to sound critical of his niece, who seemed fragile, like a delicate piece of glass that might shatter with the slightest nudge. "Is the makeup and short top something new?"

Kaylee looked embarrassed and nodded. "Alan buys those clothes for her and gave her a makeup kit for her birthday last year. She didn't touch them for almost a year until a few months ago. Then she started wearing makeup and those sexy clothes. I told her not to, but Alan said I was being old fashioned. A week ago I found a pack of cigarettes in her coat pocket. She said she was carrying them for a friend."

"Why did you decide to tell me about this?"

"I can't tell my father. He's only been sober for five years and I don't want to upset him. Besides, he never liked Alan."

"Do you want me to talk to Alan?"

"What would you say?" Her expression was trusting, reminding him of when she was younger.

"I don't know." He felt protective toward her, duty-bound to take some action, as if it was his own daughter who was asking for his help. He had no children and Kaylee was as close to a daughter as he had ever come. "I could just talk about how it feels for him to be a stepfather, what he thinks about Katherine. Maybe I'd get a sense of whether you've got something to worry about or not."

There were tears at the corners of her eyes, but she was looking across at him with the old look he'd been used to when she was younger. "Would you?"

He reached across and put his hand back on hers and smiled at her, though it was a struggle to keep the sadness from showing on his face.

His cell phone rang, startling them both. It was William Phelan. Tim Russell had been murdered and the police were on their way to Father Tom's house to question him. Phelan was requesting Nyles' help.

# Chasing Tales

## Chapter 7

Detective John Spaulding of the Boston Police Department felt unequipped for what he knew he had to do, as if he were a meatmarket butcher being asked to do microsurgery. Despite more than 30 years on the force, whenever he could arrange it, the aging, massive detective delegated to another officer, preferably one of the women on the force, the task of speaking to the relatives of a murder victim, especially when those victims included children, such as was the case with Tim Russell's two boys. Spaulding knew his hard, rough edges weren't what were needed to talk to children at a time like this. The boys had found their father's body, soaked with blood, when they'd entered the apartment to commence their overnight stay. Fortunately their mother was only steps behind them as they burst through the front door, like a pair of rambunctious puppies, and came to a horrified stop in front of the crumpled body of their father. Neither child had been willing to touch the body, but Bonnie Russell, a nurse, had reached down and felt the carotid pulse, noting that his skin was still warm, though her husband's heart had stilled.

When Detective Spaulding arrived, Mrs. Russell was in the kitchen, serving her two boys juice and comforting them as best she could. Both boys looked frightened and the younger boy, Kevin was sniffling, his cheeks still wet with tears. His older brother, Ronnie was more stoic, although he avoided looking directly at any of the adults in the room, including his mother. Spaulding was no expert on kids, but to his eyes, the older boy looked angry, whether at his father's killer or at his father, Spaulding wasn't sure.

# Chasing Tales

"He's HIV positive," Bonnie Russell had announced to the first officers on the scene. Being a nurse, she knew that both the police and the paramedics routinely took precautions such as wearing latex gloves when they dealt with bodily fluids, but in the case of touching her husband, they needed to be more than routinely careful. Even she had been conscious of avoiding touching any blood when she had checked his pulse for some sign of life. Now, perhaps like her oldest son, she couldn't shake the thought that her estranged husband's bisexual lifestyle was responsible for not just the ruin of their marriage and family life, but his own violent death.

Detective Spaulding could sense Bonnie Russell's unspoken anger, like a seething volcano beneath the surface of her controlled exterior. He hesitantly pried her away from her children so he could question her further about her husband's death.

"God knows what kind of people he had visit him, now that he didn't have us at home with him anymore," Mrs. Russell said. She was a short, attractive woman in her late thirties, comfortably overweight and well-dressed in a pair of dark wool pants and a matching sweater. She cast a distasteful glance toward the living room where the coroner was still examining her husband's body and when she did so, her anger faltered and she put her hands up to her face to cover her tears.

Spaulding shifted uncomfortably and waited until the woman stopped sobbing. "What do you mean, Mrs. Russell?" His voice had a rough quality, like a gruff football coach, even when he was trying to be soft. He knew the woman was in shock, but he couldn't seem to alter the way he talked to her, even when he wanted to. He was a bull in a china shop and he knew it. His manner came in handy when he wanted to bully suspects or even his fellow officers, but at times like this he felt at a loss as to how to alter his approach. Where was Detective Rhonda Jackson? She was usually his partner on these cases and she knew how to talk to a grieving widow.

Mrs. Russell wiped the tears from the corners of her eyes and self-consciously rubbed the back of her hand across her moist upper lip. Her face was red and she looked embarrassed and glanced toward the kitchen, as if to make sure her sons weren't listening and when she resumed speaking, she spoke in a hushed voice. "My husband was gay. I left him because he had been visiting male prostitutes. That's why he's HIV positive."

Spaulding knitted his brow in a disgusted frown. Goddamn queers, he thought. He never liked working on cases involving homosexuals. It made him angry no matter whether the gay person was the victim or the suspect. "You don't live here?" he asked the wife.

She looked around the apartment with an expression of revulsion. "He's lived here three months. The boys and I live in Braintree. They come to visit him and stay over on Saturday nights."

There had been no sign that Russell had been entertaining anyone. In fact, a cursory examination of the premises had suggested that he had been watching television by himself. A glass of Coca-Cola sat, half finished, on the table next to the chair in front of the TV. The TV had apparently been on – tuned to a Celtics game - when the two boys had entered the house. The position of the body suggested that Tim Russell might have gotten up to let someone in the front door and then had been killed almost immediately.

"There's no sign anyone broke in. Whoever did this was either someone he knew or someone who was able to talk himself into the house. Nothing was taken, either from his person or from the house, so far as we can tell." Spaulding was trying to be helpful, but he couldn't keep the habitual scowl off of his face.

Bonnie Russell wasn't really listening to the detective "Can I go back to my house?" she asked. "This isn't a good atmosphere for my boys."

Spaulding nodded his large head. "Be sure one of the officers has your phone number so I can contact you. We'll need to ask a lot of questions about your husband – but later, when things have settled down." He looked into the kitchen at the two boys, sitting wide-eyed at the table and he had a momentary thought of his own two boys at that age, even though they were now both grown up. The thought brought on a wave of anger and he too, wasn't sure if he was mad at the victim or the perpetrator.

A wiry, red haired man with a crew-cut edged his way in the front door. Spaulding stared as the man peered down at the body on the floor, shook his head, then looked around the room.

"Jesus fucking Chris," the man muttered, loud enough for everyone, including both Spaulding and Bonnie Russell and her two boys to hear.

"Can I help you?" Detective Spaulding growled, stepping in front of the man and sticking out his chin, pugnaciously.

The man looked unfazed by the detective's belligerent attitude and flashed a badge. "Randy Colton, Special Task Force. You in charge?"

Spaulding nodded. "What task force?" He remained in the man's path and continued to scowl.

"Sexual abuse cases." He looked down at the body on the floor. "Looks like we just lost a witness."

"You mean Russell?"

"He made accusations against a priest. I came out today to talk to him. What did you say your name was?"

"Spaulding."

They shook hands and Spaulding moved aside.

"What do you think happened?" Colton asked.

"Looks like he let someone in the front door and whoever it was stabbed him with a kitchen knife."

"You've got the weapon?"

Spaulding nodded.

"From his kitchen?"

Spaulding shook his head. "His wife was here. Said she'd never seen the knife before and it didn't match anything in the kitchen. But who knows? Sounds like he turned gay on her and she left him a while back. She thinks maybe it was one of his queer boyfriends who did it."

Colton shrugged and rubbed his chin. "Whoever did it, I guess my priest is off the hook on any sexual abuse charges."

"You mean Russell was your only witness against him?"

"So far."

"I guess I'd better have a talk with your priest."

Chapter 8

Father Tom and Bill Phelan were sitting in the living room in Molly O'Flannery's house talking to a large, heavyset man with a florid face, dressed in a wrinkled gray business suit. The stranger was introduced to Nyles as Detective John Spaulding from the Boston Police, Homicide Division. Father Tom told Spaulding that Nyles was a former Dorchester cop himself, and a retired LAPD detective who was helping Phelan with the abuse case.

"When were you with the Boston PD?" the detective asked. His voice was gruff and he asked the question as if it was a challenge.

"Back in the seventies," Nyles answered. His calm blue eyes met Spaulding's directly, giving no sign that he was intimidated by the detective's harsh manner.

"What did you do with the LAPD?" Spaulding still seemed to be challenging him.

"I was a homicide detective." Nyles' statement was matter-of-fact and devoid of emotion.

Spaulding nodded and seemed to be thinking. "You ever work for Raimey in Dorchester?" he asked suddenly.

Nyles nodded. "He was a watch commander when I was there. Heard he made Captain. Tough old fart, as I remember."

Spaulding's face broke into a broad smile. "He was Captain when I came on board. You're right about the tough old fart business."

Nyles was relieved that the detective had recognized a mutual connection between the two of them. He'd had enough experience with Spaulding's type of cop to know that he could make things difficult if he wanted to.

"Detective Monahan probably knows why I'm here." Spaulding said, directing his gaze to Father Tom and his lawyer. His expression was serious again. "It's a routine part of a murder investigation. Russell was a witness against you, Father, and we have to ask you a few questions."

"You mean I'm a suspect?" Father Tom asked.

Spaulding frowned. "No one's a suspect at this point – or everyone is, depending on how you want to look at it." He shot a quick glance over at Nyles, as if to see if he was going to make a comment. "The main thing I need to know is where you were earlier this afternoon between about 3:00 p.m. and 5:00." The detective had a pad and ballpoint pen out, poised to take notes.

Father Tom looked uncertainly at Phelan as if to see if he was going to give him any direction, but the lawyer's gaze was directed at the floor, as if whatever was being said didn't concern him. "I was out walking. Monsignor Hurley came by about 2:00 and woke me from a nap. After he left I went for a walk to think some things through."

"By yourself?" Spaulding was scribbling hurried notes on the small pad.

"By myself."

"Talk to anyone, stop to visit anyone? Go in any stores or shops?"

"I stopped at Shaughnessy's Bar on the way back, about 4:30 and had a beer."

Spaulding jotted a few more notes on his pad. "You didn't visit Tim Russell during that time?"

"No. I've never been to Russell's house. I don't even know where he lives."

Spaulding put his writing pad in his breast pocket. "You mind if I look around?"

Father Tom glanced at his attorney, who shrugged, as if it was none of his business. "I guess not."

"How was Russell killed?" Nyles asked.

"Stabbed, in his living room. Someone used a kitchen knife, apparently not Russell's."

"An intruder? Was it a robbery?"

Spaulding stood up, groaning as he rose from his chair, as if it was an effort to raise his heavy body. "No robbery, no struggle, no B & E. Whoever it was, Russell let him in the apartment." He turned to Father Tom. "Can I see the kitchen?"

The priest led Spaulding into the kitchen and Nyles followed, while Bill Phelan retreated further into the couch, as if he hoped to be left out of whatever was transpiring.

The detective went straight to the wooden block that held the knives. There was an empty slot in the butcher block. "One knife looks like it's missing." The detective's tone was matter-of-fact, but he cast an accusing glance at the priest.

"I'll have to ask my sister," Father Tom answered, his voice uncertain. He called his sister from upstairs.

"Did you find the murder weapon, Detective," Nyles asked.

"We're not sure it's the weapon until forensics runs their tests, but I'd say so."

"And?" Nyles asked.

"My guess is it matches the knife that's missing," The detective's voice was flat and emotionless. "Same handle as the rest of these." He looked at Nyles as if waiting to be challenged.

# Chasing Tales

Nyles directed a noncommittal stare back at the detective. There was no point in challenging evidence at this stage of the investigation.

Molly O'Flannery entered the kitchen. She was wearing loose Capri pants and a sweatshirt. She looked as if she'd been cleaning upstairs and her eyes widened in fright when she saw the crowd in the kitchen.

Father Tom asked her about the large kitchen knife.

"You mean it's not here?" Molly asked, looking guilty, as if she thought they were accusing her of stealing it.

"I looked in the dishwasher," her brother said. "I thought maybe you were using it for something." His voice was confident and gentle, as if he was trying to reassure his sister that there wasn't a problem.

Molly's eyes widened. "Of course. I was using it to cut the cake. It's under the cake lid." She strode across the room and removed the cover on the cake dish. There was no knife.

"When did you last use the knife to cut the cake, Molly?" Nyles asked. His voice was soft and gentle, as her brother's had been.

"This afternoon, when I served the Monsignor," she answered, her eyes darting from one to the other of the people in the room.

"I'll have to take the whole block of knives," Spaulding said, flatly. "We'll see if we have a match."

Father Tom's face was ashen. "This makes no sense. I'm sure the knife is around here somewhere." He turned toward this sister. "Think, Molly. After you cut the cake with the knife, what did you do with it?" He was trying to control his anxiety, but the tension in his voice was obvious .

Molly looked as if she was about to burst into tears, or run, frightened, from the room. "I thought I left it on the cake dish. If I would have done anything, I would have put it in the dishwasher." She bent down and pulled the tray from the dishwasher all the way out and frantically sorted through the utensils, then ran her hand over the bottom of the machine. She came up with nothing and stood up, looking frightened at her brother. "I don't know. Why is it so important?" Her voice was on the edge of hysteria.

"It's alright, Molly," Nyles stepped in, putting a reassuring hand on her shoulder. She flinched at his touch but then looked at him, her expression confused. "You can look again later. I'm sure that it will turn out not to be very important anyway," Nyles said. He wished he believed what he was saying.

"I'll let you know about the tests," Spaulding said. "I'll either be back or ask you to come to the station. You'll want your lawyer, I would imagine."

"There must be a lot of kitchen knife sets that match this one," Nyles said.

"That's probably something I'll have to find out," Spaulding answered.

"I guess so," Nyles said.

# Chasing Tales

## Chapter 9

Alan Demme enjoyed patronizing what he thought of as "classy" restaurants, and this definition especially included ones in which he thought he might be seen by potential clients or neighbors who would be impressed that he had the good taste and money to afford visiting such an establishment. The new Flemings Steak House at the East End Mall, just off of highway 37 leading out of Stoughton, with it's expensive menu and valet parking, was just such a restaurant. The Stoughton Courier had run a story about the restaurant's highly touted wine list and its art deco bar where local thirty somethings mingled until late in the evening on Friday and Saturday nights.

Alan was dressed in a subdued tweed jacket and dark woolen slacks and wore a V-necked Navy blue cashmere sweater over his shirt and tie, the colors of the latter matching the tiny flecks of blue and gray in the weave of his jacket. He was dressed to impress and had spent almost as much time supervising Kaylee's evening ensemble as his own. After more than a half hour spent rejecting various outfits, Kaylee was finally given permission to wear a tight-fitting, short, black, sleeveless evening dress, which made her feel faintly exhibitionistic, but pleased her husband. Since Alan had been Kaylee's life preserver, pulling her out of a downward spiral of drugs and alcohol, even as she was trying to raise a small child, she dared not challenge his opinions, even about what she wore.

Alan had insisted on arriving at the restaurant forty-five minutes ahead of their reservation so they could enjoy the bar and socialize with the other young couples and singles who were mostly their age or younger. Kaylee didn't know anyone and she drank only soft drinks, so she

47

sat quietly while her husband consumed three quick martinis and rubber-necked around the room, hoping to see someone he knew or at least be seen himself. When they were called to their table for dinner, he was already tipsy.

Kaylee was used to her husband's drinking, but, unlike her own pattern of heavy drinking or her father's, Alan only drank on social occasions and rarely at home, although he was woefully poor at holding his liquor. He wasn't an angry drunk, just an expansive one, which was in fitting with his personality. At dinner, he ordered a bottle of wine, taking great pains to explain to the waiter in a loud enough voice that the patrons at nearby tables could hear him, why he had chosen that particular red Zinfandel to go with his steak and why he considered price no object when it came to selecting the right wine.

Kaylee fidgeted, as she always did, and tried to intrude into her husband's monologue about potential choices for his next car, by talking about how Katherine was doing at school and how they needed to find a day in which they could arrange another visit at her parents' house before her uncle Nyles returned to California. Finally they hit upon the mutually agreeable topic of where they would take their spring vacation and Kaylee ate her steak, sipped her Sprite, and watched her husband get drunker and drunker as he finished the bottle of wine.

There was no argument about who was going to drive home from the restaurant, nor about who was going to take the babysitter home. Joanna Reeves was a fifteen-year-old high school student, who looked young for her age and was also a good companion to Katherine, despite their difference in ages. Joanna's parents were strict enough to not let her go out on Saturday nights unless she was attending a chaperoned event, so she was often available for babysitting, although Katherine was nearing the age where she would need no sitter.

Alan was too inebriated to drive Joanna home and when they sat in the living room chatting briefly with Joanna while she gathered her things together for the ride home, Kaylee noticed her husband so obviously leering at the teenager that she stood up to hasten the process of getting the babysitter out the door. Katherine was not yet asleep, but she was in her room watching television, which, her mother reminded her before she left with the babysitter, would need to be shut off at the conclusion of the show she was watching because, Saturday night or not, it was time for Katherine to go to sleep. Alan flipped on the television in his and Kaylee's room and with a seductive wink, told his wife he would be waiting for her when she returned. Kaylee imagined, given the amount he'd had to drink, he'd be fast asleep by the time she got back.

When she entered the house, after depositing Joanna Reeves at her parents' front door, Kaylee still heard the television from her bedroom and wondered if Alan had fallen asleep watching it or if, true to his drunken promise, he would be waiting for her to join him in bed. He was neither.

Turning off the bedroom television, Kaylee heard no other sound in the house and, her anxiety mounting, she set off toward her daughter's bedroom, the thoughts that were running through her mind horrifying her.

Katherine's bedroom was empty, the light was on, the bed had been slept in, and the television was turned off. The row of stuffed dogs across the top of Katherine's chest of drawers seemed to mock Kaylee in their innocence and she tore frantically down the hallway.

When she rounded the corner to the upstairs bathroom she almost stumbled across her husband, sitting, in his underwear and socks, outside the closed bathroom door and snoring loudly, looking like a drunk sleeping it off in a back alley.

Kaylee knocked softly on the bathroom door. When there was no answer, she whispered her daughter's name, trying not to rouse her husband. After a few seconds, the door cracked open and she saw Katherine's face, dried tears staining her cheeks, like smudges of grease paint, peering out with wide eyes at her mother.

"Come out," Kaylee whispered. "He's asleep."

Carefully, Katherine opened the door, then, as if avoiding a dangerous animal, she stepped over the legs of her stepfather, and fell into her mother's arms. "He came into my bedroom," she whispered through her sobs. "He said crazy things. I ran away and locked myself in the bathroom. He kept saying things through the door. He only stopped a few minutes ago."

"Did he touch you?" Kaylee's whole body tensed, waiting for her daughter's answer.

"No, but I was afraid of what he would do."

Kaylee let out her breath. At least nothing had happened - only what had happened wasn't nothing. "Let's get some things," she said. "We're going to Grandma and Grandpa's house."

## Chapter 10

Kaylee sat at the kitchen table with her father and mother and Nyles. Katherine was in the den watching something on television.

"Tell us again what Katherine told you Alan said to her," Millie said. She was much calmer than her husband, whose large, round face was scarlet and who sat with his eyes narrowed in anger, as if he was contemplating mayhem.

"She said he told her he loved her, that she had a beautiful body and that he wanted to kiss her and touch her."

Nyles' face registered no emotion. His brother exhaled loudly and shook his head in disgust.

"But he didn't actually do anything? Touch her in any inappropriate way, I mean." Millie asked. Just asking the question caused her face to redden.

"She said he 'pawed' at her, wanting to hold her hand, put his hand on her shoulder, hug her – but nothing terrible, though she ran from the room and locked herself in the bathroom after only a few minutes."

"The son-of-a-bitch," Sean exploded. "You hear about these things but you never think it will happen in your own family." He pounded one of his ham-size fists on the table. "You need to file charges against him," he said to his daughter.

Kaylee had her hands cupped around a mug of coffee, as if she was seeking security from its warmth. "Alan was drunk… I mean really drunk. He was waiting for me to come home. Maybe he thought it was me he was talking to." She looked uncertainly at her mother, then in an embarrassed way at her father.

"You had your suspicions about him before," Nyles reminded Kaylee.

Kaylee looked frightened and she glanced at her parents to see how they'd reacted to her uncle's words.

"What are you talking about?" Millie asked, looking first at Nyles then at Kaylee.

"I told Uncle Nyles that I was worried about how Alan acted around Katherine, that was all. He said he'd talk to him."

"Why didn't you tell me?" Her father's expression was a mixture of hurt and anger. "Why tell Uncle Nyles and not your own mother and father?"

"Because I didn't want to worry you or make you against Alan. You don't like him anyway. I thought maybe Uncle Nyles was more neutral."

Sean shot an irritated glance at his brother.

Nyles understood his brother's feelings but he also understood Kaylee's reasons for not telling her father. "Have you talked to Alan this morning?" he asked.

"Only to tell him where we were. He was hung over. I don't think he remembers what he did last night. He just said to come home in time to fix dinner."

"For Christ's sake. The man's got no pride," Sean said.

"I'm still willing to talk to him," Nyles said. Before his brother could object, he added, "I know it's your place, Sean, but you may be too angry right now." Though he wasn't giving his brother an order, there was a note of authority in his voice.

"I want him arrested!" Sean said. "The only talking I want to do is to tell him I'm going to see his ass in jail." His face was red and the artery in his neck was throbbing like a taut wire that had just been plucked.

"I think you'd better talk to him," Millie said to Nyles while putting a hand on her husband's arm.

"He hasn't committed any crime," Nyles said measuring his words. "What he's done horrifies all of us and it's probably caused some damage to Katherine. If we call the police, they'll just refer the case to social services, at least that's what would happen in LA. Social Services will probably just file a report at this point, maybe recommend counseling, which would probably be a good idea, anyway."

"Counseling for whom?" Kaylee asked suspiciously. Her parents had taken her to a number of counselors when she was young and none had helped her.

Nyles shrugged. "That's out of my domain. Maybe all of you."

"You're not suggesting that Kaylee stay with that psychopath?" Sean said.

"That's up to Kaylee."

Kaylee looked at each of them, then stared down at her cup of coffee. "He's not a demon... I just don't know."

Sean slapped his hand on the table. "It's out of the question."

"Can't Uncle Nyles talk to him and find out what he has to say?" Kaylee asked in a pleading voice.

"I don't care what the son-of-a-bitch has to say. I think it's dangerous to have him around my granddaughter. He's a goddamn pervert and you've got no business being married to him."

Kaylee looked at her mother and Nyles for support.

"Your father has a point, Kaylee," Nyles said. "This kind of behavior crosses a line most people wouldn't even think of crossing – ever. Whatever Alan says, won't change that."

Kaylee looked directly at her father. "I've done things none of you would ever do when I was drunk or high. You don't know about those things Dad, because when you drank too much, you only got happy or angry. You were unpredictable but not out of bounds. I've been out of bounds and I know it was the booze and the drugs that were responsible. If I started using again, I'd do the same things. Maybe Alan has a problem. Maybe he's an alcoholic. He sure can't hold his liquor. Let Uncle Nyles talk to him and give us a more objective opinion."

Nyles wasn't sure he could be objective, in fact he was pretty sure he couldn't be and from what Kaylee had told him when they'd met before, her husband's behavior was suspicious even when he hadn't been drinking. But he was willing to talk to Alan for whatever it was worth.

Sean shrugged. "Go ahead, Nyles. I'm too mad to talk to him. Maybe it's better that you do it."

"Kaylee and I had both better do it – together. She needs to confront him with what Katherine told her." Nyles looked over at his niece. "Can you do that?"

She nodded. "I have to."

"What about Katherine?" Millie asked.

"I guess I should try to contact a counselor," Kaylee said, reluctantly.

"Goddamn that man if he's hurt my granddaughter," Sean said. But his expression was less angry than it had been earlier.

\*\*\*

# Chasing Tales

Nyles and Kaylee didn't say much on the drive to her house in Stoughton, other than for her to give him directions once they left the main road. Nyles was feeling very much like a parent with Kaylee. He and Cloris had never had children and when they'd finally tried, when Cloris was in her forties, she'd had to abort a defective child. Following that episode, she had begun drinking heavily and overusing her medications - a situation that had finally resulted in her stroke. Their lack of children was still a source of pain for Cloris, although Nyles didn't let himself think about it, except now, when he was sitting next to his niece in the car.

Alan Demme greeted his wife and her uncle as if everything was perfectly normal. He was dressed more casually than usual, in fact, almost sloppily, compared to his usual attire. He had on a pair of baggy jeans and a T-shirt and his hair was only vaguely combed, as if he'd only recently crawled from bed. He had made a pot of coffee and, upon their entering, he asked Kaylee to bring them each a cup. "Where's Katherine?" he asked, his voice full of forced cheerfulness.

Kaylee was still pouring the coffee, but Nyles felt he had to say something. "It's Katherine we need to talk to you about," he said, trying to keep his tone neutral.

"What - both of you? Katherine is Kaylee's and my daughter." There was an edge of belligerence in Alan's voice.

Nyles was hesitant to say anything until Kaylee was in the room. "We're both going to talk to you about her." He sat down on one of the living room chairs. Alan was staring at him and Nyles returned his gaze, his face revealing nothing of what he felt.

"What's going on?" Alan asked his wife when she entered the room carrying three cups of coffee on a tray.

"Some kind of discussion about my drinking?" He stared angrily at his wife. "Why is your uncle involved? Am I going to get a police interrogation?" His voice had risen and he took the coffee but didn't sit down and instead paced back and forth in front of the couch, reminding Nyles of an agitated jail inmate. Kaylee had sat down in the chair closest to Nyles.

"Settle down, Alan," Nyles said, his voice surprising both Alan and his niece by its authority. He leaned forward in his chair and spoke directly to his niece's husband. "You got very drunk last night and made lewd comments to your step-daughter and tried to assault her. Your wife had to rescue her from the bathroom where she'd locked herself in to get away from you. You've got a problem and we're here to find out what you're going to do about it."

Alan stared at him. "What are you talking about?" He looked mystified, as if what Nyles had just told him had been spoken in a foreign language.

"You don't remember?" Kaylee asked, unable to conceal the hopefulness in her voice. She wanted him to not remember so she could consign her husband's behavior to a blacked out drunken fugue.

Alan's face twisted into a caricature of disbelief and anger. "I couldn't have done anything like that. I don't even remember what happened after I got home, except I woke up this morning on the floor outside the bathroom." His expression segued from anger to horror. "If I did anything that could be misinterpreted as inappropriate, especially with our daughter, I'm deeply sorry. The truth is I don't remember anything." He hung his head, as if admitting either innocence or guilt, it wasn't clear which.

"You have a drinking problem, honey. That's all we're saying," Kaylee said, her voice expressing both relief and concern.

"It's never happened before," Alan said, sitting down on the couch. He held his head in his hands.

"What you did suggests you have sexual interests in Katherine. That would be something you'd be aware of even when you're not drunk," Nyles said, his voice matter-of-fact.

"What are you suggesting?" Alan looked offended and ready to erupt into anger again.

"Katherine says you've walked in on her in the bathtub. You've made comments about her body even when you weren't drunk."

Kaylee moved a hand toward her uncle, as if to stop him from saying more. The look she directed at her husband was filled with anxiety. "Alan, I was worried, I had to talk to Uncle Nyles."

Alan shook his head slowly "If you were worried, honey, you should have talked to me. There's nothing we can't talk about. We don't need to share it with strangers. I'm just trying to get along with Katherine. I never meant anything wrong."

"But you *have* done things that are wrong," Nyles said, his tone steady and insistent. "What are you going to do about it?"

"I think that's between Kaylee and me, don't you?"

"If you behave the way you did last night, the next time it will be between you and the police." Nyles said, his blue eyes fixed steadily on Alan.

For a moment, Alan looked afraid, then his expression turned angry. "Is that why you're here; the great detective here to threaten me?" He stood up. "I've heard enough. I'm going to take a shower." He stomped out of the room, like a victim of a grievous affront. His footsteps could be heard climbing the stairs.

"He didn't know what he did last night," Kaylee said to her uncle, her voice pleading.

"I think your daughter is in danger if you bring her back in the same house with that man," Nyles said. He knew he was presenting his niece with a horrible dilemma, but he felt he had no choice. He had to protect her and Katherine, just as if Kaylee was his own daughter.

# Chasing Tales

## Chapter 11

Only his inurement to the sight of countless men dressed in orange prison jumpsuits saved Nyles from a feeling of shock when he confronted Father Tom in the Suffolk County Jail. Even so, the retired detective felt overwhelmed with sadness when the priest was led into the visitor's interview room, his face twisted into an awkward, forced smile. Bill Phelan, the priest's lawyer had explained that the lab results had not only shown that the kitchen knife found next to Tim Russell's body, was from the set in the priest's sister's house, but that both Molly and Tom O'Flannery's fingerprints were on the handle. The physical evidence, combined with an obvious motive was enough to justify Father Tom's arrest.

"There is a purpose in this," the priest said, sitting in obvious discomfort on a hard wooden chair across the table from Nyles in one of the rooms reserved for prisoners to visit privately with their counselors. "I'm a priest, regardless of what the Church says, and God uses me to work his will."

"I'm not going to argue with you," Nyles said, partly in reference to the long-standing debate he and Father Tom continued to have about religion. "But someone else besides God has a purpose in this and that's why you're in jail."

Father Tom shook his head and, despite his earlier words of faith, his face had an expression of defeat. "Who?"

"Let's think," Nyles answered. "Molly used the knife to serve Monsignor Hurley a piece of cake. That was the last time she saw the knife." He knew Molly blamed herself for the missing knife, although taking on such responsibility made no sense and Nyles had told her so.

59

"So are we supposed to think the Monsignor took the knife and drove to Russell's house and stabbed him? I can't make sense of that," Father Tom said, looking discouraged. "I left the house right after the Monsignor's visit and Molly went upstairs to clean. No one was downstairs for more than three hours. Anyone could have come in and taken the knife."

The possibilities were nearly endless, Nyles thought. "The killer had a complex motive. He not only wanted Russell dead, he wanted you blamed for it. What would that accomplish for someone?" Nyles was thinking aloud, hoping he and the priest together could make some sense of things.

Father Tom appeared mystified. "I have no idea."

"OK," Nyles continued. "Let's be even more concrete. Whoever it was knew how to find you. How many people knew you were at your sister's house?"

"Anyone connected to the Church or to the police... or I suppose to Bill Phelan."

"If we stick with the obvious, I'd have to say the Monsignor had the greatest opportunity. He was there the same afternoon the knife was stolen. Do you have any history with Hurley?"

Father Tom shook his head. "Until he called me into his office to tell me I was stripped of my duties, I'd never met him - never even heard of him. He comes across as a bit of a zealot when it comes to going after abusing priests and he can be very unpleasant, but I don't think he had it in for me personally."

Nyles began gathering his coat and gloves. "I think I'll have a visit with the Monsignor. I'm also going to talk to the detectives who were gathering evidence on the molestation charges against you. They probably got to know Russell as well as anyone. I'm also curious who else they've found who might be able to say who really molested Tim Russell. They're supposed to have a list of altar boys from the time when you were at St. Aloysius."

"Isn't that beside the point at this juncture?"

"Maybe. But if Tim Russell really was molested and he didn't imagine the whole thing, then eventually he might have remembered who really did it. Whoever that person is, he's someone else who might not want Russell to remain alive."

"You mean another priest?"

"Exactly."

Chapter 12

Sister Mary Agnes had the task of managing the administrative and clerical functions for the Archdiocese of Boston's office of Canon Law and, as Monsignor Andrew Hurley's administrative assistant, she ran a tight ship. Her intimidating demeanor was legendary and many would-be complainants who felt the Church had violated its canons in some way that had caused them damage, turned away from their enterprise after being thoroughly and exhaustively questioned by Sister Mary Agnes.

Mary Agnes greeted Nyles Monahan with a penetrating gaze before rising from her chair, brushing past her desk and opening her arms wide. "Nyles Monahan – from Dorchester High School – you don't remember Mary McDonald, Cloris Needham's best friend?" The solid rock of a woman in a gray skirt and dark sweater with a cross hanging prominently from a chain around her neck, beamed with pleasure.

The memories that came rushing back to Nyles threatened to overwhelm him -  images of two young teenage girls shyly walking home while he and his friends pestered them with taunts - memories of a high school dance when he had to find a date for Cloris' friend Mary or else Cloris wouldn't go to the dance with him.

Nyles hugged the large woman as tightly as he was able, almost suffocating when she bear-hugged him back. "I had no idea you worked here," he said, breathlessly, when they separated.

"I told Cloris, nine or ten years ago, when I took the job."

"Cloris has been virtually incapacitated until the last couple of years and anything that happened around the time of her stroke was totally wiped from her memory,"

Nyles explained, realizing that friends, such as Mary MacDonald, who hadn't kept up regular contact with he and his wife, could have no way of knowing the seriousness of Cloris' illness.

"And now?" Sister Mary Agnes' expression was serious and concerned.

"She's better, much better. She's almost back to her old self."

"She's here with you?" Her tone was hopeful.

"No. I'm here on business."

"With the Monsignor's office?"

"Uh huh."

Sister Mary Agnes moved back behind her desk, and sat down, straightening her glasses, then peering at her computer screen. "You're here about Father Thomas O'Flannery?"

Nyles remained standing. "I'd like to talk to the Monsignor about Father O'Flannery's case."

"What is your connection to Father O'Flannery? I know you're with his lawyer's office. Mr. Phelan called to tell us that. But you came all the way from California for this. I don't understand." She didn't sound accusatory, only curious.

"Father Tom is Cloris' priest. He's our best friend. He was there every minute during her illness and recovery."

She sat for a moment, looking thoughtful. "I'll tell the Monsignor you're here."

\*\*\*

Monsignor Andrew Hurley was a tall, slim man with glasses, who wore his priest's collar with a pride that suggested that he felt that his religious calling had elevated him above the plane of mere mortals. He came around his desk, extending his hand to Nyles when he entered the office. "I understand you're working with Attorney Phelan for Father O'Flannery." "How can I help you?" His face was a mask.

"I'm interested in getting the names of the other altar boys at St. Aloysius during Father O'Flannery's tenure as priest... and the names of any other priests who might also have provided services out of St. Aloysius during that time."

The expression on Monsignor Hurley's face hardened. "I hardly think the abuse charges against Father O'Flannery will be pursued, now that the only witness is dead." There was a dismissive tone to his voice.

"I'm not concerned about the abuse charges. I'm helping defend him against the murder charges."

"I don't understand." The look on the Monsignor's face could only be described as suspicious. He shifted in his chair.

"Russell had a recollection of having been sexually abused by Father Tom – Father O'Flannery. The police theory is that Russell was killed in order to prevent him from testifying against the Father. It's possible that he was killed so he wouldn't remember who the real abuser was. If that's the case, then one of the other altar boys may have been abused by the same man and it may have been another priest from St. Aloysius."

"I think you're grasping at straws, Mr. Monahan." The monsignor's tone was disdainful.

Nyles met his gaze with a hard stare. "Perhaps, but I'd like those names."

"They might be difficult to retrieve. That was many years ago." He made it sound as if he was being asked to dig into the ancient past.

"You must have a record of which priests served in which parish."

"Of course we have a record of parish assignments. I meant the records of who was an altar boy. I'm afraid those records are quite limited. Not every parish kept good records."

"I'd like what you've got. And since you do have a record of the priest's assignments, I'd like that."

"I already gave what information we could find on the altar boys to the police. If you're working for Father O'Flannery's lawyer, you'd need to request those records from them… or get a subpoena."

Nyles had always had his police authority on his side when he requested evidence as a detective. Hurley might be within his rights to withhold Church records, especially when there were no longer any charges against the Church in this case. "I can ask the police for the names of the altar boys and I can get a subpoena if I have to, but surely the names of the priests who were at St. Aloysius isn't confidential information."

"I'll have my assistant give you the list of priests, but you'll have to ask the police for the names of the altar boys. I'm sure you can understand."

"No I don't understand. You seemed to be quite animated in pursuing the sexual molestation charges against Father Tom. Why aren't you equally committed to finding out the truth, now that he's charged with murder?"

The Monsignor's expression was stony and his piercing gaze seemed to look right through Nyles. "Molesting a child while serving as God's emissary is a transgression against the Church. It is my job to see that priests who commit such sins are punished to the full extent of the law and stripped of their Holy Orders. If Father O'Flannery committed murder, even when he was suspended by the Church from his priestly duties, he has committed a sin and although, despite his suspension, he remains a priest, he has committed a secular crime and secular authorities are quite capable of solving it."

"But if he is innocent of the murder don't you want to help him?" Nyles found the Monsignor's reasoning incredible.

"My duty to the Church was to find out the truth about what Father O'Flannery did when he was functioning as a priest within his parish. With Mr. Russell dead, I can do no more. Whatever else happens is up to the police and I would urge you to go to them for help."

Nyles could see he wasn't going to get anything except the list of priests from Monsignor Hurley today. He hoped he'd get more cooperation from the police or if not, that Bill Phelan would be able to convince a judge that the names of the altar boys were needed for Father Tom's defense.

"You came by Molly O'Flannery's house to see her brother the day of the murder," Nyles said.

The priest stared back at him without saying anything.

"You seemed quite involved in the case at that time," Nyles said.

"Really? That was my job, wasn't it? I have just told you that it is my duty to the Church to investigate these abuse cases... that's what this was at the time." He continued to stare at Nyles, as if waiting to see where he was going with his comments.

"The murder weapon disappeared from Molly's house soon after your visit."

"What are you suggesting?" The Monsignor's eyes narrowed in suspicion.

"I'm not suggesting anything. I'm sure the police will leave no stone unturned looking for clues in this case."

The Monsignor's smile was cold. "I believe they think they've already got their man."

"Things can always come up to change the course of an investigation."

The two of them sat across the Monsignor's desk and stared at each other, like a pair of prizefighters sizing each other up before a bout.

"Is that all, Mr. Monahan?"

"For now," Nyles answered.

Chapter 13

"You're beating a dead fucking horse." Nate Hilton sat, scowling, in his chair in his cramped office while Nyles sat in a hard backed chair in the middle of the aisle separating the detective's desk from the row of file cabinets lining the opposite wall. Randy Colton leaned back in his chair, watching his partner and the older, Irish ex-detective with an amused expression.

This was Nyles' first experience sitting in a police station and not being the one in charge, and he was acutely aware of what it felt like to be powerless in that situation – something he'd tried to keep in mind when he was the one sitting at the desk, but the full impact of which he'd never realized until now.

"I'm not worried about the molestation charges against Father O'Flannery," Nyles explained, swallowing his irritation. Detective Hilton had a chip on his shoulder and Nyles wasn't sure why. "Father O'Flannery wasn't the one who molested Russell, but someone else did. I want to talk to the other altar boys and see if they can tell me who that person was. There's a chance that that person is Russell's killer."

"You LA cops really live in La La Land, don't you?" Nate said. "Spaulding has an open and shut case against your priest and you think you can pin things on some mysterious second priest who abused the kids at O'Flannery's church - behind the Father's back, I guess - and then stole a knife from O'Flannery's house and killed Russell. Sounds just like a Hollywood movie." Hilton laughed derisively. "Doesn't it sound like Hollywood, Colton?" he asked, looking over at his partner.

# Chasing Tales

Randy Colton scratched his head and squinted bored eyes. "Detective Monahan here used to be a member of our department, Nate, let's cut him a little slack."

Nate's mouth curled in a sneer. "He may have been a member of your department, but not mine. I wouldn't doubt if Monahan here harassed me or my family when he was a Boston cop. Isn't that what you Irish cops used to do for fun in Dorchester?"

Nyles leveled his gaze at the Black detective. "That wasn't what *I* did. The attorney I work for can go to court and ask for a subpoena, but I figure you've already got the information I need, and if you'd share it with me it would save me some time."

"Why would I care about saving you time?" Hilton asked.

Nyles looked across the desk at the Black detective. He didn't like to stoop to the level of Hilton's kind of cop, but if he were going to get any help from him, he'd have to switch tactics. "Spaulding's an Irish cop and he's gonna get a lot of credit for doing nothing. He thinks he's got an open and shut case against Father O'Flannery, and I've got thirty years of homicide experience telling me he's wrong."

Nate Hilton narrowed his eyes and thought about what Nyles had said. Nate didn't like John Spaulding, whom he considered a loud-mouthed, bigoted, bully and if this skinny little ex-LA detective knew what he was talking about and wasn't just grasping at straws in order to save his friend, this might be a chance to frustrate Spaulding and show the captain that Nate was a good enough detective that it was a mistake to leave him languishing in the no-man's land of the sexual abuse task force.

"You really think you might be able to prove O'Flannery didn't do it?" Nate asked.

"I know I can," Nyles answered.

Nate eyed the skinny ex-detective. Then he seemed to come to a decision. "OK. We'll share what we've got with you but you have to keep us informed about what you find out. I wouldn't mind showing Spaulding that he's got his head up his ass."

Nyles didn't allow his satisfaction to show. "Then you'll help me find the real killer?"

"Why not?"

"Geez, Nate, what are you talking about?" Colton said, coming back to life. "We're not working for homicide any more," There was a look of alarm on his face.

"So what?" Nate answered. "Nobody said we have to stop working on the abuse case, just because one witness is dead. Somebody abused Tim Russell and it's our job to find out who it was. If we dig up his killer at the same time, so much the better." Nate smiled. How could he lose, he thought. This LA cop would do the legwork and he'd take the credit if he found out that O'Flannery wasn't the killer. And Spaulding would eat crow. It was all good as far as he was concerned.

"Jesus Christ," was all Detective Colton had to say.

# Chasing Tales

## Chapter 14

Nyles didn't want to intrude on his brother and Millie, who were having a heated discussion with Kaylee in the living room. Earlier in the week Kaylee had made the difficult decision to return to Alan, but without Katherine, who had stayed behind with her grandparents. Millie ferried the eleven year old to school in Stoughton each morning. Sean and Millie wanted Kaylee to leave her husband, but their daughter only wanted him to agree to go to AA and stop drinking, which so far he hadn't agreed to do. Nyles hadn't been invited to join the conversation and he was just as glad he hadn't been. He decided that the most gracious thing he could do, would be to go into the den and watch TV.

He hadn't realized that Katherine was in the room. She was watching a re-run of *Friends*, looking bored. Nyles almost turned away, then decided to enter the room anyway. "How you doin', kiddo?" he asked, sitting down on the leather couch. Katherine was sitting in her grandfather's favorite chair directly in front of the TV, slouched into a reclining position with one leg thrown over the arm of the chair, as if she was using it as a couch.

"OK," she answered, sitting up and taking her leg off the arm of the chair, while she continued to stare at the TV. He noticed her eyeshadow, but she wasn't wearing any lipstick and she wore an oversized shirt – perhaps her mothers - and jeans.

Nyles tried to make sense of what was happening on the TV show. He was familiar with the characters, since Cloris, formerly a regular on a daytime soap opera herself, had loved the show when it was still airing in prime time. The plot had something to do with a misunderstanding about who had slept in Rachel's bed the previous night when she was away from the apartment. Nyles couldn't understand any of it.

"Do you miss being at home?" he asked Katherine.

"I miss my room." She didn't look away from the TV and her voiced sounded petulant.

"Would you like to go back?"

She looked away from the TV, but not at Nyles. She stared out the window. "Not if Alan is still there." Her voice was angry.

"Have you told your mother that?"

Katherine was still looking out the window. "She says he's going to change. She thinks he's an alcoholic."

"What do you think?"

"I hate him." She glanced at her uncle as if daring him to say something.

The intensity of her statement surprised Nyles, but he found it understandable. "I imagine you do," he said.

Her face showed her surprise. "Mom says I'm not supposed to hate him."

"You feel the way you do because of what he did," he said.

"Do you want to watch the Celtic's game?" Katherine asked, still looking at him. Her voice had lost its challenging tone.

"Don't you want to watch Friends?"

"I've seen this one."

"OK," he said.

She changed the station. The Celtic's led the Nets by four points. There were still eight minutes to go in the first quarter. "Good, they're ahead," Katherine said.

"Do you like watching basketball?" he asked.

"I like the Celtics."

"Me too. I miss them out in California."

They watched in silence as the Celtics built their lead to eight points.

'Do you mind if I stay in here and watch with you?" she asked, looking at him uncertainly.

For the first time he thought she sounded like an eleven year-old girl. "I think that would be great," he said. He settled in to watch the game with his grandniece.

## Chapter 15

North Quincy was just across the Boston line from Dorchester, and the drab, wooden row house architecture of the city's working class neighborhoods changed little until you crossed the old Coast Highway and reached the edge of the bay, at which point a conglomeration of beach restaurants, marinas and warehouses lined the edge of the harbor, looking as if the remains of a strip mall had washed onto shore. Mickey Ryan's one bedroom apartment was tucked behind a dilapidated diner, whose fading sign advertised bargain-priced breakfast and lunch deals to the local workers. He lived on the second floor, which was accessible only by ascending an outside wooden stairway, which, although covered, was still slippery with ice when Nyles made his way, gingerly, up to the second floor to ask Mickey if he'd ever been molested by Father O'Flannery or anyone else when he was an altar boy at St. Aloysius, thirty years before.

Ryan was a short, skinny, pale, man in his early forties. He was dressed in a pair of corduroy pants and a sweatshirt that said *Harvard* across the chest, although he had never attended Harvard or any other college in his life. When he came to the door he was wearing a pair of brown faux sheepskin slippers with a hole in one toe.

"I'm off work because of disability," Ryan said, apologetically, as if he owed Nyles an explanation for why he was home on a weekday. "My chiropractor says I can't go back to work for another six months at least."

"I'm sorry to hear that," Nyles said. He took a seat on the couch and his host eased himself into a large, worn, easy chair, wincing as he sat down. The living room was neatly arranged, although almost barren of furniture. Besides the sofa and chair, there were a TV set, a fishtank along the wall opposite Ryan's chair, and a tall lamp with a dented shade standing behind the chair. A folded Boston Globe was on the end table next to the chair and Nyles could see a tiny kitchen just beyond a nook containing a table and four chairs. A toaster and a stack of paper napkins sat on the table.

Nyles reiterated that he was working for Father O'Flannery's defense, which he'd already told Ryan on the telephone when he called him on Sunday afternoon from Sean's house. "You know who Tim Russell is?" he asked.

Ryan picked up the paper and tapped it with his finger, as though he was offering it in evidence. "I read about him in the paper. He was murdered. Father Tom is in jail for it. I don't believe it, myself. That's why I said I'd talk to you." Although he was doing his best to be friendly, the young man's eyes shifted around the room nervously, as if seeking to avoid engaging Nyles directly.

"Russell was an altar boy for Father Tom – so were you. You must remember Tim Russell – from more than just reading about him in the paper."

"Sure, I remember him. We weren't really friends, but I knew him. We both came from the same neighborhood. He was younger than me by a couple of years. Why would anyone think Father Tom would kill him?"

"Russell accused Father Tom of molesting him when he was an altar boy."

Ryan's eyes widened. "Father Tom? I don't believe it."

"Why don't you believe it?"

"Cuz..." Ryan seemed at a loss for words. He cast his gaze about the room as if marking time until he could get his thoughts in order. "He wasn't like that – not Father Tom," he finally said. "I was his altar boy for more than a year and he never touched me – I mean in that way – he never touched me in that way. None of the other kids ever said anything about him either."

"Maybe Russell had Father Tom mixed up with someone else," Nyles suggested. "There were other priests besides Father Tom at St. Aloysius weren't there?" He pulled the list that Sister Mary Agnes had given him from his pocket. "Father Riordan? Father Jennings?"

Ryan looked as if he was trying to remember. "Riordan maybe. I think so, but I'm not positive. I think Jennings took over when Father Tom was sick a couple of times and he had something to do with the school - I don't remember what."

Nyles knew that Father Tom had gone through two long bouts of bronchitis, both of which had progressed to pneumonia and put him in the hospital. His fragile lungs were what had finally forced him to move to California for the warmer climate.

"Did you ever hear about either Father Riordan or Father Jennings bothering any of the boys? Any rumors? I assume neither of them bothered you."

Ryan shook his head. "Nobody bothered me. I never heard anything directly about either of those priests either." He hesitated, as if weighing whether to continue. "Kids used to make comments, though. Parents warn you, you know – even though they respect the priests. They say don't let him get too friendly. Don't let him touch you in ways that don't seem right. My parents told me that. So did some of the other boys' parents because we talked about it sometimes."

"Had it ever happened to any of them?"

"A couple of boys said it did. But not with Father Tom. I don't think it was either of those other two priests, either.

"Do you remember those boys' names?"

Ryan looked over at the door while he fidgeted with his hands. "I remember Billy Norris saying something. And Jimmy Gleason. Don't tell them I gave you their names."

"I'll leave you out of it, Mickey. You have my word. Do you still see either of them?"

He shook his head. "Not since high school." He took a deep breath, as if he was relieved that they were almost done. "I hope you can get Father Tom off. He was a good priest. Everybody missed him after he left."

Nyles realized he had almost missed the obvious and he looked down at the list in his hand. "It says here that Father James took over after Father Tom left. Could that have been who the other boys were talking about?"

Ryan shook his head. "Father James didn't come right away. There was another priest who came next."

Whoever it was, there was no other name between Fathers O'Flannery and James on Nyles' list. "Do you remember his name?"

"Father Hurley."

"Hurley? The same one who's Monsignor Hurley at the Archdiocese office?"

Mickey Ryan's expression was blank. "I don't know. I didn't know there was a Monsignor Hurley at the Archdiocese. Father Hurley only stayed at St. Aloysius a few months. Then we got another priest. I don't remember his name. I kind of dropped out by then."

"Why was that?"

He shrugged. "I don't know. It wasn't the same without Father Tom. And I got busy. I was a teenager by then. I was too old to be an altar boy. My parents stopped making me go to Mass." He smiled. "I got a girl friend. On Sunday mornings she told her parents she was going to my church and I told my parents I was going to her church and we both skipped church to see each other. We just walked around."

Nyles had a flashback to the days when he and Cloris had gone for walks, sometimes without letting their parents know they were seeing each other. His parents didn't care, but hers did. They'd heard stories about Nyles' father's drinking. It was funny how many different things brought back memories to him these days. Maybe it was being back in Boston... or just growing old.

He thanked Mickey Ryan and wished him luck and a quick recovery. As he descended the stairs he thought about how difficult it must be to get in and out of the apartment with a bad back when the stairs were covered with ice. He dismissed his worries. He couldn't do anything about Ryan's problems. He had to quit worrying about everyone he came in contact with. The same tendency had plagued him most of his career. Father Tom had encouraged the tendency in him. He needed to get the priest back his freedom.

# Chasing Tales

## Chapter 16

For the first time in as long as he could remember, Billy Phelan felt good about himself. He'd woken at six that morning and drunk a cup of instant coffee, shaved, and arrived at his South Boston office by 7:00 a.m., just as a weak winter sun shone its first morning rays on the dirty grey snow piled along the edge of the street. With a second cup of coffee from the Starbucks just down the street, he re-read the police reports on the fingerprint analysis of the knife found at the scene of Tim Russell's murder.

After more coffee and another hour gleaning whatever else in the police report might help his case, Phelan got a call from Nyles Monahan. The ex-detective had gotten the list of altar boys from the police and a list of former St. Aloysius priests from the Archdiocese and he was going to interview one of the altar boys that morning. Billy decided to review some of the previous Boston clergy cases of child abuse and see what he might find that could be of help in Father Tom's case. For the first time in years, he felt as if he was back to being a real lawyer. By eleven thirty he'd decided he'd earned himself a drink. He headed for the Hibernia Pub in Dorchester for a beer, a Bushmills and lunch.

The drive from his South Boston office to the historic pub on Adams Street in Dorchester took less than fifteen minutes, but Billy's thirst had continued to grow the closer he got to his destination. He parked his car on the street, and as he walked toward the front door of the pub, he gazed at the neon signs advertising Guinness, Harps and Smithwicks in the windows. The signs seemed to him as if they were bright beacons welcoming him home. On the way in he passed several local businessmen and workmen, many of whom greeted him with a smile and a, "hey Billy, how they hanging?" Billy was well known to the regular lunch crowd at the pub.

Tommy O'Donald, dressed in a white shirt, tie and an apron, which fit under his protruding pot belly, poured Billy a Harp and a Bushmills chaser as soon as he sat down at the bar. "We thought you'd taken sick," the sixty year-old bartender said to Billy as he said down. "You're past your usual hour. Alf here was getting antsy."

O'Donald was referring to the skinny older man, dressed in a wrinkled suit and a white shirt with a frayed collar, sitting next to Billy at the bar. Alf spent his days as a counselor working out of the office of one of the local psychiatrists, the physician himself an over-the-hill hack who provided medications to referrals from the state Medicaid program and tacked on an extra half-hour's fee for every client who would accept "case management" from Alf. His job was the one source of pride in the old alcoholic's life, but it wasn't enough to keep him from drinking every evening beside Billy in the pub. In fact, some days, such as this one, when he had no cases in the afternoon, Alf started his drinking early and didn't stop until the bar closed. He and Billy often closed it together. Billy was a friendly, if insecure drunk, who loved to regale anyone who'd listen, which was few, with stories of his ambitions to find the perfect big case that would get him back on top in the field of law. Alf, on the other hand was a curmudgeon, who, when he got talking, usually ranted against what he referred to as the authoritarian, dark ages mentality of the Catholic Church. Only they listened to each other, anymore.

"I've been working," Phelan said, not able to conceal the pride in his voice. "I've got a big case, remember?" He was talking to Alf now, since Tommy O'Donald had gone into the kitchen to put in his order for

# Chasing Tales

a corned beef sandwich, but he spoke loud enough for anyone within earshot to hear because he was in an expansive mood. Sometimes Tommy joined Billy and Alf in their conversation and sometimes, especially when the thread of their stories became difficult to follow because they had each become too drunk to keep a coherent story line, Tommy left them to themselves.

"I thought your client was charged with murder," Alf said, looking surprised. "Didn't the witness against him get killed?" He lit a new cigarette off of his old one, scattering ashes across the top of the bar and into his lap without seeming to notice. His hand shook, dropping more ashes into his beer.

"Now I'm defending Father Tom on the murder case," Phelan answered, his voice containing more than a hint of pride, as he took a long sip from his Harp.

"You ever defended a murder case before?" Alf asked, the skepticism evident in his gravelly, smoker's voice. He had a critical look on his wrinkled face.

"It's not any different than defending Father O'Flannery against the abuse charges, except the evidence isn't thirty years old."

"Jesus Billy, you didn't have a chance in hell when it was just an abuse case. What makes you think you've got a chance of winning now that its murder?"

Billy turned toward his drinking friend, his expression a mixture of anger and hurt. "Why don't you fuck yourself, Alf? You don't know anything about it. I used to be pretty good in court... in fact really good. I could get almost anyone off." As soon as he said it, Phelan's expression clouded over. He was remembering the last real criminal case he'd had, nearly fifteen years ago. He'd been successful all right. He'd been on top of the world after getting off his rich, powerful client, who'd been charged with assault against his ex-wife. Billy's whole firm thought he was a genius... until the client murdered his pregnant wife two months later. Billy hadn't taken a criminal case since. He downed the shot glass full of Bushmills and raised it toward Tommy O'Donald for a refill.

"OK, Billy, you're a good lawyer; what do I know anyway?" Alf said, patting Phelan on the shoulder, his tone apologetic. "The paper said they found the weapon on the scene and it had Father O'Flannery's fingerprints on it."

Billy had the feeling that Alf was hoping Father O'Flannery would be found guilty. He thought he could hear it in Alf's voice. He wasn't surprised, because every misfortune that befell the Church seemed to please Alf. But Billy wanted to share his enthusiasm about what he'd learned from the police fingerprint report that morning and Alf was his only audience. He looked around as if the pub might be filled with spies from the prosecution. The bar was already a third full and Tommy O'Donald was serving someone at the other end of the bar after bringing Billy his second Bushmills. "I've found some flaws in the police reports. The prints showed that the killer wore gloves but didn't wipe off either O'Flannery's or his sister's fingerprints."

"So?" Alf asked, a blank look on his face. He had followed Billy's lead and downed his own shot glass of Bushmills. He took a long drink from his beer, though he looked as if he was already drunk.

"So why would Father O'Flannery wear gloves and then leave his and his sister's fingerprints on the knife?"

"Maybe he forgot about the fingerprints."

"But he's careful enough to wear gloves?"

Alf took another sip of his beer. "You really think that's important?" He was holding his shot glass up to get Tommy O'Donald's attention. The pub contained a number of lunchtime customers and Tommy and the other two waiters were busy moving back and forth between the bar and the tables.

Billy did, in fact, think his insight about the fingerprints might be enough to raise a question in a jury's mind and derail any impression the district attorney was trying to give that it was an open and shut case. "It's exactly what someone who wanted the cops to pin it on Father O'Flannery would do."

Alf didn't look convinced, but Billy wasn't done. "Remember my private investigator?" he asked Alf, a smug look on his face.

"You mean the cop from Los Angeles?"

"Ex-cop but he's good. He's digging around for me. If we can find out that somebody else – another priest – was molesting kids, including Russell, then maybe that's our real killer."

Alf was still holding his shot glass and his face showed he was getting impatient. He always was a bundle of nervous energy, but now he seemed close to exploding. None of the bartenders or waiters had seemed to notice him or else they were deliberately letting him wait. Sometimes it was necessary to try to pace Alf. "How's the cop gonna pin it on another priest?" he asked.

"He's got a list of other priests who worked at St. Aloysius and he's talking to all the altar boys. If somebody molested Russell, he probably molested some of the other boys, too. Perverts like that don't just stop with one kid."

Alf slammed his glass down on the bar. "Jesus Christ can't a man get a drink in this place?" he shouted in the direction of Tommy O'Donald. The effort provoked a fit of coughing and his skinny frame was wracked with ugly, rasping coughs.

O'Donald hurried over to Phelan and Alf. "For Christ's sake Alf, are you ok? Christ almighty can't you behave yourself? " Tommy had seen Alf's temper before, but usually at night after more drinking than this. He took down the bottle of Bushmills and poured Alf another shot. One of the other waiters came up and put Phelan's sandwich in front of him. "Another beer, Billy?" Tommy asked.

Phelan nodded. He hadn't paid any attention to his friend's temper and coughing fit. "I think we've got a chance, Alf," he said before he bit into his sandwich.

Alf seemed mollified by getting his whiskey, a quick sip of which quieted his cough. He nodded in a distracted way at Billy's comment. "Good for you, Billy, good for you. Go get 'em." He took a long sip on his beer and then a light sip of whiskey. He closed his eyes and savored the taste as the liquid ran down his throat. A thin smile replaced his irritated scowl and stayed on his face as he treated himself to another long drink. "You're gonna be a hero, Billy," he mumbled.

## Chapter 17

When his cell phone rang, Nyles was on his way back to the Archdiocese office to ask the Monsignor why the name of Father Hurley was absent from the list he had been given of priests who had worked at St. Aloysius. The terrified voice on the phone belonged to his niece, Kaylee. Alan had come over to her parents' house to demand that Katherine come home. Katherine was due home from school in another half hour and Millie had called Sean to deal with Alan. Now the two men were out in front of the Sean's house yelling at each other.

Milton was only a short distance from North Quincy. The sky, which had earlier been bright and clear, had become grey with low hanging clouds, which were piled on each other like angry waves in a storm. The temperature had dropped by ten degrees. Nyles was at his brother's house in eight minutes. Sean and Millie and Kaylee and Alan were all standing on the front sidewalk and Sean and Alan were facing each other and looked as if they were about to square off. Everyone but Alan seemed relieved when Nyles got out of his car.

"Somebody called the cops – hooray," Alan said, casting an angry glance at Nyles as the ex-detective approached the tight little group.

Everyone was dressed in a heavy parka to ward off the cold.

"I called Uncle Nyles," Kaylee said. "I was afraid you and Dad were going to get in a fight."

Alan glared at his wife. "You're supposed to be on my side. You're my wife and Katherine's my daughter. Now that she's over here, everybody is poisoning her against me and you're on their side."

"Nobody is poisoning her against you, Alan," Millie answered. "We're just keeping her until everything settles down."

"You poisoned her against yourself," Sean said. In his parka he looked like the Pillsbury doughboy, but his voice was filled with rage and he stared accusingly at his son-in-law. "She's afraid of you. You ought to be in jail for what you did and it's only because of Kaylee that we haven't gone to the police." He moved toward Alan, his eyes flashing with anger, like an enraged bull.

Alan stepped closer to his father-in-law. His arms were at his sides but they were tensed, with his gloved hands balled into fists, as if he was ready to exchange blows with the older man.

Nyles stepped between the two men, as if he were a referee in a boxing match. "Everybody will go to jail if you have a fight out here on the street. This needs to get talked out, but not on the lawn." His voice was quiet but it carried enough of an air of authority to cause the two men to step back from each other.

"We don't need to talk," Alan said. "Kaylee and I both want Katherine back today. She's our daughter and these people have no legal right to keep her here." He was addressing Nyles as though he acknowledged him as their arbitrator.

"You can demand to get Katherine back," Nyles said, looking at Alan, "and Sean and Millie can refuse. The case will go to court. Do you really want all this brought out in court? Regardless of how it's settled it will be in the papers."

Alan's expression sobered. "I don't want anything in the papers, I have a reputation and a career to consider." He looked over at Kaylee. His expression was angry, but he also looked helpless.

Kaylee turned to Nyles. "I'm in favor of us having a talk, just like Uncle Nyles said."

"There's nothing to talk about," Sean said, still glaring at Alan.

"You haven't got a choice, Sean," Nyles said, quietly. "Katherine's Kaylee's daughter."

Sean turned his glare on Nyles. "Whose side are you on?"

Nyles held his brother's gaze. "I'm on Katherine's side – and all of yours," he answered. "Let's set something up. Maybe even get a mediator, if we can – a counselor or something. We need to have ground rules so this doesn't happen again." He turned to Kaylee. "And you need to talk to Katherine to find out what she thinks." He knew Katherine didn't want to go back to living with Alan but he wasn't sure she'd tell her mother that.

"I have to pick up Katherine from school," Millie said, sounding nervous. "It feels like it's going to start snowing pretty soon."

"Kaylee and I can pick her up," Alan interjected, his tone belligerent.

Kaylee looked at her uncle. "No, Alan. Let mom and me pick her up. We need to have this conversation before we bring her home."

Nyles nodded.

"What a bunch of bullshit," Alan said, looking angrily at all of them. He turned and stomped back to his car. "I want you home in time for dinner," be shouted over his shoulder at Kaylee.

"Will he take out his anger on you?" Nyles asked his niece, unable to conceal the worry in his voice.

"Only in words," she answered, looking sad. She managed a smile. "Thanks, Uncle Nyles."

"Me too," Sean said, a sheepish look on his face. "Thanks for being the level head."

"I'm going to pick up Katherine," Millie said.

"I'll drive," Kaylee offered and they headed toward her car in the driveway.

# Chasing Tales

## Chapter 18

Jimmy Gleason folded his newspaper and laid it down on the floor beside his chair, then picked up the tall whiskey and soda from the table next to him and sloshed the ice a few times while he gazed ruminatively at the wall before taking a long, slow sip. He could hear Tracy, his wife, on the telephone in the kitchen, talking to one of her friends about a shopping trip they were planning for the next day. Then he heard quick footsteps bouncing down the stairs from the second floor of the spacious Weston Colonial and he heard his 12-year-old daughter's cheery greeting to her mother as she removed something from the refrigerator to take upstairs with her to eat while she continued doing her homework. Jimmy didn't remember getting as much homework from St. Aloysius when he was in the sixth grade as his daughter, Kimberly, was getting from the public school in Weston, but she was a good student and the amount of homework never seemed to be a burden to her. He heard her skip back up the stairs, taking them two at a time, like a young doe full of youthful energy, on her way to her bedroom, where she had her own computer and television and stereo – a child's life Jimmy would never have dared dream of when he was her age and growing up as one of four children of an industrial machinist father and a waitress mother in Dorchester.

He couldn't stop himself from staring down at the headline in the paper next to him on the floor. Father Tom, his priest from childhood, was accused of murder and Jimmy could hardly believe it, even though it was right there in the paper. The story said that he was charged with killing Tim Russell, another name from Jimmy's past. According to the newspaper, Tim had accused Father Tom of molesting him as a child and the police claimed that the priest had killed the young man in order to keep him from testifying against him.

If Tim Russell had been molested by a priest at St. Aloysius, Jimmy knew that it hadn't been Father Tom. But it was that knowledge that made him anxious enough to pour himself a second, and larger, whiskey before he finished reading the story in the paper.

Jimmy looked around at the room. The wainscoting on the wall was dark brown walnut, with a beautiful soft sheen, more like silk than wood. He remembered finding a picture of the paneling in a magazine when he and Tracy had just moved into the house and were planning how they wanted to remodel it. He had never seen such a rich, satiny texture on the walls of a den and, in order to match the picture in the magazine, he and Tracy had painted the ceiling white and papered the walls above the wainscoting with a pale, Federalist blue paper. Beyond the open French doors, which separated the den from the hallway, he could see a corner of the sunken living room with its blue carpet, which matched the paper in the den. Outside, through the window, the snow was falling softly on the Currier and Ives landscape of pine trees and picket fences.

He had a good life. He had a good job as vice president of one of the largest independent banks in Eastern Massachusetts. The job had earned him his beautiful house. Maybe the job, or the money it brought him, had even earned him his beautiful wife – at least it hadn't hurt. Could he afford to risk any of what he had, to save Father Tom? His memories of the priest were filled with warm feelings connected to the encouragement Father Tom had given him as a child, the haven he had made his church for all the children who endured such hard, often mean and violent lives at home – although the safe haven had disappeared with Father Tom's leaving.

Why was it his responsibility to make the truth known? He took another long sip from his drink and let his gaze wander the room again. He still went to Mass every Sunday, often because it was expected of a bank vice president in his community, but sometimes to pray and to hope he was doing the right things in his life to insure his salvation when he died and to keep his family safe. He swirled the ice in his drink, then took another sip and pondered whether his piety was a sham. Even as the thought surfaced in his mind, he rejected it, more out of distaste than reason.

He was as good as the next man, he told himself, and besides, where were the others? He couldn't be the only one who had read that story and realized that Tim Russell had made a mistake. There had been other boys back then who were now grown men and knew the truth about what had happened at St. Aloysius. Others who, like him, knew what had happened in the presence of Father Tom's successor.

He forced himself to get out of his chair and walk into the kitchen where his wife had just hung up the telephone and was putting glasses in the dishwasher. She still wore her pink warm-up outfit from having gone to the gym earlier that day and her blonde hair was tied back in a ponytail. Jimmy stared at her. Even in the loose fitting gym clothes, her hips were shapely and her long legs, flat stomach and high, round breasts gave her the appearance of a movie starlet. He still felt the stirrings of desire when he looked at his wife, even after thirteen years of marriage.

She looked up at him and smiled. "Are you drunk? You've got a silly grin on your face."

"I'm just enjoying looking at my beautiful wife. You make me smile."

"Good. Then all this exercise at the gym is working."

Her playful expression turned serious. "Are you alright?"

He nodded.

"You look so serious, almost sad." She walked the four steps until she was directly in front of him and put her arms around his waist and gazed up at him, a look of concern on her face. "Everything's OK at the bank?" She worried about his position at the bank almost more than he did.

He nodded. What would she say if he told her he was considering doing something that could jeopardize his career, maybe even change the way she thought about him?

"Sure?"

"Everything is fine. I'm just a little tense tonight. A friend of mine from childhood was killed. The story was in the paper tonight. The priest from our church has been charged with killing him."

She stepped back, her mouth open in shock. "My God, that's terrible."

"Yes it is." And I know that it's not true, he thought.

"What worries you about it?"

He hesitated, looked around the room before answering. "Nothing. It just makes me feel bad. I knew both Tim Russell and Father Tom. It's hard to believe."

She took the glass from his hand, even though it was still one-third full. "Don't think about it. You can't do anything. Come to bed."

The alcohol had dulled his anxiety and raised his libido. He smiled crookedly at his wife. "I know how to take my mind off such troubling thoughts."

She jabbed him in the ribs. "Let's wait till Kimberly is done with her homework and has gone to bed."

He smiled at her and winked. "I'll be waiting." He turned and went back into the den and picked up the paper. If someone asks me about it I won't lie, he thought, but I'm not going to volunteer any information. He turned to the sports page and began reading about the Celtics' chances for a playoff spot.

# Chasing Tales

## Chapter 19

"The Monsignor couldn't have been a priest at St. Aloysius," Sister Mary Agnes said to Nyles. They were meeting at a Starbucks a few blocks from the chancery, because Sister Mary Agnes had said it would be better if they talked away from her office. The snow the night before had stopped by midnight and this morning was bright and clear with the promise that always followed a winter snowfall, although the temperature remained in the low twenties.

"How do you know?" Nyles was having a straight coffee and it amused him that Sister Mary Agnes had ordered a caramel latte with whipped cream. There were only a few other customers in the Starbucks at that time of day, each of them huddled over their steaming hot coffees as they enjoyed a respite from the frigid temperatures outside. Nyles had a momentary thought of the Starbucks near his house where he often stopped for a coffee in the morning, even now that he was retired. Everyone there was usually in baggy shorts and Hawaiian shirts. The Boston crowd wore overcoats or parkas over suits and ties.

"I've had to mail out his biography countless times when he spoke at conferences or when he testified for the church in court. He graduated from seminary and worked for the Archdiocese for a couple of months, then they sent him to law school and when he graduated he began working in the Canonical Law Office where he's been ever since."

"Mickey Ryan, one of the former altar boys said Father O'Flannery was replaced by a Father Hurley. He said Hurley only stayed a few months."

Sister Mary Agnes looked startled. "The list the Monsignor gave me to give to you didn't list any Hurley.

It's a pretty common name among Irish-American priests so it could be someone else," she said hopefully.

"Or the Monsignor could have left a few months at St. Aloysius off his resume."

She frowned. "Well – maybe. If he was only there a few months, he might not have thought it was important enough to put on his resume, but that's not like him. The Monsignor is scrupulously accurate in every detail of everything he does."

"Except the list of priests he had you give me."

She looked confused. "I don't know what to say."

"Can you find out if he was there? Or if not, is there another Hurley in the Archdiocese who served at St. Aloysius?"

She sipped on here latte. "You don't think the Monsignor was the one who abused those boys do you?" There was a note of dread in her voice.

"I know Father Tom didn't abuse anyone."

She looked thoughtful. "I'm having to go behind my boss' back. That's why I wanted to meet here."

"I hate putting you in that position, but I need all the help I can get."

"You and Cloris are both special to me." She looked thoughtful again "Most importantly, though, I know you believe in Father O'Flannery, so I do too. I don't want an innocent priest convicted of murder. I don't think the Monsignor would want that either, if he thought about it." A look of uncertainty crossed her face. "At least I hope he wouldn't." She finished her latte. "Good thing I don't ccme here very often. I'd be even bigger than I already am," she joked.

"I guess you'd better get back. If you find anything let me know."

"This isn't a substitute for dinner. You promised to take me, remember?"

"Of course. How about Thursday night? Would you know about Hurley's background by then?"

"I should. It's just a matter of checking records. I've got a favorite restaurant, if you're interested..." she left the offer dangling.

"Will I need a reservation?"

"I'm not sure."

"Better tell me the name then."

"Simco's."

Nyles choked, blowing coffee out of his mouth. "Simco's in Mattapan? On the bridge? On Blue Hill Parkway?"

"I haven't been there since high school, have you?" Simco's On the Bridge was a legendary hot dog stand that had been in the Mattapan section of Dorchester since Nyles' childhood. It was open till the early hours of the morning. When he was in high school everyone went there after whatever was going on Friday or Saturday night.

"The last time I was there was when I was a detective in Dorchester. That was more than thirty years ago."

"Well I've never lost the urge for one. O.K?"

"O.K. It's a date."

## Chapter 20

"I already talked to Gleason and Norris," Nate Hilton growled, "neither of them told me anything about being molested." He sat hunched over his desk, his thick forearms crossed and a wide scowl on his face, making him look like an angry Sumo wrestler.

"You asked them if they'd been molested by Father O'Flannery, not whether they'd ever been molested by *any* priest. Besides, they might not want to tell you the truth." Nyles sat opposite the Black detective and he was still in his overcoat because Hilton had made no offer to either take his coat or indicate where he should put it. He thought the detective hoped he'd just leave.

"You mean because I'm Black?" Hilton asked, his eyes narrowed while he waited for Nyles' answer.

"I mean because you're a cop." The race issue was a constant wedge between Hilton and him, but Nyles was determined to not let it preclude their working together.

It wasn't the answer that Hilton had expected... or even wanted. He gazed sourly at the skinny ex-detective across from him. "You're a cop, too." Even as he said it he knew that there was almost nothing about Nyles Monahan that reminded him of a policeman – other than that he was Irish. He was too small, too skinny, and two soft-spoken and thoughtful to be a detective. Maybe Monahan *would* have better luck with the two former altar boys than Nate had had.

"I'm not a cop anymore," Nyles answered.

"You want me to come along?"

Nyles looked over at the large, scowling, Black detective. "No. I can handle it; just give me their addresses."

"You Irish stick together – right?" Nate looked through a pile of papers inside a file folder on top of his desk. He pulled out a sheet of paper, looked it up and down, then tore another, smaller piece of paper from a pad on his desk and began copying down the two names and addresses.

"If that's your list of the altar boys and their addresses, why don't you just Xerox the whole thing and give it to me. Then I don't have to keep coming back for every address."

"Why don't you just get the fucking addresses yourself? I did the legwork for this information, so you can damn well get yourself down here to get them from me."

Nyles stared at the detective. "I'm just doing my job, Sergeant. Why are you giving me a hard time?"

"This was my case and now that asshole Spaulding has got it. By rights I ought to be investigating the homicide charge." Hilton looked embarrassed that he had revealed his jealousies.

"Spaulding is gonna botch his case," Nyles answered. He sensed the Black detective's vulnerability. Hilton wanted to prove he was as good as any White cop. Nyles could sympathize with his feeling, given the history of the Boston PD. "Father O'Flannery didn't kill Russell. I'm going to prove that either with your help or without it. I suspect I'll even find out who really did the killing. If you want to be part of that, then give me a hand."

Nate heaved himself out of his chair. "I'll copy the fucking list for you."


\*\*\*

Billy Norris looked embarrassed, then his expression changed to anger. "You cops have already

98

asked me about this," he said, stepping outside onto the porch of his one-story ranch-style house in South Weymouth. Billy had on a wool shirt and a pair of jeans. The sunlight had faded to a gray haze and the temperature was in the mid-thirties and dropping.

"I'm not a policeman," Nyles answered, although it still felt odd for him to say it. "I'm a private investigator and I work for the lawyer who's defending Father O'Flannery."

Norris stared at him, his jaw set, but a look of uncertainty in his eyes. "So why are you asking me about what happened when I was an altar boy?"

Nyles shivered. He marveled that Norris wasn't shivering in the frigid evening air. Maybe his anger was keeping him warm. "I know that Father O'Flannery didn't molest you, Billy. I'm trying to find out if any other priests who worked at St. Aloysius bothered any of the boys. I'm talking to everyone, even if they already talked to the police."

Norris looked as if he'd suddenly become aware of the cold. He shivered dramatically and hunched his shoulders, as if trying to hide himself from the freezing night air, then looked longingly at the door to his house. "What's that got to do with anything now? The past is the past. I'm married; I've got three kids, a good job. I'm not trying to stir up any trouble for the Church."

"You want to go inside and talk?" Nyles asked. As long as they remained outside on the porch, he knew that Norris would try to end the conversation. Inside they could keep talking until Nyles learned something.

"My wife's inside," Norris said, as if in explanation.

"Then maybe you just want to tell me what happened."

Norris looked around, stamping his feet, as if to stay warm, but he seemed angry as he did it. "I haven't got anything to say." He stuck out his hand. "Pleased to meet you Mr. Monahan. I'm going back inside."

Nyles pulled one of Billy Phelan's business cards out of his pocket. "This is Father O'Flannery's lawyer. My cell phone number is on the back. If you want to say anything give me a call – or talk to Mr. Phelan. Even if you won't appear in court, we're interested in what you've got to say. It could be the information that gets Father O'Flannery off, even if it never comes up in court."

Norris looked hesitant, but then he took the card. "Nice to meet you," he said, turning his back and opening his front door.

Nyles walked back out to the street and got into his car.

## Chapter 21

Nyles couldn't put his finger on what the difference was, but he noticed something had changed as soon as he walked into his brother's house. Sean was watching television in the den, as usual, and Millie was cutting carrots for the salad in the kitchen and the dining room table was already set. Staring at it, Nyles suddenly realized what the difference was: there were only three places.

"Katherine's not here tonight?" he asked Millie, while he hung up his coat.

There was a moment of silence. before Millie answered. "She's gone back to Kaylee's house."

"For the evening or for good?"

"For good – or at least for awhile." She hung her head and sighed. "Kaylee insisted. We couldn't do anything."

Nyles' anger was muted by the defeated look on Millie's face. Who should he be mad at? A memory of the eleven-year old's vehement statement of hatred against her stepfather leapt into his mind but he reminded himself that he was only Katherine's great uncle. Decisions belonged with the girl's mother and grandparents, not with him.

Nyles wanted to ask Millie what Sean had thought - what had happened to his brother's threats to call the police if Alan took Katherine back? But he could ask Sean himself. He finished hanging up his coat and walked into the den, where Sean was watching the Bruins lose to the Pittsburgh Penguins. Sean was sitting in his favorite chair in front of the TV and he had a coke on the table next to him. Nyles sat down on the couch.

"Kaylee took Katherine back home," Nyles said, leaving his comment hanging in mid-air.

Sean took a long sip from his coke before he answered. "We tried to talk her out of it. She wouldn't listen to either of us." He looked over at Nyles. "She's afraid Alan will leave her."

Nyles didn't respond, except to look back at his brother, his eyebrows arched in question.

Sean shifted uncomfortably under his brother's unwavering gaze. "What did you want me to do? Call the police?" Sean's tone was defensive and when he looked at his brother, his eyes revealed his dismay.

"Nobody's committed any crime," Nyles answered.

"What then?"

"Call social services. Tell them you think Alan may be endangering Katherine and ask them to open a case."

"Will they?"

"I don't know. It can't hurt." He stared at the television. Boston had scored another goal and the score was now 3-2 in favor of Pittsburgh. "Was there a fight between you and Kaylee?"

"She wouldn't fight. She just had her mind made up. I would have had to do something physical to stop her. She knew I wouldn't do that."

"Then keep talking to her. In the long run, Kaylee's got to be convinced that being with Alan is the wrong thing for her daughter."

"You mean she should leave Alan?"

"I thought that was what you wanted."

"I'm not sure anymore. I've always been against divorce."

Nyles had never been religious because of his father's influence, but Sean had been raised by their mother and Nyles knew what his brother's religion meant to him and to Millie. Divorce was something to be ashamed of in their family. "She has to think of her daughter," he said.

"She says Alan has a drinking problem."

"He probably does, but that's not why he bothers your granddaughter."

"Booze can make you lose control. I know that from experience"

Nyles knew his brother was rationalizing "His behavior toward Katherine was out of line even when he was sober."

His brother rubbed his hand through his thinning hair. "Maybe not. Maybe if he stops drinking…"

Nyles was acutely aware of how little expertise he had when it came to such intimate family matters, but he was used to making decisions under difficult circumstances and he was probably more objective than either his brother or his wife. "Kaylee doesn't want to see the truth because she may lose her marriage if she does. You and Millie don't want to see Kaylee hurt. But all of you need to keep Katherine's safety in mind. She's in danger and she can't defend herself. She's a kid and she's counting on the adults in her life to protect her."

"Jesus Nyles. I can only do the best I can do. She's my granddaughter, but she's Kaylee's daughter. I can't fight my own daughter can I?" Sean's voice was pleading.

"If Kaylee isn't able to see the situation clearly, then you have to fight her. Katherine has to depend on someone."

Sean shook his head. "I can't figure it out right now." He reached for his glass of coke and took a long slow sip. "I hear you, but I have to think."

Nyles was frustrated by his brother's ineffectualness, but the expression of pain on Sean's face stopped him from pressing any further. "O.K. Just don't think the problem is going to go away. There's a little girl's future at stake." He couldn't help but think that his brother's granddaughter was in danger and he was frightened.

# Chasing Tales

## Chapter 22

The redheaded woman three seats down the bar was listening to him, a fact of which Billy Phelan was acutely aware. Unescorted women at the Hibernia were a rarity and when they were there, they were usually drinkers on a mission – often newly divorced middle-aged women looking for companionship – something to replace the vacuum that had opened up in their lives when their marriages had ended. Billy was past middle age, but he wasn't too old for the woman at the bar and he was a lawyer. Women were attracted to his profession because they thought it meant he had money, which he knew wasn't true, but he wasn't going to advertise the fact.

He'd been talking about his case to Tommy, when the bartender had time between serving other customers, and Alf, who had an irritating habit of hanging on Billy's shoulder when he was drunk, and another man Billy didn't know, but who seemed immensely interested in a story about a priest who was accused of murder. Among the crowd at the bar, it gave Billy a certain stature to be the priest's lawyer and he knew that and milked it as much as he could. Tonight, he wanted to let the woman sitting down the bar know that he was involved in an important case.

"I've got an investigator who's doing my legwork for me," Billy said, expansively. He'd had three beers already, each of them chased with a shot of Bushmills. "My investigator has found out that there was another priest fooling around with those altar boys back then. He's even got a name. That other priest could be Tim Russell's real killer. Imagine if I spring that on the jury..." He risked a glance down the bar. He had the redheaded woman's attention.

"You mean you think you can throw the blame on another priest? For both the abuse and the murder?" the stranger asked.

"That's how it's shaping up. If this other priest molested a bunch of altar boys at St. Aloysius back in the early eighties, then he's probably the one who killed Russell in order to keep him quiet."

"But I thought they found the murder weapon at Russell's house," Alf interrupted. He was drinking Harp himself, though it wasn't clear how many he'd had, since he'd been drinking well before Billy Phelan had arrived at the pub. He fidgeted in his usual, wound-up nervous way, as if a coiled spring inside was letting go in fits and starts. Billy Phelan's agitation always left after his first drink, but Alf's was a permanent part of his personality.

"They did," Phelan answered. He raised his voice so the woman sitting down the bar could hear him. "Remember, I figured out that somebody else – the killer, I assume – left the knife at Russell's house to frame Father O'Flannery. The killer's own fingerprints weren't on the knife because he wore gloves. But O'Flannery and his sister's were. They were left on the knife in order to frame the Father."

"So who's this other priest?" the stranger asked. The woman at the bar had moved one seat nearer to hear the conversation. She appeared to be captivated.

Phelan had a sly expression on his face. "I've got an idea who it is – from something my investigator told me." He caught the woman's eye and winked and she smiled at him in return. "I'll let you know after Thursday. That's when my investigator is going to tell me for sure who it is."

"Your investigator is going to tell you who killed Tim Russell?" Alf asked. His words were a little slurred.

# Chasing Tales

"Why wait till Thursday? What's so damn important about Thursday?" He was clutching at Billy's arm.

"Calm down, Alf." Billy said, pulling his arm away. "Thursday is when my investigator's contact in the Archdiocese tells him if the priest he's identified as a possible killer was ever assigned to St. Aloysius"

"Why not tell you now? I don't see why you need to wait till Thursday," Alf said. His words were followed by a series of hacking coughs, which he countered with a long swallow of beer.

Billy leaned his head toward Tommy, who was listening across the bar, then looked toward Alf. Before he said anything he raised his eyes and smiled at the redhead, hoping she'd move closer to hear what he had to say, but she didn't move. "Someone pretty high up in the Church might be involved. He's trying to conceal the fact that he was a priest at St. Aloysius."

"You'll be a hero," Alf said, smiling uncertainly. His fingers were drumming nervously on the top of the bar as he talked.

"The Church will be out to get you," Tommy O'Donald said from behind the bar. "A priest is one thing, but if you're accusing someone in the Archdiocese hierarchy, they'll fight you tooth and nail."

"They don't scare me," Billy answered. "I'm just interested in getting at the truth." He stole another glance down the bar. The woman was still smiling at him - a kind of half-smile - but he could tell she was impressed. He looked around, first at Alf, then at the stranger, who was taking a long drink from his pint of Guinness, then he looked over at Tommy, who was straightening up to go attend to someone else at the bar. "Tommy, bring me another one and bring another one for this lass over her." He nodded at the woman who sat a few barstools away from him. She nodded back, smiling.

Billy got up from his seat and moved around Alf and sat down next to the redheaded woman. He amazed himself with his boldness. The Father O'Flannery case was giving him confidence and he could feel it. He was going to be back on top pretty soon and when he was, he wouldn't give the time of day to some bar broad like this redhead, but for now, why not enjoy his success?

"You look lonely," Billy said to the woman.

"I'm not lonely, I'm fascinated. I didn't know lawyers came into this place."

"We get all kinds in here," he said, taking a sip of the new beer Tommy had set down in front of him. "I don't mind entertaining some of the boys with my stories, but I'm working on a pretty important case. I don't really tell the details to anyone here at the bar."

"You mean you know who the person in the Archdiocese is?"

"You were paying attention, I see."

"I couldn't help it. You make the case sound so interesting."

Billy beamed. "Have this drink on me. Maybe we can go somewhere more private and I can tell you more about the case."

# Chasing Tales

## Chapter 23

Nyles was impressed by the opulence of Jimmy Gleason's house, although, since the house was located in the upscale suburb of Weston, he wondered why he was surprised. The home was relatively new, but it had the look of an antique Colonial, with tall pine trees lining the winding driveway leading up to the front door He reminded himself that not everyone who grew up in a working class neighborhood such as Dorchester remained working class. It was the American tradition to outdistance one's parents in the upward mobility race, but in the last twenty years that scenario had been the exception more than the rule and Jimmy Gleason was one of those exceptions.

Nyles knew that Gleason hadn't been receptive to Nate Hilton when the detective had questioned him earlier, but Jimmy's reaction might have been to Nate's race, or just to the fact that he was a policeman and if Hilton had been as hostile as he'd been so far to Nyles, it might have been the detective's attitude that had fostered the cold shoulder from Gleason. I'll soon find out, Nyles thought to himself as he pressed the bell to Gleason's front door. When Nyles had phoned yesterday, Gleason had indicated he would be working at home until noon today and that he preferred talking to Nyles there, rather than at the bank where he held the position of vice president.

Gleason was dressed for work, with a nicely starched, light blue shirt, a conservatively striped tie and dark slacks, but no coat. The look on his face conveyed the message that he had sacrificed a morning at work in order to comply with Nyles' request for an interview and he wasn't happy about it. He was a tall, well-built man, good-looking with a ruggedly handsome face and when he

109

smiled he showed white, even teeth, but the wrinkles in his brow and the squint in his eyes suggested he was uncomfortable with the visit. He brought Nyles into a beautifully paneled office-den off of the living room and offered him a seat in one of two large, well-stuffed leather chairs, which reminded Nyles of a banker's office.

"I'm having coffee, would you like some?" Gleason asked before he sat down.

Despite having already had two cups that morning, Nyles accepted his host's offer. Gleason would tell him more if the conversation was informal and if they had a cup of coffee together their talk would less resemble the interrogation to which he suspected Detective Hilton had subjected the potential witness. He heard Gleason talking to someone outside the room and then the man returned, saying the housekeeper would bring Nyles coffee and explaining, although Nyles hadn't asked, that his wife was out for the morning, donating time to a charity she sponsored.

"You must remember Father O'Flannery," Nyles said, as a way of opening the conversation. "I'm working for the lawyer who is representing him. He's on trial for murder."

Gleason's expression became grim and he shook his head, sadly. "Of course I remember Father Tom and I've read about the case, but I assumed it would all get cleared up; it couldn't be true."

"What couldn't be true?"

"That Father Tom would kill anyone – Tim Russell in particular – but anyone. Father Tom was a wonderful priest and a positive influence on all of us who went to St. Aloysius."

"Tim Russell accused the Father of molesting him. That's one of the reasons Father Tom is a suspect in his murder."

Gleason appeared incensed. "I told the police that that was ridiculous. Father Tom was always perfectly well behaved around us boys, including Tim Russell. He wasn't that kind of priest."

"But some were," Nyles said, his voice flat as if he were stating a fact.

"Some were what?" There was an edge of anxiety in Gleason's voice.

"That kind of priest. Some priests did molest boys. Tim Russell, for instance, may have been molested by a priest; it just wasn't Father Tom."

Gleason looked startled by Nyles' statement, but just then someone the banker addressed as Juanita entered with a tray on which was laid out a cup of coffee and two small china bowls, one filled with milk and the other sugar. She set the tray down on a table next to Nyles and he picked up the coffee and took a sip.

"I wasn't a good friend of Tim. He was a lot younger than I was," Gleason said. He had recovered his composure but there was a defensive tone to this voice that hadn't been there before.

"Do you remember Father Hurley?" Nyles asked.

Jimmy stared at the floor. Nyles was getting ready to repeat the question when Gleason suddenly spoke. "He was one of those priests you mentioned."

Nyles waited for him to elaborate

"He molested some of the boys," Jimmy said, looking away from Nyles' penetrating gaze. His voice was barely audible.

"How do you know?"

Gleason took a long breath then he sank into his chair in an attitude of defeat. "I was one of them. I made a complaint to the Church – or my parents did." His tone made it sound as if the admission had been forced from him.

"Can you tell me about it?

"It was an unpleasant episode in my life. I prefer not to talk about it." Gleason didn't look embarrassed, but his expression was resolute.

"Father Tom's future may depend on it."

"What does Father Hurley have to do with Father Tom's case?"

"I think it may have been Father Hurley who molested Tim Russell. If I can show that, or at least make a strong case for it, it will lessen the evidence against Father Tom."

Gleason looked around the room. He appeared irritated. " Goddamnit. I don't like to talk about this and I sure as hell am not prepared to say something in court about being molested as a child. I'm a bank vice president, for God's sake. I can't look like my past life was a soap opera."

"You wouldn't have to testify unless you wanted to. I just need information right now. I'm trying to find Tim Russell's killer so Father Tom can go free."

"You mean you think Father Hurley killed Tim Russell?"

"I think whoever molested Russell killed him and tried to make it look like it was Father Tom."

Gleason took another deep breath. He got out of his chair and opened a drawer to his desk. He pulled out a pack of cigarettes and a lighter. "I hope you don't mind. I'm trying to quit – since New Years – but this merits a cigarette."

Nyles nodded.

"Father Hurley was one of those priests you were talking about. He put his hands all over me and most of the other boys. He brought me up to his bedroom a few times. At first we just talked but then he wanted us to take a nap together. We did that a few times, but nothing happened except he put his arm around me, and things like that. Then he started saying we needed to get undressed to be more comfortable. I still didn't know what he was doing. I went along with it. Finally, he began to touch me. When I got frightened he told me it was all right – that he did it with lots of the boys. When I finally figured out that what he was doing was wrong, I told my parents. I also told some of the other boys and I found out I wasn't the only one. Most of the boys I talked to said they told him to fuck off or ran away from him. I was embarrassed that it took so long for me to figure out what he was doing. I still am."

"What happened after you told your parents?"

"They complained to the Bishop. I guess a lot of people did. Father Hurley got transferred or sacked; I don't know what, but reading about how Cardinal Law handled things back then, I guess he probably just got transferred."

"No one brought a law suit against the Church?"

"My parents were faithful Catholics. They wouldn't even have considered a lawsuit. It would have brought shame on the Church. Things were different back then."

"Did you ever hear anything more about Father Hurley?

Jimmy shook his head. "Nothing."

"Do you know Monsignor Hurley with the Archdiocese offices?"

Jimmy shook his head and his face showed his surprise. "Is that him? Did they kick him upstairs?"

"I don't know. There's a man by that name in the Archdiocese hierarchy. In fact he's the one in charge of abuse cases for the Church. But I don't know if it's the same person."

Gleason's anger flared again. "Jesus. That would be just like the Church wouldn't it? Put the fox in charge of the hen house."

"I don't know if it's the same person or just a coincidence of names. If I brought you the man's picture, would you be able to identify him?

Gleason's face showed his alarm. "I can't do that. I'm not going to get involved. I'm an important person in the business and social world, Mr. Monahan. I don't want Father Tom hurt, but I can't jeopardize my position. It could even hurt my marriage and I don't want that."

"You'd let an innocent priest go to jail to protect your reputation?"

"I've put that episode behind me and I've made a success of my life. I'm not going to put that in danger. You'll have to find another way to help Father Tom. I hope you understand."

Nyles did understand and it made him wonder about the value of Gleason's Catholic education. He was a faithful churchgoer, yet he was more concerned with his own financial position than the welfare of Father Tom and he was willing to turn his back on the truth if revealing it compromised his reputation. But then the Church, in the person of Father Hurley and Cardinal Law had never given Jimmy Gleason a clear message on the value of truth.

Nyles stood. "Don't make a decision right now. Think about it for a while. I'll be back in touch. Thank you for your time and candor, Mr. Gleason."

# Chasing Tales

## Chapter 24

Nyles hung up the telephone. After talking to Jimmy Gleason the day before, he had been encouraged, but just now, after hearing Sister Mary Agnes say she had important information about who Father Hurley was, he was exhilarated. He picked up the phone and dialed Cloris in California. It was only noon in Los Angeles and she wouldn't expect his call until evening – late night in Boston – but he wanted to share his thoughts with her.

Cloris was surprised and pleased to hear his voice. He told her about his upcoming date that evening with her old friend, Mary MacDonald.

"At Simco's? You mean it's still there?" Cloris asked. They had visited the hotdog stand many times together during high school.

"I hope so. Actually I don't think either Mary or I checked to be sure it is. But we'll find out. Besides, it's an institution. It's got to be there."

"Are you making progress?" Cloris' voice betrayed her concern.

"It's all circumstantial but I'm building a case for the killer being someone else who molested that boy and then killed him and blamed it on Father Tom."

"I have faith in you, Nyles. I'm sure Father Tom does too."

"Mary is a big help. She's got some information for me that she says could change everything for Father Tom."

"Really? Oh that's wonderful." Nyles could hear the relief in his wife's voice. Father Tom was as close to her as he was to Nyles. Maybe closer.

"I know you can help him, Nyles."

"I hope so." He was feeling more confident than he had been at any time since arriving in Boston, but he knew that he was fighting an uphill battle against almost overwhelming circumstantial and physical evidence.

"You can, dear."

They said good-bye.

*\*\*\**

Monsignor Andrew Hurley sat as expressionless as a stone statue, listening to Sister Mary Agnes telling him why she couldn't stay late and finish the report he had asked her to work on. Her mother was waiting for her, she said, Mary having promised to take her to dinner that night. Finally the Monsignor gave a curt nod, providing his administrative assistant permission to leave. Not everyone put the Church ahead of everything else, he thought, then he caught himself. I'm indulging in the sin of pride, he thought to himself and I am the last one who has a right to feel proud of myself, knowing the terrible sins in which I have taken part. He put his head in his hands and then straightened up again and began to pray. "Father forgive me for what I have done and for what I'm about to do."

*\*\*\**

Sister Mary Agnes stepped out into the frigid evening air, shivering as she drew her coat up around her neck. It was already dark outside. She walked across the dark, glistening pavement of the parking lot, which resembled the surface of a dark pond in the light from the bright lampposts, feeling a mixture of fear and excitement and stealing glances to either side to see if she was being watched. She gave a small prayer of thanks for the

# Chasing Tales

Chancery parking lot being well lit. She was being silly, she admonished herself, because she was doing nothing different tonight than she did every night. No one else could know that instead of driving home to be with her mother, she was headed for the Brighton T-stop, where she would take the Green Line, then transfer to the Red Line and travel to Lower Mills to meet Nyles Monahan.

She started the car and pulled out of the parking lot. Behind her, another car started a moment later, hanging back until Sister Mary's Volkswagen pulled onto Commonwealth Ave and then following a discreet distance behind.

At the T-station, a closely packed throng of office workers and evening shoppers pushed toward the open door of the train, engulfing Sister Mary in their midst. She felt uncomfortable at the crush of bodies, which moved forward like cows being herded toward a waiting cattle car and obscured her view of anyone except those passengers immediately next to her, keeping her from being able to identify who else was entering the train. She searched her mind for why she should be feeling anxious and realized that she had always sensed something ominous in the Monsignor's manner, which now caused her to fear his discovery of what amounted to her theft of documents from the Chancery. Her surreptitious assistance to Nyles Monahan, behind her superior's back, had seemed noble and even adventurous when she'd agreed to participate in it, but now she felt a growing sense of dread. She tried to reassure herself that she had no reason to be afraid. No one but Nyles was aware of the information she had taken from the Archdiocese record room and she had kept it especially secret from the Monsignor, since it was information that was directly related to him.

# Chasing Tales

She took a seat at the end of the car, leaning her back against the intersection of the side and the end of the car then anxiously leaning forward and craning her neck to survey the other passengers. After a moment she leaned back again and closed her eyes, reassured that she knew no one on the train. Another wave of anxiety caused her to reopen her eyes and she thought she saw someone whose momentarily glimpsed profile looked familiar, as they started to get up and then sat back down, at the other end of the car. She craned her neck again but could not see anything except a man, his overcoat collar pulled high up on his neck and his face completely obscured. She considered whether to get up and walk forward, giving herself a better view, then realized she was acting silly. There was no reason to act like a fool, she thought, behaving like one of those disturbed old women who sometimes rode the train, pacing and muttering to themselves. Instead, she reassured herself that her imagination had played a trick on her and she leaned back and closed her eyes again.

By the time she had transferred to the Red Line at Downtown Crossing, Sister Mary Agnes had dismissed her earlier fears and she had managed to doze for a few minutes before waking with a start to look around anxiously, and then feeling reassured that no one had approached her in any threatening way. She no longer could see the vaguely familiar head of the man with the coat pulled up around his chin and she assumed he had innocently disembarked at one of the stops along the route. When she boarded the Red Line train she picked a similar seat at the end of the train and lay back, closing her eyes for the long trip to Lower Mills station. She did not see the tall man with the glasses, his long overcoat fastened securely beneath his chin, slip into her car just as the doors were closing. And falling into a light doze, she was unaware when, after the first stop, he rose from his seat and began moving toward the sleeping nun at the end of the train car.

*\*\*\**

Nyles pulled up into the parking lot of the Red Line T-stop at the edge of the Milton-Dorchester town line. Sister Mary Agnes had not wanted him to pick her up at her work, just in case someone might see the two of them together. The information she'd gathered was not something Monsignor Hurley, her immediate superior, would want her to give to Nyles. They'd agreed that taking the T would be the best method of concealing her destination and they both remembered the Lower Mills stop where the two of them and Cloris used to catch the train into downtown. It was only a short drive from there to Simco's, where they were planning to treat themselves to Boston's best hotdogs.

The T-stop had changed little since when Nyles had come there to catch the train for Southie with his father or to catch a lift up to Mattapan or into downtown. There was a large parking lot that hadn't been there before, but the covered benches were still next to the tracks in the shadow of the bridge, which carried the automobile traffic above them, and within view of the old brick Baker's chocolate factory, which stood like a medieval castle on the bank of the rushing Neponset river – a river that had provided power to the first chocolate mill in America. The chocolate factory had been the defining landmark in the area and had now been turned into apartments.

Nyles left his car and walked to the wooden platform at the side of the tracks. The small group of people who shared the stop included African-Americans of mixed ages and several older Whites. The racial groups were separated like distant islands, divided by an ocean of suspicion and standing apart from both groups were three or four young white people in their teens, with backpacks and faded jeans, leather coats and spikey metal jewelry, probably heading into town for an evening's entertainment. The young people were laughing and horsing around with each other, while members of the other two groups stood as isolated, silent individuals within their respective circles, apparently gaining security from the sense of belonging within their own racial group, but not enough security to risk socializing with one another. Nyles stood apart from all of them, memories of his younger years parading across his mind like an army of ghosts, while he gazed hopefully up the track for a sign of the approaching train.

The train came rattling down the track, looking as if it was going to barrel right past the T-stop, then suddenly it decelerated and came screeching to a stop in front of the knot of people standing on the dock. At the same time, a Boston PD car and an ambulance, each of them with its multicolored lights flashing, came careening into the parking lot and jammed to a halt next to the train. The waiting passengers were wide-eyed and Nyles tried to quell the feeling of dread that had begun to spread, like a cancer in the pit of his stomach, as he watched the officers clear a path through the passengers and enter the train car. Nyles elbowed his way to the door of the train.

Sister Mary Agnes was seated on a bench at the end of the car, her head leaning against the side of the train. Her feet were splayed wide and the front of her coat was wet with blood, as was the floor beneath her seat. Two policemen and a train guard stood in front of her.

# Chasing Tales

Behind him, Nyles could hear the jangle of the wheels of a stretcher as it bumped across the pavement. He pushed himself through the passengers gathered at the door, who were pushing and shoving each other to get a look inside the car. He didn't need to ask if Mary MacDonald was dead, he could see that she was, from twenty feet away. Even as he hurried to her side, he snapped at one of the uniformed cops, "For God's sake don't let any of those passengers who were in the car leave." He had gone into his police detective mode without thinking but beneath the automatic actions he was overwhelmed by the thought that a person he cared deeply about was dead because of him.

The authority in Nyles' voice caused the young policeman to automatically obey, until he stopped to look at Nyles and realized he wasn't a police officer. "Who the fuck…?" the young policeman sputtered.

His older partner, a fortyish uniformed officer with a lined, red face and a sizeable paunch, turned to the young cop. "The man's right – go do it," the older cop said. "Now who the hell are you?" he asked Nyles.

Nyles put aside the guilt that Mary's death provoked in him and explained that he had been waiting for the nun and that they were friends. He told the older cop that he was a retired policeman himself and a former member of the Boston PD, hoping that the information would have a positive effect on the man's attitude toward him.

"This hasn't happened on this run in a couple of years," the cop said, shaking his head. "It's always these old women who these damn perps prey on. The bastards don't even care if it's a nun. They just want her money."

"She's still got her purse," Nyles said.

The older cop just looked at him.

The EMTs were checking Sister Mary Agnes. The older cop told them to leave her on the train. They couldn't hold the train at the station indefinitely because another train would be coming down the same track in another twenty minutes, but they didn't want to disturb the body until the crime scene investigation team had examined it.

The train departed, rattling and swaying down the tracks with the car in which Sister Mary Agnes had been murdered sealed off with crime scene tape. The younger uniformed cop and one of the EMTs rode along with the body in the empty car. The crime scene crew would examine both the body and the car when it arrived back at the yard and could be separated from the rest of the train. Nyles waited with the older uniformed officers and the herd of passengers, who all seemed to be talking on cell phones and getting more irritated by the minute. Finally an unmarked car pulled up and two detectives emerged.

Neither detective was familiar to Nyles. The older uniformed cop handed over his clipboard to the younger detective, who seemed to be in charge, filled him in on the bare bones of the case and the state of the body, then introduced Nyles, mentioning his background as a detective. Nyles told the young detective who Mary MacDonald was, where she worked, and why she had been on the train. When he was asked if he knew anyone who might want to kill the nun, he didn't hesitate.

"She had found out some information relevant to a murder case on which I'm doing some private investigating," he told Detective Arnold Leeper, a young, good looking detective whose earnestness was almost disarming and who seemed impressed that Nyles had spent over thirty years with the LAPD as a homicide detective. "The person she was keeping that information secret from was her boss, Monsignor Hurley, with the Boston Archdiccese."

"Christ almighty," Detective Leeper said, shaking his head. "You don't think someone like that had something to do with this?"

"He wasn't among the passengers. I already checked that out. And from what I've heard people saying, Sister Mary Agnes was alive until at least one stop before this one. Assuming the killer didn't stay on the train, in which case he or she would be among these people, then he got off at the previous stop. I'd ask if any of these people saw anyone who looked like a priest if I were you."

The young detective nodded. His partner, who was about the same age, was still questioning people and he went over and talked to him. A small, elderly, Black woman had come forward, volunteering that she had seen a man talking to the victim.

Nyles followed Leeper, staying close enough to overhear the old woman telling him that she hadn't thought the man who had been talking to Mary was a priest, but that she couldn't be sure because his clothes were covered by an overcoat. When Detective Leeper noticed that Nyles was shadowing him, he gave him a long, pointed look , sufficient to convey the message that he was not welcome. Reluctantly, Nyles moved away.

They all turned when another car came screeching into the parking lot and when it stopped, Nate Hilton emerged, an eager look on his face.

"Hilton? What are you doing here?" Detective Leeper asked, sounding irritated.

Hilton nodded toward Nyles. "Monahan here is involved in a case I'm working on. I heard his name mentioned on the radio."

"This isn't Task Force business," Leeper said, looking suspicious.

"I'm already involved, so don't get on your high horse," Hilton said, scowling at the younger detective.

Leeper narrowed his eyes and his voice was even when he spoke. "The murder is mine. You need information from this crime for something you're working on, fine, you go through me. You find out anything, you give it to me – OK?"

"Can't we just all get along?" Hilton said, his face twisted into a sarcastic grin.

"Those are the rules," Detective Leeper said, unsmiling.

"OK. Just let me talk to Monahan here." He motioned for Nyles, who was waiting to see who won the little fight over authority between the two cops, to move over near his car. "This connected to O'Flannery's case?" he asked when they were out of earshot.

"I'm willing to bet whoever did this is the same person who killed Tim Russell," Nyles said, hoping such candor wouldn't come back to haunt him.

A satisfied smile crossed Hilton's face. "Then you and I are gonna scratch each others' backs on this one, Monahan. You know the old saying, 'you show me yours and I'll show you mine.' Tell me what you know and I'll tell you what else I know."

"I thought you already told me everything you knew," Nyles said, even though he knew it wasn't true.

Hilton leered at him. "You Goddamned Micks always underestimate Black cops."

# Chasing Tales

## Chapter 25

Roseanne Compton was a tiny, bird-like Black woman in her early seventies, who, despite her age, still worked as a nurse for the Boston Head Start office, which was downtown near Chinatown and the City Hospital. She had been the only witness who had gotten a good look at the man who might have murdered Sister Mary Agnes, but she had been so anxious to get home to her husband that she had given only a cursory description to Detective Leeper at the crime scene and he had scheduled an interview with her at her home later in the evening.

Mrs. Compton rode the Red Line home every evening to her house in Lower Mills where she lived with her disabled husband and her forty-one year old daughter who was in-between marriages and had come home to live with her parents until she got back on her feet, financially. Mrs. Compton had followed the same routine, coming home on the train, every weekday, except holidays, for the last 5 years, which was why she hadn't wanted to talk to the police at any great length while she was still at the train station.

Detective Arnold Leeper found out all this information within the first two minutes of their conversation. He also found out that the elderly African – American nurse, who had been sitting across the aisle from Sister Mary Agnes when she was stabbed to death, had no hesitation in giving her account of who she thought had killed the nun.

"They were both already on the train when I got on," Roseanne said, eyeing Detective Leeper with distrust, although as far as he knew he had done nothing to make her suspicious of him. Maybe she looked at everyone that way, he thought; or maybe it was because he was cop.

# Chasing Tales

They were sitting in her living room on the first floor of her three-story home in Dorchester. The house was furnished in old, but well-kept furniture with a large television set occupying one side of the room. Roseanne's husband, who was in wheelchair, had been in the living room watching the television when the detective had arrived, but he'd wheeled himself into the kitchen within the first few seconds of the interview without so much as a hello to Leeper. Mrs. Compton had explained that her daughter wasn't home and, despite still seeming wary, had offered the detective a cup of coffee, which he had accepted and was drinking while they talked.

"But they were talking to each other?" the detective asked.

"He was doing most of the talking. Finally, she turned away from him, as if she didn't want to talk any more."

"What did he do?"

"If you let me continue, I'll tell you," the woman said, as if she was chiding a child.

The detective almost laughed. He was reminded of conversations he'd had with his grandmother.

"He just sat there with his hands in his pockets looking at the floor," she continued. "For awhile he even had his eyes closed. I didn't want to stare so I didn't watch them all the time, but when we got to the Mattapan stop he got up and left. There were a lot of people getting on and I was paying attention to my bag, but when the train started off again I looked over at the woman and I saw the blood all over the seat and the floor. Some other people saw it about the same time."

"So someone called the conductor?"

"Um huh. With that red phone at the end of the car."

"But nobody came?"

"No. But when we got to Lower Mills, the police were there."

Leeper looked down at his notes. "You said he was tall and slim, wearing an overcoat. You thought his pants were dark, maybe black and his shoes, also. He didn't wear a hat and he had thinning hair and wore glasses. He might have been in his fifties or older. Is that right?"

She nodded and looked impressed that he had gotten her description down almost word for word. "That's exactly right, detective."

Her description corroborated those from other witnesses, though hers was the most complete. "You're very observant, Mrs. Compton. Why do you think you're able to remember so much about the man?"

"I'm an old woman, detective. I can't fight back if I'm attacked so the only thing I can do is be alert when I'm on that train. I've learned to look at everyone. If someone takes my bag, I'll be able to give the police a complete description of them, believe me." There was a note of pride in her voice.

He smiled, despite himself. "Could you tell if the man you observed could have been wearing a priest's collar underneath his overcoat?"

Her eyes widened in surprise. "You think a priest killed that nun?"

He shook his head. "We don't think anything yet, but if she knew the man, he might have been a priest, since she worked for the Church offices."

"He had his coat buttoned all the way up. I didn't notice anything at his neck, but I remember that he looked like he must have been cold, even though it was warm inside the train, because he had his collar on his coat all up around his chin." She looked down at his coffee cup. "You want more coffee?"

"No thank you. I think I've got all the information I need. It's been very good of you to talk to me, Mrs. Compton. I'm sorry to have inconvenienced you and your husband."

Her wary expression softened. "You've been very polite, young man. I want you to catch the man who killed that poor woman. I don't mind saying that I'm glad the killer was a white man. I'm not prejudiced against Whites but we don't need to have Black people blamed for more violence in this city – and especially in this neighborhood. We're all getting along right now, but below the surface there's still a lot of anger."

"From both sides?"

She looked at him as if his question was naïve. "Of course from both sides. The White people are afraid of every Black person they see and they still think we're invading their territory after all these years of Black folks living in Dorchester. And Black people know they're gonna be blamed every time something happens to a White person."

Detective Leeper thought about what she said. He had grown up in upstate New York in a mostly White suburban neighborhood and now he lived in Brookline where the Blacks who were his neighbors were middle class. But in his job he dealt with Black crime all the time and he saw the attitudes of his fellow police officers. Racism wasn't as rampant in the Boston PD as he'd heard it had been, but it was still apparent and, in some of his colleagues, even some of the younger ones, quite blatant.

"You've witnessed a lot of the race problems in this city. How do you feel about things, yourself?" He hoped he wasn't treading on forbidden territory with his questions.

"I work with children every day and I want those children to grow up feeling part of this city and this country. I have to overcome my anger or I'll pass it on to those kids and that's not fair to them."

"But you're still angry?"

She glanced toward the kitchen. "My husband was shot by a policeman twenty years ago. He didn't do anything wrong, but they thought he was somebody else."

Her answer had caught him off guard. "I'm surprised you let me come here at all. Does my being here upset your husband?" He already knew the answer to his question from the way her husband had left the room as soon as he had introduced himself.

"He agreed that I should talk to you. He's had to move on. We can't dwell on the past."

"Did the city pay you for his injuries?"

She looked around at the modestly furnished house. "I couldn't afford a house like this on what I make as a preschool nurse. He got a settlement from the city but it doesn't compensate for what he's lost – except living with his disability has taught him a lot. He's a better man now because of it." Her old eyes had misted over as she spoke the words and she looked away in embarrassment.

"I have another request, I'm afraid," the young detective said, his tone apologetic.

She looked at him inquiringly.

"I'd like you to describe the man you saw to a police artist, so we can draw a picture of him. We can send the artist over here to your house, if that would be more convenient."

She looked thoughtfully toward the kitchen. "I'll come to the station. It will be easier for Robert."

The detective nodded. "I'll be going, Mrs. Compton. You've been very helpful."

She nodded and wiped her eyes, then got up to show him out. "I feel bad about that nun. I hope you catch the man who did it."

"Me too."

# Chasing Tales

## Chapter 26 .

Monsignor Hurley had at first thought the request from the Boston PD for an interview with one of their detectives was related to the death of his administrative assistant, Sister Mary Agnes, and he didn't appear happy to see Detective Hilton and find out that the policeman was here to question him about the molestation accusations against Father O'Flannery.

"Since Tim Russell is dead and Father O'Flannery is accused of a much more serious crime, what exactly is the point of going ahead with your case, detective?" the Monsignor challenged the detective. "Your department certainly has more important cases to solve, such as finding Sister Mary Agnes' murderer, for instance." The Monsignor sat, ramrod straight, behind his desk, looking down his nose at Detective Hilton and looking like a stern magistrate whose valuable time was being wasted by a misguided petitioner.

Nate felt a delicious taste of satisfaction that the Monsignor was irritated by his being there and he pulled a thick notepad from his breast pocket and put on a show of leafing through several pages before answering the Monsignor's question. "Sister Mary Agnes' death is being investigated, you can depend on that. I'm still working on the accusations against Father O'Flannery. You know how these investigations are, Monsignor – since you've been involved from the Church's end before – one thing leads to another and you turn up things you never expected." His smile suggested he knew more than he was saying. "It could even turn out that the Sister's murder is related to Tim Russell's. You never know." He looked down at his notepad as if checking something, then looked up again, a pleased expression on his face.

Monsignor Hurley sat stiffly behind his desk, frowning. "What are you saying, detective? What is the relationship between Sister Mary Agnes' murder and Father O'Flannery's case?"

Nate shook his head, as if there were things he couldn't say. "We'll have to wait to find out. Meanwhile we've been trying to corroborate Russell's report of abuse by looking for other victims. We interviewed all of the other altar boys who served under Father O'Flannery at St. Aloysius. I believe your office gave us that list."

"Of course we did. We're just as interested in getting at the truth as you are."

"I'm sure you are." Nate couldn't help but let a smile appear on his face as he said it and the sarcasm was evident in his voice. "Well that list was very helpful. We didn't find any other reports of abuse by Father O'Flannery, but we did find a few young men who claimed to have been abused by another priest – in fact the one who followed Father O'Flannery at St. Aloysius after he left."

"You mean Father James?" The Monsignor's voice was steady, but Nate detected a look of fear in the priest's eyes.

"Actually, they mentioned a Father Hurley." Nate left the smile on his face. "That wasn't you was it?"

The Monsignor's scowl was indignant, but his eyes were frightened. "Of course it wasn't me. I was never at St. Aloysius. There was never a Father Hurley there at all, according to the records." He looked suspiciously at the detective.

"That would have been 1982." Hilton said. "Can you tell me what you were doing at that time?"

"You still think it was me?"

"I just need something for the record."

# Chasing Tales

The Monsignor shook his head, as if in sad disbelief. He pointed to the wall over his left shoulder. There was a large plaque with the insignia of Catholic University School of Canon Law. "If you examine the date on that degree, Detective Hilton, you will see that it is 1983. I was a full-time law student in Washington DC in 1982 – hardly a parish priest in Dorchester."

"You lived in Washington?" Nate's face showed no emotion, but beneath his mask of detachment he was furious. Nyles Monahan had misled him.

"For two full years from 1981 to 1983. I'm sure there are university records to prove it."

"Then I guess someone's mistaken."

Monsignor Hurley smiled, icily. "It seems so."

## Chapter 27

Mrs. Edith McDonald was a widower who had lived alone with her daughter, Mary, in the family home in Roslindale for the past six years, since the death of her husband. Now she was alone and the impact of the loss of her daughter was palpable to Nyles as he was led into the living room of the old, two story row-house in what had once been a working class neighborhood but had recently been gentrified with coffee houses, art galleries and upscale restaurants. The McDonald home, with its old fashioned, comfortable furniture, looked as if it had remained the same for many years, although, when Nyles was a teenager and had known Mary as Cloris' best friend, the McDonald family had lived in Dorchester.

"We moved here soon after Mary got her position at the Chancery. She no longer had to live at the convent and we thought we could be closer to her." She eyed him fondly. "I remember you, Nyles. You were her friend, Cloris' boy friend. Didn't you visit our house in Dorchester when you were young?" The woman, who must have been at least in her mid-eighties, was trying her best to act sociably, trying to conceal her sadness, although it was evident in the moistness of her eyes and the trembling of her lips.

"Yes. The three of us, Mary, Cloris and myself, did many things together back in those days." He fought the urge to apologize to Mrs. McDonald for causing her daughter's death, but he knew that such an act of contrition, though it might salve his own conscience, would only confuse and disconcert the elderly woman.

The old woman's expression had a far away look. "Cloris was like a second daughter to Jim and myself. We were so sorry to see her leave Boston and move to the

West." Her face brightened. "We followed her career. I used to watch every episode of *Ordinary Lives*, when she was on it." Her expression became concerned. "I know she had to leave the show because she was sick. Mary said she was better now, though."

"Cloris had a stroke, but she's recovering. She would have loved to see Mary again." He felt a pang of regret as soon as he said the words.

Mrs. McDonald smiled bravely and gazed fondly at him. She seemed to be struggling to keep her composure.

"Mary and I were working on something together, Mrs. McDonald. Did she talk to you about it?"

The old woman smiled politely. "Mary said you and she had talked but not about what. She told me you were going to dinner that... that night." Her face had become troubled and Nyles could see she was trying to control her emotions.

"We were going out for hotdogs, in fact, but she also was bringing me some information for an investigation I'm involved with." He didn't want to say that Mary had information she didn't want her superior at the Archdiocese offices to know about. Her mother wouldn't have understood.

"I still can't believe it happened." The topic of her daughter's movements the night she died had triggered the old woman's thoughts about the younger woman's death. "What kind of person wants to kill a nun?" She paused and her face took on a momentary hardness. "It's such a shame. The other reason Jim and I moved here was to get away from the violence those people brought to our neighborhood. We got away for all these years but when Mary returned for just one evening, they did that to her."

Nyles felt certain that "those people" Mrs. McDonald was talking about were the Black families who had moved into Dorchester, frightening away many of the white families such as the McDonalds. He also was certain that the so-called Black crime Mrs. McDonald was fearful of had nothing to do with her daughter's death, but he didn't want to get into that with the old woman. It would all come out anyway when they caught Mary's killer – an outcome he was determined to make happen.

"Mary was bringing me some information that was important for the case I'm working on."

"She said you were helping a priest." Mrs. McDonald appeared to have recovered her composure. She sounded curious.

"A priest who's been falsely accused, I'm afraid. Mary was trying to help out."

"Mary? Did she know the priest?"

"Not really, but she had access to some Church records that were helpful to the case. I think she was bringing me a copy that night. Did you find anything like that in her belongings?" It bothered him to be asking the woman such questions when she was still mourning the loss of her daughter, but it was important and he was sure Mary would have wanted him to track down the information she had been trying to bring him.

"I haven't been able to look through them. The police brought me her purse but I just put it on her bed in her room and haven't even gone back inside." She looked apologetic. "I know Mary's next to God right now, but I'm still struggling with losing her."

Nyles nodded. "Of course you are. Would you mind if I looked through her purse? I believe she would have wanted me to get the information if she had it with her."

# Chasing Tales

She said she had no objection.

Mrs. McDonald gave him instructions as to where Mary's room was on the second floor and he left her in the living room and went up by himself. The door was closed and he had to stop himself from knocking, before he hesitantly opened the door.

The room was small and neat, and seemed to suggest that Mary only used it for sleeping, which was natural, given that she had the run of the house, with only she and her mother living there. There was a dressing table, but no desk or computer. A small TV set was on a stand in view of the bed and a portrait of Jesus was on one wall and one of St. Mary on another, both pictures being inexpensive copies of famous renaissance paintings. On another wall was a photograph of Mary and Cardinal Law, taken several years earlier, no doubt when he was still Archbishop of Boston. On the floor next to the bed was a pair of fuzzy slippers, pointing expectantly toward the bed. Nyles felt the emotion rising in his throat as he thought about Mary's life being cut short and his own role in causing it to happen. For the nth time he put aside his guilt, knowing that to be swallowed by it would prevent him from finding her killer.

On the center of the bed lay a black leather purse. Nyles resisted sitting down on the bed, feeling as though doing anything to mar the pristine atmosphere of Mary's room would be disrespectful. He picked up the purse. The contents were jumbled, as if they had been dumped into the purse, which he imagined they had been after the police looked through them. He didn't really expect to find anything, since the police had already searched through the purse, but perhaps what he was looking for hadn't seemed significant to them. He turned the purse upside down and, with reluctance, emptied it onto the bed.

# Chasing Tales

Nyles had learned years ago that purses were a lot like well-used kitchen drawers. At the bottom of most of them was a collection of scraps of paper, business cards, pens, paper clips and small change. He doubted that Mary had written any message on one of those scraps of paper, but he would check each of them after he went through the larger items and the content of her wallet.

There were several large pieces of folded paper – a train schedule, an old announcement for a Christmas concert, a notebook paper with a list of groceries to be bought, but nothing about priests who had been assigned to St. Aloysius. The wallet yielded forty-five dollars, but no information. Nyles stared at a younger picture of Mary on a Chancery ID card and a more recent one on her driver's license. He always had an eerie feeling when he saw a picture of someone recently deceased – making him wonder what had been going through the person's mind when the picture had been taken and how the event that had led to his or her death was not even on their horizon. Looking at Mary's picture he felt an overwhelming sadness.

Whatever information Mary had been bringing him on the night she'd died, she either hadn't been carrying it in her purse, or her killer had removed it. Nyles thought the latter possibility was unlikely, since the easiest thing would have been to take the entire purse, rather than going through it on the train next to the body of a woman he'd just stabbed to death. Maybe he had talked her into giving him the information before he'd stabbed her.

Nate Hilton had informed Nyles that Sister Mary Agnes had been carrying nothing of importance in her coat pockets. The coat itself was still in the custody of the police and being subjected to lab analysis, which might yield evidence that could lead to establishing the killer's identity. Perhaps Mary had committed her information to memory

Nyles rejoined Mrs. McDonald downstairs. She was sitting in the living room, holding a framed picture of her daughter and she appeared to have been crying. Caught with her guard down, she looked even older and more fragile than she had before, but she forced a smile when Nyles entered the room. "Did you find what you were looking for?"

Nyles shook his head. "I'm afraid she was not carrying the information with her."

She nodded. "I've been looking at an old picture – when Mary was in high school. Would you like to see it?" Without waiting for his answer, she held out the picture to him.

He took the picture and gazed at it. It was a black and white photo of Mary in high school. She was wearing a calf-length skirt and a dark sweater with a round, white collar showing at the neck. Her face carried a broad smile as if she was about to break into laughter. The picture triggered a series of images in Nyles' mind – images of Mary and Cloris walking arm in arm down the sidewalk toward him as he met them from school, images of the three of them in his old car, driving down to Nantasket Park to spend a day at the beach. "She was a wonderful person. I'm going to miss her…" He was unable to say more without his voice cracking with emotion and he handed the picture back to her.

The old woman took the picture and held it against her chest, as if she was giving her daughter a final hug. "She always did what she thought was the right thing."

"I know that," he said. And doing the right thing was what killed her, he thought.

.'

Chasing Tales

Chapter 28

Jimmy Gleason pulled out of his driveway, turned onto the main road, and pointed his car in the direction of the highway 128 on-ramp. In the summer months he took the side roads past Brandeis University to his office in neighboring Waltham, but at seven in the morning in midwinter, it was almost pitch-black outside and some of the side roads still had a treacherous covering of snow and ice. He preferred the highway on a winter's day.

Turning off at the exit of Route 20 he headed for Waltham Center, where his bank's offices were located. Bankers' hours were a myth, he thought to himself. They no longer even applied to the hours a bank was open to its customers. Even with ATM machines that were available 24 hours a day, people wanted the convenience of using their bank in the evenings and on weekends. Jimmy's position as Senior Vice President in charge of the mortgage loan department didn't require meeting customers and he didn't have to work evenings or weekends, but he was at his desk by 7:30 every morning, ahead of even the office staff.

The Waltham Savings Bank's building occupied half a city block and was four stories high with another two levels of parking garage below it. The attendant for the garage didn't arrive until seven-thirty but Jimmy's magnetic access card raised the gate on the entrance to the garage so he could enter. The garage was well-lit by lights that came on automatically at six a.m. and Jimmy wound his way along the labyrinthine route among concrete posts, past the lonely lines of empty stalls, looking like a subterranean city from which all the residents had fled, to the reserved parking area near the elevator entrance to the bank. Being a Senior Vice President earned him a short

# Chasing Tales

walk from his car to the elevator. This morning, the overhead lights near his parking stall and over the entrance to the elevator were dark. Jimmy noticed broken glass on the concrete floor and swerved his car to avoid it, silently swearing at the pointless viciousness of vandals who would do such a thing.

He parked his car in the stall marked with a chrome-plated sign bearing his name and title, leaving his headlights on for a few extra moments while he got his briefcase from the back seat and removed his key card that would let him into the elevator this early in the morning. Then he switched off the headlights with the button on his car key and turned to walk to the elevator.

"Jimmy?" The voice was vaguely familiar but it startled him so much that he nearly dropped his briefcase. He hadn't seen anyone else in the parking lot. Looking around, he could see nothing but the vast emptiness of the concrete structure, then he noticed the outlines of another car in a darkened parking stall about fifty yards away. The voice must be that of a fellow worker, he thought, but he nevertheless began to move cautiously back toward his car, feeling in his pocket for his car keys.

"No point going back to your car," the voice said. Jimmy spun around and saw the outline of a figure, like a dim specter, moving slowly toward him through the shadows on the other side of his automobile. The man must have been concealed behind the concrete pillar next to Jimmy's parking stall.

"Who is it?" Jimmy asked, trying to keep the anxiety out of his voice. He had suddenly realized that the broken lights were not the work of vandals. Someone else had been waiting for him – someone who knew his name.

The figure kept moving silently toward him. Jimmy's eyes were beginning to adjust to the darkness and

141

he saw that it was a slim man in a heavy overcoat. The man wore a hat – and old-fashioned fedora – glasses, and in his hand he held a gun.

"What do you want?" Jimmy asked.

"Nothing, really," the man said, a note of sadness in his voice. "I'd like to see you better." He moved closer, the gun held in front of him.

"I know you," Jimmy said, though even as he said it, he realized he couldn't place where he had seen the man before.

"That's the shame of it," the man said. "You remember too much, Jimmy, though in truth, I don't really remember you. You were just one of a number of boys. Your parents got me removed from my position at the church."

"Father Hurley?" As the words left his mouth, Jimmy felt a sharp shock of recognition. The face was only faintly familiar, especially in the dark, but when he put it together with the voice, the man's identity was clear to him. He had never expected to meet Father Hurley again in his life.

"You shouldn't have told that private detective anything, Jimmy. Why get involved like that?" In the shadows, the man turned his head and looked around, as if he was surveying the parking structure around him. "You've got everything you could ever want, why not just leave well enough alone?"

"How did you know I talked to Mr. Monahan?"

The man with the gun shook his head. "It doesn't matter. I can't let you identify me, I'm afraid." He held the gun a little higher and pointed it directly at Jimmy's chest.

"I'm not going to testify against you, I told Monahan that," Jimmy said. His hands were sweating and his heart was beating so hard he could hear the blood poundirg like loud drums in his ears. He looked to both sides, wondering what his chances of getting away would be if he started to run.

"I'm sorry," the man said and fired the gun.

Jimmy felt as if he'd been hit in the chest with a sledgehammer. The force of the bullet knocked him backward and he dropped his briefcase to the floor. For a moment, he regained his balance and felt amazed that he was still alive. Maybe there was still time to run, he thought. Then the energy seemed to drain completely from his body and he felt his legs turn to rubber. He no longer could stand and he felt himself falling to the ground, but he was too tired to put out a hand to break his fall. By the time he hit the concrete floor of the parking garage he was no longer conscious. The blood that had gushed from his body like water from a hydrant, now leaked languidly from his stilled heart, creating an ever-widening pool across the concrete floor.

The man in the shadows put the gun into his coat pocket and turned away, his shoulders slumped forward in a posture of defeat as he walked toward his car. What had he become? What else would he have to do to save himself? He knew the answer and as he trudged toward his car, he thought about Nyles Monahan, the investigator who had brought all of this upon him. If it weren't for Monahan, Jimmy Gleason would still be alive and so would Sister Mary Agnes. He slowly shook his head. He was targeting the wrong people – the innocent ones. It was Monahan who needed to be killed before any more deaths were required.

## Chapter 29

Katherine was missing.

Kaylee was in tears. Both Sean and Millie were in the process of reassuring their daughter that everything would be fine, but their expressions betrayed their anxiety.

"Have you called the police?" Nyles asked. They were all in the kitchen of Sean and Millie's house - Millie having been in the midst of preparing dinner when her daughter had appeared on her doorstep, looking like a lost child herself, her message about Katherine being missing tumbling out of her mouth in a jumble of words. Kaylee's first thought had been that her daughter had returned to her grandparents' house and she had driven the twenty miles between her house in Stoughton and theirs in Milton, scouring the shoulders of the road for her daughter, whom she suspected might be either walking or hitchhiking.

"We were hoping she'd turn up here," Millie told Nyles.

"How long has she been gone?"

"She didn't come home from school," Kaylee answered her uncle's question, "and when I checked her room, thinking she might have come in without me seeing her, I saw that she had taken clothing and her toothbrush and shampoo and all those things. She must have had them in her backpack when she went to school."

"Call the police," Nyles said, the authority in his voice leaving no room for questions. "Then call all of her friends. She's probably staying with one of them."

"I think we should go out looking," Sean said. "It's getting dark and if she's outside, she'll freeze."

Nyles looked at his brother and Millie and Kaylee and he felt a wave of protectiveness. God forbid anything tragic should happen to Katherine. "Did anything happen that might have caused her to leave?" he asked his niece.

"Alan came home from a meeting with clients… drunk." She looked at her parents. "But he didn't do anything to her. I made sure she was in her room and he was with me."

"Maybe it just frightened her," Nyles said, gently.

"Christ, Kaylee," her father exploded. "You need to leave that man. You have to make a choice between Katherine and him."

Millie put a hand on her husband's shoulder. "Not now, Sean. Let's concentrate on finding Katherine."

"Make your calls – to the police and to her friends," Nyles said, his voice commanding, yet gentle, as he patted his niece's shoulder.

They all waited in the den, feeling like anxious relatives waiting for news of a disaster, while Kaylee made her calls The Stoughton police told her to go home and wait there and they would send an officer over as well as put out a notice to all of their patrol cars. It wasn't time to issue an amber alert, since there was nothing to suggest that Katherine had been abducted.

"I'll go with you," Millie said to her daughter.

"And I'm going to drive around Stoughton and see if I can spot her," Sean volunteered. "I can't just sit here and wait."

"I'll stay here," Nyles volunteered. "She still may come here and someone needs to be here."

They each went their separate ways and Nyles was left to his own thoughts as he waited in his brother's house – just he and Ranger - for some word or the appearance of Katherine on the doorstep. The waiting gave him time to think about the situation. He suspected that what he had told Kaylee was right – that Katherine had been frightened by her stepfather's drinking and had left, probably to go to a friend's house. Finding her was the first priority, but he knew that something needed to be done after that. Katherine would only have left if she'd lost faith in her mother's ability to protect her from Alan. Remembering that Kaylee had said that Katherine was doing less well in school and had been caught with cigarettes, suggested to him that she would soon lose all faith in the adults around her and he knew that that was the first step toward her becoming alienated, delinquent, and prone to all sorts of negative influences. Nyles had been glad to hear his brother finally echo his own thoughts – Kaylee needed to show Katherine that her safety was more important than her mother's marriage. It was time for Kaylee to leave Alan.

His cell phone rang and the caller ID indicated that the caller was the Boston Police Department. Had Katherine gone into the city? He felt a stab of anxiety, but when he answered the phone he found it was Nate Hilton.

"You're information is fucking dead wrong," Hilton said, by way of a greeting.

"What are you talking about?" Nyles snapped. He didn't want to talk to Hilton right now and he certainly didn't want to put up with the surly cop's anger.

"Monsignor Hurley was never at St. Aloysius. He was in Washington, DC, going to law school in 1982 and he stayed there until the middle of 1983. He's got the fucking plaque on the wall to prove it."

"He's lying," Nyles said. "Both Ryan and Gleason remembered Father Hurley being at St. Aloysius. Gleason said he was molested by Hurley."

"Gleason didn't tell me anything about being molested."

"It was hard to get him to talk about it."

"You mean he didn't want to talk to a Black cop."

"Maybe you're right – though I think your attitude probably has something to do with it. But anyway, trust me, there was a Father Hurley at St. Aloysius and he's the key to this – probably to both Russell's killing and to Sister Mary Agnes'."

"Fuck my attitude. It's done me just fine up to now. What do we do next, genius?"

"I'm going to talk to Father Tom tomorrow. Maybe he remembers Hurley. Do you want to come along?" Nyles had misgivings about asking Hilton along, but he needed to keep the Boston detective on his side.

"You don't think me being Black will interfere with getting the truth?" His tone was sarcastic.

"Not with Father Tom. He told me he liked you. I guess he's a forgiving priest."

"Fuck you, Monahan. I'll see you at the jail."

Nyles hung up and his thoughts immediately went back to Katherine. He checked his cell phone and saw that no one else had called while he'd been on the call with Detective Hilton. The Stoughton police would call the home phone anyway, if they had any news. He felt powerless just sitting and waiting and he stood up and went into the kitchen. Maybe a cup of coffee would focus his attention. He didn't want to have a beer in case he had to drive somewhere to help out in some way. He realized he was feeling completely overwhelmed by his inability to do anything – a feeling he wasn't used to in his former role as a cop. Everything was different when his own family was involved.

He had just begun a search for instant coffee when Ranger jumped up and ran to the front door. Then he heard the door open. Sean must be back. "Any luck?" he called.

"Hi Uncle Nyles," Katherine said, standing in the doorway to the kitchen, Ranger nuzzling against her side. She had on her parka and her backpack, but was shivering and she looked tired and frightened and even younger than her eleven years.

"Thank God you're safe," Nyles exclaimed. He threw his arms around his tiny grandniece and felt the coldness of her body even through her parka. "There's a fire in the living room. Let's go stand in front of it. I need to call your mother and your grandfather and tell them you're OK."

Katherine didn't move. Her eyes had teared up. "I'm sorry. I didn't mean to worry anyone."

"We'll worry about that later. The important thing is that you're safe. You're mother's got to know. She's terribly frightened."

"I'm not going back, Uncle Nyles." She sniffed and rubbed her nose with the sleeve of her parka. "My mother only worries about me now when she's scared because she can't find me – not when I'm at home and *he's* around." She reached down and rubbed the dog's ears.

Nyles helped her off with her backpack and parka and guided her into the living room, then pulled a footstool up in front of the fire and sat her gently down upon it. "I was looking for instant coffee and I saw some hot chocolate. Can I get you a cup? It'll warm you up."

She nodded and he went into the kitchen and fixed a cup of hot chocolate for her. When he brought it back, she was sitting on the footstool with her feet extended toward the fire. Although he knew she was safe, she still looked tiny and defenseless to him. He handed her the chocolate.

"Did your stepfather do anything to you?"

"I kept my door shut, but I heard him. He was saying all those things again outside in the hallway."

"Did your mother know?"

"He only did it when she went downstairs. He whispered very loud so I could hear. I don't think she knew."

"Would you be willing to tell someone from Social Services or the police about what Alan does?"

She looked frightened. "My mother would kill me. Alan would too."

"Your mother already called the police. If you tell them what you told me – and about the earlier times it happened – they will help you. Your mother wants to do the right thing for you, but she needs to hear it from someone else – like the police."

"What will happen? Will they take me away from her?"

"If they did, it would only be to come here, with grandma Millie and grandpa Sean. If it goes to court a judge would probably ask your grandparents to take care of you." Nyles knew that a relative was always the first choice for a living arrangement when a child was removed from home.

"Mom will be really upset." Kaylee looked down at the floor. "She might start drinking or using drugs again."

He shook his head. "I don't think so. Your mother just needs a nudge. She'll do the right thing. I think if a judge says you can't live with Alan, then your mother will leave too."

"Really?"

"Let's call her and get the ball rolling, shall we? You're safe and no one in your family is going to let you be in danger again."

She looked at him with big, trusting eyes. "OK. Let's call mom."

# Chasing Tales

## Chapter 30

For the second time in only a matter of days, Nyles found himself possessed by the sense of powerlessness that accompanied being interrogated by the police. This time, his interrogator was Detective Arnold Leeper, the officer in charge of the investigation of Sister Mary Agnes' death. Detective Leeper was a smallish, handsome, blonde man in his mid-thirties, whose mild manner and thoughtful questions had nothing in common with the belligerence of Nate Hilton nor even the coarse directness of Detective John Spaulding, the man who was investigating Tim Russell's murder.

"Tell me again about the message that Sister Mary Agnes was delivering to you, that you think may be the reason she was killed," Detective Leeper said. They were seated at his desk in the Dorchester District Headquarters, which didn't look much different from Nyles' old desk at the LAPD station, except Leeper had a laptop computer instead of the ancient desktop that Nyles had had in his office. The wooden desk with the scratched surface and the hard wooden chair in which Nyles sat could have been transported from LA.

Nyles had decided to be as open as possible with the Boston Police, reasoning that they had many more resources to devote to finding Mary MacDonald's killer than he did. "She was bringing me information about priests who had worked at St. Aloysius Church here in Dorchester during the time that Tim Russell would have been an altar boy. I thought that the information might be helpful to Father O'Flannery's case."

Leeper nodded. "And Detective Hilton was involved, because he's in charge of the molestation case against Father O'Flannery."

"Yes. Detective Spaulding is investigating Russell's murder, which Father O'Flannery has also been charged with, but Detective Hilton is still investigating the molestation charges. I think the two crimes are related."

Leeper looked thoughtful. "So you think someone else besides Father O'Flannery molested Russell – and killed him also?"

"Yes." Nyles tried to read the expression on the detective's face but it was impossible to tell what he was thinking.

"And I take it that Hilton thinks you might be right, but Spaulding doesn't, so you're working with Hilton, is that right?"

Nyles didn't want to paint a picture that placed him too close to Detective Hilton, suspecting that Nate's relationship with a lot of his fellow officers was an antagonistic one. "Detective Hilton is giving me access to the names of other altar boys who served at the same time as Russell."

"And how did Sister Mary Agnes fit into all this?"

"Like I said, she was bringing me the names of more priests who had served at St. Aloysius. The official list given to me by Monsignor Hurley was incomplete. Several former altar boys identified a Father Hurley as the priest who succeeded Father O'Flannery but Hurley's name wasn't on the list he gave me."

"But Sister Mary Agnes worked for the Monsignor, isn't that right?"

"Yes."

"So she was bringing you information about him without his knowledge?"

"Yes."

"Why would the Monsignor's administrative assistant go behind his back to bring you evidence against him?"

"She helped me because she was an old friend and I asked her to. I think that's what got her killed." Nyles felt his face reddening and he had to swallow hard to keep his composure.

"I'm sorry," Leeper said, as if he sensed Nyles' guilt. He leaned back in his chair and chewed on the end of his pen. His eyes were narrowed in concentration and his face had momentarily lost its boyish appearance. "So what do you think is going on that would lead to Sister Mary Agnes being murdered?" He leaned toward Nyles with an intense look on his face.

Leeper reminded Nyles of himself thirty years earlier, always seeking more information before jumping to conclusions. "I think it's at least possible that Monsignor Hurley is both the real molester and the killer and that he found out that Sister Mary Agnes was bringing me information that might incriminate him and he killed her."

To Nyles' surprise, Leeper wasn't shocked by his suggestion. "You only said it's possible that Hurley is the killer. Does that mean you've got reservations?"

"Other than the same name, there is nothing to suggest that Monsignor Hurley was ever assigned to St. Aloysius and, in fact, there's a pretty good reason to think that he wasn't. He was in school in Washington DC during the time the molestations were supposed to have occurred and when a Father Hurley was the priest in that parish."

Detective Leeper looked surprised. "So if the Monsignor couldn't have been the one who molested Tim Russell, why do you still suspect him?"

Nyles shook his head. "He hasn't been open with me and I got the feeling from Mary – Sister Mary Agnes - that whatever information she was bringing me, it involved him."

"She said that?"

"No, but she made it clear that she felt it was necessary to go behind his back."

Leeper straightened up and breathed a sigh. "I'll be talking to the Monsignor today or tomorrow and I'll have to ask him about these same things."

Nate Hilton wouldn't be happy that Nyles had given so much information to a rival detective, but Nyles welcomed any assistance he could get. "Good," he said. "What have you found out regarding the description of the man who sat next to Sister Mary Agnes on the train?"

"It fits the description of thousands of Bostonians. He was too well covered in his coat to tell if he was wearing a priest's collar. I'm having a police artist make a drawing from some of the eyewitness descriptions and, after what you've told me, I'll be asking the Monsignor for a photograph of himself to show witnesses."

"Will you keep me informed? I'm still working on Father O'Flannery's defense."

The young detective chewed on his lower lip. "If I have any information that I think is relevant to the charges against Father O'Flannery, I'll present it to Detective Spaulding. You have access to his evidence through the court."

"I was a close friend of Sister Mary Agnes." Nyles felt awkward having to plead with the detective.

"Since I know you're looking for material to use in court in defense of your client, I need to be careful that I don't tell you things I shouldn't."

Leeper was playing things safe and close to the vest, just as Nyles would have in the same situation. "I understand," the older detective said.

The detective looked surprised that Nyles hadn't tried to argue with him. Something in the ex-cop's manner made the younger detective trust him. "If there's other information not pertinent to Spaulding's case against your client, then I'll be happy to share it," he said.

Nyles figured that pressing the young detective any further would be counterproductive and he still had Nate Hilton as a listening post within the department anyway. "That's good enough for me, detective. I hope you find Sister Mary Agnes' killer soon."

## Chapter 31

The picture on the front page of the Boston Globe stared out at him like an accusing judge. Nyles recognized the handsome face of Jimmy Gleason, the prominent Weston businessman whom, according the story in the newspaper had been shot to death in the parking garage of his bank in Waltham the previous morning. The Waltham Police Department, which was investigating the murder, was at loss as to the motive or, for that matter, any suspects and had only declared that the crime did not appear to be motivated by robbery.

Nyles sipped his coffee and fought against the sense of guilt that threatened to overwhelm him. Had his own investigative activities been responsible for another death? How could anyone have known that he'd talked to Jimmy Gleason? Only Nate Hilton and Billy Phelan were even aware of Gleason's role in the case against Father Tom. Then Nyles remembered that Gleason had told him that his parents had filed a complaint with the Church against Father Hurley. The Monsignor would have had access to those records.

Nyles put down the paper and picked up the telephone. His knowledge of Gleason's role in Father Tom's case could be of help to both the Waltham Police Department and to Detective Leeper. It might help one of them connect the dots in what was now a string of murders.

He called Leeper first. The detective had read about the Gleason murder in the newspaper but had not made any connection to the case he was working on.

"How long ago did you talk to Gleason?" Leeper asked.

The question rekindled Nyles' recriminations regarding his role in causing Jimmy Gleason's death. "Two days ago, but he wasn't planning to testify against anyone. He wanted to be left out of the case."

"But Gleason would still have been linked to Father Hurley in the Church's records if his family filed a complaint against the priest."

The young detective had jumped to the same conclusion that Nyles had. "Those records would be in the possession of the Monsignor's office," Nyles reminded the young detective.

"You mean the record that maybe Sister Mary Agnes might have been carrying when she was murdered," Leeper said flatly. "That doesn't necessarily implicate the Monsignor. Whoever Father Hurley is, he might have seen his name linked to Gleason, if the history of the complaint was part of the record that he stole from the Sister."

"You can contact the Waltham PD and say I'll be glad to tell them anything I know, although I've told you everything I can think of."

"With any luck, there will be some physical evidence that can connect the two crimes," Leeper said. He sounded as if he was ready to hang up. "Thanks for giving me a heads-up on this Monahan. One favor deserves another. If I find anything that might help your client, I'll let you know – so long as it doesn't violate any rules of evidence."

"Fair enough," Nyles said. He was glad to get the pledge of help from Detective Leeper, but if Jimmy Gleason's death was the price that had been paid for it, he knew it wasn't worth it.

\*\*\*

Father Tom's round and usually jovial face was lined with fatigue, though he tried his best to smile and feign an upbeat attitude. He was surprised that Nyles was accompanied by Detective Hilton, but greeted him with an open friendliness, as if he assumed the Black cop was there to help him and not to make more accusations. Nyles explained that he and Hilton had combined forces to try to find the real child molester and he told him about Sister Mary Agnes' and Jimmy Gleason's murders.

Father Tom closed his eyes and muttered something, though whether it was a prayer or a curse, neither Nyles nor Nate Hilton could say. "That my case is responsible for the deaths of two more people is terrible," he said aloud.

"I'm the one who got Mary involved in your case. She was coming to tell me who followed you in your post as the priest at St. Aloysius," Nyles said. His guilt about Mary's death weighed heavily on him.

Father Tom looked surprised. "Why would that information get her killed?"

"Because the priest who succeeded you at St. Aloysius may have molested Tim Russell and then killed Russell to keep him from identifying him. That could also be why Jimmy Gleason was killed."

"I can't believe it," Father Tom looked aghast.

"If priests can abuse kids, why not commit murder?" Detective Hilton asked, not making any effort to conceal the sarcasm in his voice.

"Was your replacement Father Hurley?" Nyles asked, ignoring Nate's comment.

"You mean the Monsignor?" Father Tom asked, appearing stunned.

"I don't know. We've heard from two former altar boys, one of them being Gleason, that you were replaced by a Father Hurley, but the Monsignor appears to have been in law school at the time."

"I never heard the name of the person who came after me and before Father James. I'm sure that if the Monsignor would have been at St. Aloysius he would have mentioned it to me."

"Not if he didn't want anyone to know."

"There's a whole congregation that would remember him," Father Tom said.

"Your congregation moved out of town," Hilton interjected with a sour note of sarcasm. "You used to minister to Irishmen, Father, but the whole parish is Hispanic and Black now. Your good Christians decided to flee to the suburbs rather than welcome their new neighbors."

"But it's a matter of Church records," Father Tom said, ignoring Hilton's tone.

"I think those were the records Sister Mary Agnes wanted to show me the night she was murdered," Nyles answered.

"There are other records," Father Tom said, shifting his gaze between the two of them.

"What are you talking about?" Hilton asked, frowning.

"The records at St. Aloysius," Father Tom answered, still taking no apparent notice of Hilton's sour demeanor.

"What kind of records would still be at St. Aloysius after more than 25 years?" Nyles asked.

"Baptisms, marriages. Whoever was priest would have presided at the services."

Nate looked at Nyles. "Jesus Christ," the Black cop exclaimed. "That's too obvious. One of us should have been a better Irish Catholic," he said, looking accusingly at Nyles.

Or a better cop, Nyles thought. "The detective and I have a church we have to visit," Nyles said, rising.

"Let me know what you find," Father Tom said. He turned to tell the guard he was ready to return to his cell.

# Chasing Tales

## Chapter 32

Billy Phelan's confidence was abandoning him like water flowing from a leaky bucket. Tomorrow the trial against Father O'Flannery was set to open and he was scheduled to defend his first criminal case in more than ten years. He was about as ready as an adolescent suddenly finding himself alone with his first date. Nyles Monahan had told Billy that he had a lead that could break the case wide open, but now the two most crucial witnesses related to that lead were dead and the attorney was facing an armload of circumstantial and physical evidence against his client, while he was empty-handed.

Alf listened with dutiful attention to his drinking partner's confession of his insecurities. "All you can do is do your best," the wiry barfly said to the attorney. "Your client hasn't got much going for him, so it's not your fault that the prosecution has a better case than you do." He coughed into his hand, then took a quick sip of the whiskey he was drinking as a chaser to his beer.

"But Father O'Flannery is innocent," Phelan said morosely, taking another long drink from his pint of Harp. The two of them were huddled together at one end of the bar in the Hibernia Pub, like a pair of shadowy conspirators, although the rest of the bar was almost empty on a Tuesday night.

"How can you be sure?" Alf asked, sipping from his glass of Bushmills. "Because he's a fucking priest?"

Billy shook his head. "Because I've known the man since we were kids. I wouldn't have taken the case if I'd thought he was guilty." Phelan took another long sip of his beer. "It's not my fault, Goddammit. If I could afford a real investigator, I'd have enough evidence to set my client free."

"I thought you said your private eye had found out something that could change the whole trial."

Phelan burped and took another long drink from his beer. "That's what he keeps telling me, but now he says he doesn't have anything and he's got to go over to St. Aloysius to find some baptism records or something."

"Baptism records?" Alf was swaying but he managed to focus his attention on his companion.

"From back in 1982. He says those records will tell him who the priest was who really molested those kids and killed Russell."

"You mean the priest baptized the person who killed that guy?" Alf's gaze was wandering the room as if he was barely involved in their conversation. His fingers drummed on the top of the bar. The woman with whom Billy had left the other night was back and she was sitting at the other end of the bar. Alf got up and circled around his friend and placed himself in Billy's line of sight so he couldn't see the woman.

"Jesus Christ, Alf, the priest didn't baptize the killer; the priest *is* the killer."

Alf scratched his head. He held up a finger to signal Tommy that he wanted another Bushmills. "That sounds like bullshit to me, Billy. I think your private dick has his head up his ass." He giggled. "Maybe he has his dick up his ass too, or maybe he has almost no dick, like a fucking whatchamacallit... a hermaphrodite."

Billy stared at his friend. "You're a brainless loser, you know that?"

"Don't get mad at me. I'm just trying to make you feel better." Alf whined.

Billy heaved a sigh. "We're just a couple of drunks, Alf. What the hell do we know? What the hell business have I got defending a priest, for God's sake?"

"What's wrong with being a drunk?" Alf said. "It just means we're not involved in a lot of the bullshit that goes on in this world." He moved jerkily, with small nervous gestures.

Billy had seen the woman at the end of the bar. He smiled and raised his glass to her. Maybe something good could still happen tonight, he thought.

Alf had noticed that his friend's attention had been captured by the woman who'd pulled him away last week and he didn't like it. He didn't want to drink alone again. "Why are you interested in that slut?" he asked, his raspy voice low and ugly.

"Jesus, Alf, watch your mouth. You don't even know her."

"I know her type. I bet she cost you a pretty penny the other night."

"She's no whore, Alf. She's just a woman from the neighborhood."

"Give me a fucking break."

"You can take a break, all right," Billy said. He downed his beer and started moving down the bar toward the woman.

Alf shook his head. "Fucking lawyers," he said, as he began to cough then raised his shot glass to his mouth, as if the Bushmills were a life-saving medicine.

## Chapter 33

"I thought I already gave you people all the information you needed," Monsignor Hurley told the fresh-faced young detective in front of him.

"What are you talking about?" Detective Leeper asked, surprised by the cleric's comment.

"Detective Hilton, I believe his name was. He practically accused me of molesting young boys at St. Aloysius during a period of time I was in law school. He was most obnoxious."

Leeper knew exactly which detective the priest was talking about. Hilton must have been following the leads that Monahan had found regarding someone named Father Hurley being at St. Aloysius during the time that Tim Russell was molested. But Hilton had no business investigating Sister Mary Agnes' death and the thought made the young detective angry. But despite his anger he still needed to gather evidence himself. "Were you aware of any enemies of the Sister?"

The Monsignor shrugged. "Sister Mary Agnes could be gruff with people who thought they could bully the Church in one way or another, and I'm sure she ruffled some feathers, but not to the extent someone would kill her because of it."

"The night she was killed she was bringing information to Mr. Nyles Monahan, whom I believe you've met and who has been retained as an investigator by the attorney for Father Thomas O'Flannery."

To Detective Leeper's practiced eye, Monsignor Hurley didn't look surprised by the suggestion that his assistant was delivering information about a case without his knowledge, although he was making an effort to feign confusion.

164

"I don't understand, detective. There would be no reason for Sister Mary Agnes to hand carry information to Mr. Monahan, especially outside of work hours, and she certainly didn't tell me she was providing him with any additional information beyond what my office already gave him, which was quite complete."

"Actually, Mr. Monahan told me that the information he was hoping to receive from the Sister was about you."

"Me?"

"That's what I was led to believe."

"What information about me could possibly be relevant to the defense of Father O'Flannery?"

"Were you ever a priest at St. Aloysius?"

The Monsignor's face betrayed his anger. "Why does this question keep coming up? I told Detective Hilton that I was never at St. Aloysius. My entire career is a matter of Church record and I've been quite willing to share that record with anyone who is interested."

"Where were you between five p.m. and six p.m. last Thursday?"

"You mean when Sister Mary Agnes was killed?" The Monsignor's lips were curled in a sneer.

"Can you account for your whereabouts at that time?"

"I was here in my office, which was where I was supposed to be. My administrative assistant would have been here also, except she left early, to take her mother to dinner." He looked flustered. " ...or so she said - although I guess that wasn't true."

"Did anyone see you here?"

"Of course not. Who would see me? I was in my office." His voice didn't disguise his disdain.

"How about when you arrived home? I understand you live here on the grounds."

"I have an apartment here, along with several of the other priests who work for the Archdiocese administration. I don't recall exactly. I believe I worked late and got home around seven thirty or so."

"So no one saw you from roughly five o'clock until seven-thirty?"

The sneer hadn't left the Monsignor's face. "I have no alibi, if that's what you mean. The idea that I would harm my own assistant is absurd."

"I'm sure it is, Monsignor and I'm not suggesting such a thing. I have to check  on the whereabouts of everyone who is involved in the case."

"And you consider me involved?" The sneer was barely covering a look of panic on the Monsignor's face.

"I'm afraid I do."

Leeper's expression was bland when he asked the next question. "Where were you yesterday between 6:30 and 8:00 a.m.?"

"I was in the chapel praying – as I am every morning at that time. And, to anticipate your next question, I was alone. Why do you ask?"

"There was another murder yesterday. Does the name Jimmy Gleason mean anything to you?"

The Monsignor looked back at him, his face expressionless. "Only that I read about his murder in the paper last night. What does it have to do with Sister Mary Agnes' death?"

"Gleason was a former altar boy at St. Aloysius. He filed a complaint with the Church against Father Hurley for molesting him."

The Monsignor's expression was one of anger. "That's impossible. There was no Father Hurley at St.

Aloysius and there is no record of a complaint filed against someone with that name."

"Then Gleason was wrong?"

"I'm afraid so. Did he tell you that he had been molested by someone named Hurley?"

"He told Mr. Monahan."

"Mr. Monahan seems to be leading you down false paths, detective."

"Two people have been murdered. Both of them had information connected to a person you say doesn't exist."

"You only have Mr. Monahan's word for that."

Detective Leeper stared back at the older man. "But I will find out the truth; you can count on that, Monsignor." He rose from his chair. "I'd like a picture of you, if I may. We may want to show it to witnesses."

The Monsignor heaved a tired sigh and opened a lower drawer on the side of his desk. He thumbed through several folders, then retrieved a 3X4 glossy photograph of his face and upper body. "I use this for brochures when I go on speaking engagements. You're free to have it. I'm sure you will find that no one will identify me as the person you are seeking."

Monsignor Hurley's lack of reticence about giving up a copy of his photograph surprised the young detective, but he reached across the desk and took the photograph. "Thank you. I'll return this when I'm finished with it."

"Keep it detective. It will be a reminder of your folly. Good day."

# Chasing Tales

## Chapter 34

The trial of Father O'Flannery was on the front page of both the Globe and the Herald as well as on the evening news on all of the local TV stations, but Nyles and Nate Hilton missed the opening moments of the trial because they were visiting St. Aloysius Church in Dorchester.

The one-hundred fifty year-old church brought back memories for Nyles. He had gone to the parish elementary school until the eighth grade, as had most of his neighborhood friends. The grammar school was still there, across the street from the church, and it remained as the same small cluster of buildings where Nyles had attended school as a young boy. He paused before entering the church and watched the children in the schoolyard. Despite their being bundled in parkas and mittens and gloves, he could see, even from a distance, that the majority were Black and Hispanic children, reflecting the mixed racial makeup of the neighborhood. He had never seen a Black child in class when he had been a student at St. Aloysius.

"My mother wanted me to go to St. Aloysius," Nate said as they climbed the low front steps to the church.

The comment surprised Nyles. "You're Catholic?"

Nate's expression was disdainful. "Shit no, I'm not Catholic. My parents just wanted me to get a good education. My mother didn't want me going to school with all those poor Black children in the neighborhood."

"But you didn't go to St. Aloysius, did you?"

"My father wasn't going to have me be the only Black kid in with a bunch of Micks - most of whom were going to private school to avoid having to go to school with me."

"You grew up in Dorchester?" Nyles was a good twenty years older than Hilton. The neighborhood in which Nyles had grown up had changed during that twenty years.

"On Gallivan Boulevard."

"You went to Dorchester High School?"

"Uh huh."

" Me too," Nyles said, feeling a momentary sense of camaraderie before he realized that Nate's experience at Dorchester High must have been very different from his. He wondered how accepting he would have been if Nate had gone to school with him and, knowing the answer, felt a fleeting sense of guilt.

"I'll bet there weren't many Black students when you were there," Nate said, a sarcastic tone evident in his voice.

"A few, but you're right, we were mostly Irish kids… Micks, as you say."

"You go to church here?"

Nyles nodded. They had entered the large front doors of the church.

A small, pudgy, dark complected man with glasses, wearing priest's clericals, had entered the room from a side door. He greeted them with a wave and hurried across the floor, taking small rapid steps, in their direction. "You are the policemen?" He asked, introducing himself as Father Hidalgo. He had a noticeable Spanish accent.

Nate took out his badge.

"He's a policeman, I'm a private investigator for Father O'Flannery's lawyer." Nyles answered.

The priest shook his head, putting his two small hands to his face in a theatrical gesture of dismay. "A

terrible thing. I hope he didn't do what he's accused of."
The look on his round, dark face was hopeful.

Nyles felt no inclination to talk about the case.
"We're here to take a look at your baptismal records."

Father Hidalgo led them to a large room with file
cabinets lining two of the walls and bookshelves lining the
others. Father Hidalgo went to one of the walls that was
lined with bookshelves. "The baptism books are here,
arranged by dates." He scanned the dates on the backs of
the books, then stopped. "Here it is - 1982." He reached
out to take the volume from the shelf, but Nyles put out a
hand to stop him.

"Have you had this book out recently?" Nyles
asked, glancing at Hilton, whose expression showed that
he had noticed the same thing that Nyles had.

"No, why?" the priest answered.

"All of the other books are dusty –this one's not,"
Nate answered. He pulled a pair of rubber gloves out of his
pocket and put them on.

"Has anyone else asked to see these records
lately?" Nyles asked.

"No one," Father Hidalgo answered, shaking his
head. He looked flustered and guilty, as though he was
being chastised for not keeping more secure records.
"Besides me, only my secretary comes in here. I can ask
her if she's the one who looked at this book  recently. I
can't imagine who else it could have been."

"If she's here today, can you do that?" Nate asked.
He was gingerly pulling the large, leather-bound book
from the shelf. He carried it over to a desk in the center of
the room and put it down.

Hilton flipped through the pages. "Look at these
names," he said, frowning. "This was a fuckin' Irish ghetto

– even in 82. How come you people always say *we* have too many kids?"

"A lot of the families didn't live here anymore by then," Nyles answered. "They still attended church here though. It was where they were brought up. And they sent their kids here to school – even if they lived in Milton or Quincy."

"Goddamn it to hell," Nate said, exasperation in his voice. He was staring down at the book.

"What's wrong?" Nyles was trying to look past the burly detective at the pages in the book.

Nate held up the book for Nyles to see. "There's a good two or three months worth of entries cut out of the book. Look at the page stubs." He fingered the cut stubble of several pages. "The entries stop at August $18^{th}$ and begin again November $23^{rd}$.

Nyles let the Black detective hold the book in his gloved hands but put his head close so he could peer at the edges of the cut pages. "You can get your lab to examine these, but I'll bet they were cut in the last few days. Let's hope Father Hidalgo's secretary knows who visited these records recently."

Just then Father Hidalgo came back in the room, accompanied by a middle-aged Hispanic woman with gray hair. She was plump, dressed in a too-tight fitting pair of spandex pants that showed off her voluminous but shapeless thighs, and had a sweet, pleasant face, which appeared frightened.

"Who else has been in here in the last week or so?" Detective Hilton asked, staring accusingly at the secretary.

"No one… not even me," the secretary said, her voice shaking. Like Father Hidalgo, she had a distinct Spanish accent.

Nyles stepped in front of Hilton. "We don't mean to frighten you miss...?"

The woman switched her attention to Nyles. "Cabrera, Marisol, Cabrera."

"Someone cut some pages out of one of your baptismal books," Nyles continued, after giving the nervous woman an encouraging smile. He turned toward Father Hidalgo. "We'd like to have the police lab take a look at the book, maybe identify some fingerprints on it."

Nate was getting irritated. It seemed to him as if Nyles was trying to take over the case. Did Monahan think that they wouldn't cooperate with a Black detective? "You said you had other records, Father. Where are they?" His tone was angry and demanding.

"We have marriage records," Miss Cabrera answered, looking toward the set of bookshelves across the room. She looked offended by Detective Hilton's irritation.

They followed the secretary to the bookshelves on the opposite wall. The books were arranged by date, just as the baptismal records had been.

"Look at 1982," Nyles said.

"No dust," Nate growled. "I'll bet the same dates are missing." He reached up and pulled down the 1982 book of records. Leafing through it he stopped at mid August. The following several pages had been cut from the book. "Shit!" the detective exclaimed. Then he caught himself and with a sheepish look on his face turned to Ms. Cabrera. "Sorry for the language."

"Someone is determined to cover his tracks," Nyles said. "The best we can hope for is that he left some fingerprints."

"There's one more set of records from that year," the secretary said quietly. "Whatever you're looking for could be in them."

"What kind of records?" Nate asked. His tone was more cordial than it had been. His face still betrayed his embarrassment at having sworn in front of the woman.

"I'll show you," the secretary said.

The two detectives and the priest followed the woman to a corner of the room where she opened a file drawer that was labeled "construction."

"The church underwent repairs in 1982 and '83." She stopped looking and turned around to face them. "St. Aloysius is almost a national landmark, you know. It's one of the oldest churches in the country and certainly one of the oldest with this style of architecture." Her face was filled with pride.

"Great. Can we see the records?" Nate growled impatiently. The scowl had returned to his face.

Her face reddened and Ms. Cabrera turned back to the files, thumbing through them without looking up at the men standing behind her. She pulled a thick file from the drawer, then opened it. After a few moments of looking through the contents, she turned around and started to hand it to Detective Hilton, but then drew back and, changing her mind, handed the file to Nyles, instead. "You will find everything you're looking for in this file." She said, primly, as if turning in a term paper to her teacher. She cast a sidelong frown at Nate, as if to let him know that she didn't need to deal with him, if he was going to be rude to her.

Nyles resisted looking at the file. He thanked Miss Cabrera and stepped to the desk in the middle of the room, then spread the contents of the file folder out on the desk for all of them to see.

Nate pulled his gloves on tighter and shuffled through the invoices while Nyles looked over his shoulder again. Nate held up two invoices, both with Father Hurley's signature on them – *Rev. A. Hurley*. The dates were both in September of 1982.

"We're going to need to take these with us," Nate announced.

"You can make a copy for your files if you like, though you'll need to put on gloves before you handle them," Nyles told Miss Cabrera. "They may still have some old prints on them." He wondered why Detective Hilton didn't make at least some effort to gain the goodwill of a potential witness.

Miss Cabrera smiled at Nyles and looked over at Father Hidalgo for permission. When he nodded, she put on the gloves that Nate handed her and picked up the whole file and took it with her. "I'll copy all of the invoices with Father Hurley's name on them," she said, again addressing Nyles and pointedly ignoring Detective Hilton.

When the secretary returned with the originals of the invoices – more than ten in all – Niles and Nate thanked her and the priest, then left the church.

"What's the Monsignor's first name?" Nate asked as they walked along the sidewalk to their cars.

"Andrew, I think."

"I guess I'd better go see the Monsignor tomorrow," Nate said.

"Mind if I go with you?"

Nate stopped walking. He thought for a moment. "I guess it won't hurt for me to bring along a token Catholic," he said.

# Chasing Tales

## Chapter 35

Nyles reached Billy Phelan on his cell phone. It was only four in the afternoon, but Phelan was already firmly ensconced in the Hibernia Pub recuperating from a hard day in court. The prosecution had laid out its case to the jury, citing a large body of devastating physical evidence connected to the murder weapon, then describing a scenario in which Father O'Flannery had gone to Tim Russell's house, probably to try to convince him to recant his accusations about sexual molestation, and when that didn't work, killed him with a knife which he had brought with him just in case his arguments didn't work. They asked the jury to find Father Tom guilty of first-degree, premeditated murder.

Nyles offered to meet Phelan at the pub, since it was clear that the attorney had no intention of returning to his office. The invoices with Father Hurley's signatures on them were in Nate Hilton's possession in order that he could log them in as evidence in the child molestation case and have them examined for fingerprints. Phelan could then request them as evidence in the murder trial. Nyles wanted to explain to Phelan what the invoices meant so he could call Hurley in as a witness and start building a case that it could have been he who had molested Russell and later killed him. The case needn't be proven, only plausible enough to raise a doubt about Father O'Flannery's guilt in the mind of the jurors.

Parking across from the Hibernia Pub, Nyles' mind was flooded with memories. The bar was less than a half mile from where he had grown up and was almost as familiar a Dorchester landmark as St. Aloysius. It was a working class bar, but one that attracted some of Boston's most powerful Irish politicians, along with a heavy contingent of off-duty cops. Nyles' early adolescent memories were filled with evenings when he'd had to walk to the pub to collect his father. Later, when he was on the police force, he'd often come into the pub after work.

Billy Phelan was sitting at the bar, huddled in conversation with a middle aged, attractive, redheaded woman, one of whose hands rested suggestively on his thigh. On the other side of him was another man who might be Billy's age, or younger but whose face was lined and aged from drink. He was slim and wiry and wore glasses and a rumpled suit and was listening to Phelan talk, although he had an angry frown on his face while his hands nervously drummed the top of the bar.

Nothing seemed to have changed in the thirty-five or so years since Nyles had been inside the pub. The waiters still wore white shirts and ties and the worn wooden floor and long semi-oval bar with Guinness ads and Celtics, Red Sox and Bruins banners hanging above it, the tables scattered around the room, all looked the same as when he'd come in to retrieve his father ... or come in himself to do some drinking with his fellow detectives after work. He walked over to where Phelan was still talking to the woman at the bar.

"Evening Mr. Phelan, can I have a little of your time?" Nyles asked, putting a hand lightly on Phelan's shoulder. Nyles' tone made it clear that he was voicing a command, rather than a question.

The attorney looked surprised, then worried, as he redirected his gaze at the woman, almost as if he was asking her permission to break off their conversation. Phelan's other companion, the wizened little man with glasses, stared accusingly at Nyles and then at Billy. "You're so Goddamned popular tonight, Billy. No time for your old friends," the man said, savagely.

# Chasing Tales

"Fuck off, Alf," Phelan hissed. He looked at the woman. "Do you mind, honey? I'll be back in a jiff."

They took a free table in the corner.

"Why aren't you at your office working on the case?" Nyles asked, making no attempt to conceal his irritation. No lawyer worth his salt would be in a bar at this time of day with an important case going on and Phelan's presence confirmed Nyles' misgivings about the lawyer's ability to adequately defend Father Tom.

"Jesus, Monahan, don't you start criticizing me, too. The judge adjourned the trial at noon today. I haven't even presented my opening statement to the jury yet. There's nothing for me to do." He sat down at the table and looked at Nyles. "Unless you've got something for me to work with. The fucking evidence is all against my client right now."

Nyles was surprised by Phelan's feistiness. The attorney was more assertive when he'd belted down a few drinks. "I've got something for you, so you'd better quit hanging around this bar and go back to your office and work on Father Tom's defense," he said, looking Phelan in the eyes. His voice had taken on the authority of raw steel. "What I've got is important enough to be the basis for your defense, so you're going to have to revise your opening argument to let the jury know the direction you're heading."

Phelan's bravado had evaporated. He looked sheepishly at Nyles, then raised his hand to the bartender to bring him another beer. When the waiter arrived, Nyles ordered a Guinness for himself.

"What have you got? I'm already planning to say someone else planted the weapon," Phelan said. "The idea that Tom wore gloves but left his and his sister's fingerprints all over the knife doesn't make sense. It suggests a frame-up."

"We've got proof that Father Hurley was a priest at St. Aloysius. There was at least one complaint against him by a boy named Jimmy Gleason. Unfortunately, Gleason was killed a few days ago and we don't have a record of the complaint, but we've finally got proof that Father Hurley exists and he was at St. Aloysius when Russell was an altar boy."

"You're talking about the same Father Hurley who came to visit Tom the day of the murder, right? The Monsignor in charge of molestation cases for the Church?"

"I don't know. I'm having the records with Father Hurley's name on them examined for fingerprints and then we can compare them to the Monsignor's – unless he admits it to us outright."

"Holy shit. Monsignor Hurley's goose would be cooked if it could be proven he was trying to conceal the record of his having been at St. Aloysius."

Nyles looked around the bar. Phelan's two companions, the woman and the man called Alf, were sitting next to each other in heated debate. "Somebody has been tipping off Monsignor Hurley, or whoever is behind these killings, about what I'm doing. That would explain why Sister Mary Agnes was killed, and maybe Gleason, too. It would also explain why the pages of the baptismal records were clipped out before I got there. How much are you discussing this case in here?"

Phelan's astonishment turned quickly to anger. "Jesus. Don't blame me for someone knowing what you're doing. Anyway, wasn't that nun the Monsignor's secretary? He could have found out what she was up to on his own and if Gleason's family filed a complaint against him then he already knew about Gleason. And if he's trying to cover his past, then he'd remove any records whether he knew you were looking for them or not."

Phelan was right, but Nyles still didn't trust him to not have discussed the case with almost anyone who'd listen at the bar. "This is no place to conduct a law practice."

Phelan was looking over at Alf and the woman at the bar. She appeared as if she was getting ready to leave. He felt a sense of panic. "I don't need you telling me how to be a lawyer," he said, standing up. "Just keep investigating. You're doing your job. Let me do mine." He glared down at Nyles and then turned and headed back to the bar.

Nyles shook his head in dismay. Talking with Phelan had brought back memories of the times he'd tried to talk his father into leaving the pub early and the old man had refused. He took one last, long sip of his Guinness and left.

# Chasing Tales

## Chapter 36

Billy Phelan returned to the bar and was surprised to find that it was Alf, not Norma, who was the more upset with his having left to talk to Monahan. His longtime drinking partner was becoming more and more possessive and his behavior had become increasingly irritating. Now Alf was demanding to know why Billy had had to have a private conversation with Nyles Monahan.

"It's my job, for Christ's sake. I'm a lawyer and Monahan works for me. We're in the middle of an important case." Billy was sitting between Norma and Alf.

"And you're probably telling *her* every detail of the case, like you're some big-shot lawyer," Alf said in his low, gravelly voice, casting an angry look at the woman. He swayed at little. He had already had four or five glasses of beer and a couple of shots of whiskey.

"Christ, you two are like an old married couple," the woman said, her expression filled with disgust.

"We're just friends," Billy said, sheepishly. He finished his glass of beer and looked for Tommy O'Donald to bring him another.

Norma looked at her watch. "Can't we go somewhere more private?" she asked. "First it was your private investigator who wanted your time and now Alf is acting like a jealous wife. I'd like to spend some time with you alone."

Billy was more than receptive to Norma's suggestion. He was desperate for companionship and sitting in the bar with Alf wasn't what he had in mind. He suspected Norma had a husband at home – maybe one who worked nights. She had never suggested that they go to her place. Although he had at first thought of her as a one-night stand, he had become attached to her.

"Let's go," he said to the woman. "We'll go to my place."

"You're leaving?" Alf said, a hint of panic in his voice.

"We're tired of talking in public. Besides Monahan thinks I talk too much in here."

"So you're going to go to your place and tell her everything about the case?"

"What's it to you?" Billy said. He was getting more and more irritated by Alf's jealousy.

"Oh, fuck it," Alf said, shaking his head. "You've probably told her everything, about the case already, anyway."

"What the fuck do you care?" Billy asked.

"I don't. And fuck you, Billy. Leave your friends alone if you want. See if I give a shit." Alf turned his back and signaled Tommy for another beer.

\*\*\*

Billy's apartment was nothing to write home about but ever since the first time when Norma had come home with him, he'd been keeping it clean and tidy, in case he got lucky with her again. He also kept plenty of alcohol around.

"Wine? I bought some of your favorite kind," Billy said, lifting the bottle for Norma to see.

She nodded. She was sitting on his couch, smoking a cigarette with an eager look on her face. The first time she had been in his apartment she had been surprised that it hadn't been nicer, given that he was a lawyer, but she was gradually coming to realize that he wasn't a very successful lawyer, although, according to him, his current case had a chance of changing that. "What was the new information the private detective told you about today?" she asked.

Billy joined her on the couch, handing her a glass of white wine and sipping on a glass of whiskey himself. "Remember I told you that one of those former altar boys identified Father Hurley as the person who molested him?"

She sipped her wine slowly and nodded. "And the detective thinks this Father Hurley is the same priest who is now in charge of abuse cases for the Church, except he was away in Washington, DC when the abuse happened."

"Wow, you really are interested in this case. I didn't think you'd remember all that."

She shrugged. "I'm interested in everything you tell me, Billy. What did the detective tell you today?"

"Monsignor Hurley told the cops and my investigator that he'd never been a priest at St. Aloysius and there never was anyone else by that name there. But today, while I was in court, Monahan and a cop visited the church and found some documents with Hurley's signature on them as the parish priest back in 1982, right after Father O'Flannery left."

"So the story about being in law school was a lie?"

"Monahan thinks so, but he's not willing to go that far. There could be two Father Hurleys, though why the Monsignor is covering up for the other one is a mystery. But anyway it's the piece of evidence that I need in order to shake the foundation of the prosecution's case."

"Can you do that even if the altar boy who accused Hurley is now dead?"

"I couldn't win if I was prosecuting the Monsignor, but all I have to do is raise a question about my client's guilt. The evidence Monahan has found so far could be enough to get my client off."

# Chasing Tales

She smiled and raised her glass in a toast. "Congratulations Billy." Then her face became serious. "What about Monsignor Hurley? Will the prosecutor go after him?"

Billy downed the remains of his whiskey and stood to get another. He looked at Norma's glass and it was still more than half full. "Maybe," he said, as he walked to the kitchen. "The two main witnesses, Tim Russell and Jimmy Gleason are both dead, so it will require them finding another witness who will say that Hurley molested him. There's probably more out there and when they read Hurley's name in the papers as part of Father O'Flannery's trial, it may cause one of them to come forward."

Norma nodded thoughtfully, then knocked back the rest of her wine in one long swallow. "Don't get yourself another drink, Billy. I'm feeling amorous. Let's go into your bedroom." She gazed at him through half-closed eyes.

Billy put the bottle that was in his hand back on the kitchen counter. "Talking about abuse cases must make you horny. That's fine with me though." He was thinking he was luckier than he'd ever imagined he'd be.

"*You* make me horny, honey. And I have to leave early tonight. I don't want to miss any time in bed is all." She had already unbuttoned the top button of her dress.

Billy felt a tinge of anxiety at the thought of her leaving, even though he was excited at the prospect of getting quickly into bed. The truth was, he was as lonely for companionship as he was for sex and he wished she'd stay the whole night. But sex and a few hours with her was better than nothing at all – or an evening spent drinking with Alf at the Hibernia. "You're my kind of girl," he said, leading her into the bedroom.

# Chasing Tales

## Chapter 37

Roseanne Compton was the last witness to view the lineup of photographs. Six of the previous ten witnesses had been unable to identify any of the pictures as the man they'd seen in the train next to Sister Mary Agnes. Two persons, a teenage girl, who had been coming home to Dorchester from attending dance lessons in the center of the city and a middle-age businessman from Milton who rode the train to work every day, picked the Monsignor's photo, though neither was one hundred percent sure. Two others, both of them middle-aged women who had been shopping in the city, picked other photographs, though the two of them hadn't picked the same one. One of them was "absolutely sure" that the photo she picked was the man she had seen in the train. The photograph was of a detective from another precinct and was one of the foils designed to make identification more difficult. Detective Leeper was hopeful that Mrs. Compton, because of her proximity to the killer and her alertness to her surroundings, would provide the deciding vote on the Monsignor's fate.

"Take your time and look at each photograph before you answer. You don't have to identify anyone if no one looks like the man you saw on the train." Detective Leeper was doing everything he could to avoid signaling which picture was Monsignor Hurley, even unconsciously. He looked away as she gazed intently at each photograph, each one glued to one large piece of cardboard so she could view them all at once.

"I don't see him," she finally said, a curious note of defiance in her voice.

Leeper swallowed hard, trying not to show his disappointment. "Take one more look, Mrs. Compton – so you're sure."

"I can't be sure, young man. I won't say that all white men look alike to me, but all skinny, middle-aged white men with glasses look alike. They just do. He might be in here and he might not, I just can't tell."

"But you're not saying he's *not* among these men?"

"I'm not saying he is or he isn't."

"There's another way to do this. Let's say you have to pick one. Pick the picture that's most likely to be him, even if you're not sure if you're correct."

"I can't do that. My husband was shot because the police thought he was the man they were after and they were wrong, but he's still disabled. I'm not going to guess about who's a murderer."

The detective drew a deep breath. "We can't use your identification in court. We can only use positive identifications in court. This will just help me to find the man."

She shook her head, an expression of stolid defiance on her face. "I'm not going to do that. If I'm not sure, then I'm not saying."

Leeper made an effort to control his irritation. He understood her reluctance and he felt a grudging admiration with regard to her insistence on sticking to her principles, but he wasn't going to give up. "OK. You don't have to tell me who you think it might be. You don't have to identify anyone at all. Just tell me one thing. Without saying which one, do any of the pictures look like the man you saw on the train?"

She pursed her lips as if trying to decide if it was a trick question. Finally she nodded. "One of them looks sort of like the man. But I won't tell you which one, and don't ask me anymore."

He smiled and nodded. "I said I wouldn't and I won't. You've done your best and that's all I wanted you to do. Thank you, Mrs. Compton. You've been helpful."

She began to gather up her coat and purse from the chair next to hers. "Have I? I don't know how I could have been. I haven't told you anything."

He thought about how only one of the five pictures was not a Boston PD detective or a picture of an inmate already in jail. "You've told me enough, Mrs. Compton. Thank you again."

## Chapter 38

"Don't judge Billy too harshly," Father Tom told Nyles. They were in the visiting room at the jail and Nyles had just told Father Tom about his visit with the priest's lawyer in the Hibernia Pub, though he'd downplayed his negative feelings about Phelan as much as he could in an effort to avoid presenting too discouraging a picture to Father Tom. Nyles had been on his way home when he had remembered his wife's admonition to visit the priest more often and he turned around and drove downtown to the county jail, just making it inside the modern glass and steel building with about fifteen minutes before the afternoon visiting hours expired.

"It's probably a good thing that Billy hasn't presented his opening arguments," Nyles said, "since I was able to give him some new information this afternoon."

"What kind of information?"

Nyles told the priest about the discovery of documents at St. Aloysius containing Father Hurley's signature.

"But the baptismal records had been cut from the record book?" Father Tom shook his head in dismay. "I guess Hurley thought about those records about the same time we did."

"Or someone tipped him off," Nyles said.

"What do you mean?"

"Whoever this Hurley is - either the Monsignor or someone else - he seems to be one step ahead of me, either murdering a potential witness or destroying evidence. If it's the Monsignor, it might make sense because of his access to records and because Sister Mary Agnes worked for him, but I've got a sneaking feeling that Billy's talking too much to someone – either that or Detective Hilton has a leak in his department."

"Billy talks a lot, but the Monsignor would have the easiest access to everything, although I can't imagine him walking into St. Aloysius incognito and cutting up records. He'd be too easily recognizable. Anyway, didn't you say he was in law school when I left Boston?"

Nyles frowned and shook his head. "I still haven't figured that out. Either there's a flaw in the Monsignor's story – a flaw we haven't found yet – or it's simply not him." He kept shaking his head. "For someone who's innocent, he's done everything he can to conceal information that's crucial to your case. I just find it hard to believe he's not involved."

"It will be devastating to the Church if the Monsignor is the one behind these killings."

"The Church will survive. I'm worried about you."

Father Tom smiled a thin smile. "I'll survive too. That's what my faith is for."

The guard signaled that their time was over and Nyles rose to leave. He wasn't even allowed to shake the priest's hand, though he would have hugged him if he'd had the chance.

The sun had set and the evening had become frigidly cold. This close to the harbor, a stiff wind could be felt blowing off the ocean. Nyles hoped it wasn't going to snow again. He walked through the dark parking lot and got into the Jeep SUV he was driving on loan from his brother. He knew why he hadn't visited Father Tom very often; he emerged from each visit feeling beaten down by the weight of responsibility that sat squarely on his shoulders. Billy Phelan was too incompetent to convince a jury of Father Tom's innocence. It was up to Nyles to find the real killer.

188

# Chasing Tales

Within five minutes of leaving the county jail he noticed a battered Ford Taurus following him. There was enough traffic on the wet streets, which were starting to become icy, that he made two random turns onto side streets just to verify that he was being tailed, before resuming his normal route back to Milton. Whoever was following him must not know his destination or they wouldn't have followed his arbitrary deviations. That meant his tail didn't know he was staying at his brother's house and Nyles had no intention of leading him there. When he entered Milton he took the first side street and pulled up in front of a small, antique-looking cottage he'd picked at random, then walked toward the house, ducking behind a pair of twin oak trees in the front yard, just before he reached the front door. From the shelter of the trees he watched the Taurus pull up several spaces behind his car and kill its lights.

He could see a head in the dim light from a streetlamp at the end of the block, but not with enough definition to recognize who it was behind the wheel. He moved from the safety of the twin oaks to the shelter of a tall hedge near the border of the property and then, bending down, he began edging toward the street. When he reached the sidewalk he had no choice but to move into the open and dash toward the parked car. Before he could reach it, the driver, apparently seeing him coming, started the car and with a screech of tires, turned a tight U-turn in the middle of the street and drove back the way he had come. Nyles stood and watched as the taillights from the car disappeared over a rise in the street.

\*\*\*

# Chasing Tales

After entering his brother's house Nyles immediately went to his room upstairs and looked out of the window. From the upstairs vantage point, he could see the road in front of Sean and Millie's house all the way to its intersection with the main road, which led toward the center of town. He continued his vigil at the window for ten interminable  minutes and then, convinced that he hadn't been followed, he went downstairs.

Nyles had gotten used to Kaylee and Katherine being in his brother's house when he returned at night and in the past several days he had felt comforted knowing they were safe, but tonight he surveyed the scene with a different feeling. The idea that he might be leading a murderer to their doorstep unsettled him. Tonight, just like most nights,  Katherine was doing her homework at the dining room table. The eleven year-old had become more relaxed and outgoing since the Department of Social Services had prohibited her from living in the same house with her stepfather. Kaylee had had to make a decision about whether to stay with her husband or her child, whom the court had put in the custody of Kaylee's parents. Nyles could tell that Kaylee was still under pressure from Alan to come back to him, but she had made the choice to live wherever her daughter lived. Neither Sean nor Millie had brought up the issue of her marriage to Alan.

"How are you feeling about living here?" Nyles asked. He and Kaylee were sitting in the living room opposite each other in two wingback chairs, each of them holding a can of coke.

Kaylee flashed an uncertain smile at her uncle. "Mom does everything for me, just like when I was a kid. That's nice but it makes me feel like I've regressed. I don't like Katherine seeing me acting helpless."

"I suspect Millie is glad to feel that you need her again. Besides, in her house, she probably feels as if she's supposed to do the work. If you're going to stay here for awhile, you'll probably have to talk to her about it."

Kaylee put her head in her hands. "I don't know what I'm gonna do, Uncle Nyles. Alan wants me to come home but the court says Katherine has to live here."

"Alan can't be around Katherine. Not just because the judge said so, but because it's dangerous for your daughter."

Kaylee looked as if she was about to cry. "I have to choose between my husband and my daughter."

He nodded. "That's because of your husband, not because of anyone else."

"Alan saved me. If it weren't for him, I'd still be using drugs. He saw something in me when no one else did."

"Some people are attracted to a person with a weakness – they know it's going to make the other person dependent upon them and it allows them to abuse the relationship."

She was listening intently. "Do you think that's what's going on? He's using my fear of going back to drugs?"

Nyles knew he was sounding like an amateur psychologist. What did he know about overcoming drugs – or even about relationships, for that matter? His own wife had almost died of a drug and alcohol induced stroke and he had been powerless to alter her behavior ... he hadn't even tried. His voice was tentative. "Alan can't be your only reason for not using drugs. You have a daughter to raise and protect."

She shook her head. "I don't know what to do."

# Chasing Tales

To Nyles, Kaylee's choice was obvious, but he'd never been in her position. He felt obligated to guide his niece, even if he didn't know how. "You're Katherine's mother, Kaylee. You're the single most important person in her life and you probably always will be. I believe that if she feels you won't protect her from Alan, she'll turn her back on you. She's already sneaking cigarettes and falling behind in school. If you lose her, you'll be losing her to the same influences that almost ruined your life."

Kaylee's face looked stricken. "She can't get involved with drugs – not my daughter."

"She needs you. She needs to be able to trust you to put her first."

She nodded. "You're right. What was I thinking?" She blinked back tears. "Thank you Uncle Nyles."

He smiled. He hoped her resolve wasn't temporary. "Let's go check on your daughter's homework, shall we?"

She stood and hugged her uncle. They both went into the dining room where Katherine was sitting at the dining table, writing the answers to math problems.

Nyles looked over the young girl's shoulder. She was doing simple algebra and he noticed she wore no makeup or lipstick and she wore jeans and a sweatshirt, both befitting her age. "Your mom and I came to see if we could help you with your homework. You're past my level of knowledge already."

Katherine looked up at her great uncle with barely concealed pride on her face.

"We can just sit and admire what she's doing, can't we?" Kaylee said, her eyes still filled with tears, but her voice strong.

# Chasing Tales

Katherine moved the page of equations over for her mother to see. Her movements were hesitant. "I'm all done with tomorrow's assignment," she said, quietly.

"Then I'm very proud of you," Kaylee said. She reached down and put her arms around her daughter's shoulder and gave her a hug.

Millie announced time to set the table for dinner and Katherine began putting away her books. Helping her grandmother set the table had become an evening routine, which seemed to give her as much pride as completing her homework. Nyles watched his niece's daughter bring dishes from the kitchen, feeling a sense of satisfaction that the young girl seemed to be headed in a healthier direction than when he'd first met her. After a few minutes he turned and went into the den to talk to his brother.

"I'm going to move into a hotel tomorrow," Nyles announced to Sean, who was reading the evening newspaper with a Celtics game on the television in the background, the sound turned very low.

Sean looked startled. "Why the hell would you do that?"

"Somebody followed me tonight on my way here. I lost them by stopping in another part of town, but I don't want them following me here."

His brother looked stunned. "Followed you? Why would someone follow you here? What would they want?"

Nyles didn't want to alarm his brother and he didn't want to sound melodramatic, but he needed to be clear about his concern that Sean's family might be put in harm's way if he continued to stay at their house. "Someone seems to have figured out what I'm doing on Father Tom's case and whoever it is has killed two of my witnesses already. I don't want any of your family in the line of fire."

Sean's expression was sober. "Then you're in danger yourself."

Nyles' expression softened. "I've helped witnesses protect themselves before, I just didn't know it was necessary in this case, but now I do and I'm going to take the same precautions myself. I'll go to a hotel in some busy part of town, get a room that gives me a view of who's coming and going, and use a valet service to park and retrieve my car each morning and evening." He spoke calmly, as if avoiding getting killed was an everyday occurrence. In truth, Nyles wasn't frightened, but he was exaggerating his nonchalance for the benefit of his brother.

Sean nodded. "It sounds as if you've thought it all out." He took a sip of his coke and gazed at the television screen for a few seconds. "What do I tell Millie and Kaylee and Katherine?"

"I already thought of that. I'll just say that I'm working with the Boston Police on the case and we're going to be involved in some stakeouts for awhile so they're putting me up in hotel downtown. If they ask me anything more about it I can say I'm not allowed to talk about it."

Sean shook his head in wonder. "Geez brother, aren't you getting too old for this kind of cloak and dagger business?" There was a hint of a grin on his face, but his eyes showed his worry.

"I feel like I am. I thought that being a private detective would be a nice safe way to spend my retirement. I thought I'd be bored. I guess I was wrong." As he said it, Nyles realized he was feeling an almost pleasant sense of tension. If he could keep his family out of danger, he didn't mind engaging in a little cat and mouse with the killer himself. He knew it meant he'd gotten close to discovering the murderer and his leads about Father

Hurley were on the right track. "I don't think I'll be away for long," he said to his brother. "This case is about to break."

When he returned to his room after supper, the first thing he did was to look out the window. He hadn't turned out the light in the room and as soon as he parted the curtains, he regretted his mistake because a set of tail lights immediately switched on, then began to move off toward the intersection. There weren't enough houses on the street to make curbside parking usual and he was almost certain the car, which had turned onto the main road and disappeared, must have been the one following him earlier. He felt an even greater urgency about leaving his brother's house, even though he realized that he, not his family, was the killer's target. He would not only need to move, he would need to make it obvious to the killer that he had done so.

## Chapter 39

Nyles stood shivering on the front steps of the Archdiocese offices in Brighton, watching Nate Hilton lumbering toward him across the plaza in front of the massive building. The thickness of the Black detective's body, especially in the heavy overcoat he was wearing, gave him the appearance of an NFL linebacker.

"It's colder than a witch's tit," Nate said as he got close to where Nyles was waiting for him. The temperature was in the high teens that morning and clouds of vapor escaped when he spoke. The detective was carrying a manila envelope under his arm.

"Any news about the fingerprints?" Nyles asked as they entered the building.

"We got some old fingerprints off of the invoices as well as prints off of the baptismal book cover. Same prints. Looks as if Father Hurley returned to St. Aloysius recently to try to cover his tracks. I guess he didn't remember the construction invoices."

They were at the door to the Monsignor's office. Nyles hesitated. He knew he would have a shock when he opened the door and saw the empty desk where Mary had sat.

Nate stepped in front of Nyles and opened the door. A young woman in a dark suit sat at the desk formerly occupied by Sister Mary Agnes. She smiled brightly at the two men.

"Can I help you?' The young woman asked.

"Detective Hilton here to see Monsignor Hurley," Nate answered. "I left a message that we were coming." Nate hadn't bothered to introduce Nyles.

The young woman's smile faded briefly, then returned. "I'll let him know you're here. Please take a seat." She got up and knocked on the door then entered.

They had both sat down on a wooden bench along the wall in the outer office, like two kids waiting to talk to the principal. "We may have a break in the case," Nyles said. "Whoever Hurley is, he's getting more careless. I was followed back to my brother's house in Milton last night."

"Bullshit!" Hilton said loudly, a deep scowl on his face. He quickly looked around the room self-consciously.

"It's not bullshit," Nyles answered. He spoke in a low, confidential voice. "Whoever this Hurley is, he probably killed three people so far and it would make sense for him to go after me."

Nate pursed his lips. "You mean he knows what you're doing?"

"How else would he have figured out about Sister Mary Agnes and Jimmy Gleason?"

"There's other ways, but..." Hilton's dour expression had turned to worry. "Goddammit, this guy's arrogant. What are you going to do?"

Nyles spoke matter-of-factly "I don't want to put my brother's family at risk. I'll take a hotel."

"And call me if you even *think* you need help." Hilton reached into his pocket and pulled out a card and wrote a number on the back. "This is my cell phone. You can reach me anytime, 24/7."

Nyles accepted the card. "Thanks." He was surprised by the detective's gesture.

Nate shrugged as if it was nothing, but he looked embarrassed. "You're my ticket back to the being a legitimate detective. I've got to keep you safe, you fuckin' Mick."

# Chasing Tales

The door opened and the young secretary stood holding it open. "The Monsignor will see you now."

Monsignor Hurley was standing behind his desk, a brittle smile on his face. "I see you two are working together now. Are you here to make another ridiculous accusation, Detective Hilton?" He gestured for the two of them to sit in the two leather chairs facing his desk. "Detective Leeper was already here, making thinly veiled accusations with regard to Sister Mary Agnes' murder and even that recent killing in Waltham. Why am I being persecuted by your department?"

"I don't have any control over what Detective Leeper does. I'm still working on the Tim Russell molestation case," Nate answered.

"Really? I would think that's beside the point since Father O'Flannery is now charged with murder."

"I don't think Russell's molester was Father O'Flannery." Nate's tone was even, carrying an edge of warning.

Monsignor Hurley didn't say anything.

"We have an accusation against a Father Hurley when he was a priest at St. Aloysius."

The Monsignor's eyes narrowed. "I already told you, as well at that other detective, that there was never a Father Hurley at St. Aloysius. On top of that, you know where I was during the time in question." He glanced over his shoulder at the Catholic University diploma on his wall.

"I'm afraid you're wrong," Nate said.

"I'm wrong?" The Monsignor's eyes widened in surprise as he struggled to control his anger.

"We've found records at St. Aloysius from 1982 signed by Father A. Hurley."

The Monsignor's eyes widened even further. For the first time his expression was fearful. "That's impossible. What kind of records?"

"Construction invoices. We also took fingerprints from those invoices and they match prints on the book of baptismal records from 1982, which were altered to take out the name of the priest who signed them."

"The baptismal records were altered?" Monsignor Hurley looked confused.

"Destroyed, actually. The baptismal records were cut from the book."

Monsignor Hurley's expression changed from fear and astonishment back to anger. "Someone cut the records of baptisms? Outrageous. Altering the records of the Church is a sacrilege. "

"I guess that means it wasn't you who committed the sacrilege." Nate said, a note of sarcasm in his voice.

"Of course not."

"We have fingerprints."

"Fine. I told you already I was never a priest at St. Aloysius. I wasn't even in Massachusetts at that time."

"Then who is Father A. Hurley?"

The Monsignor's expression was fearful again but also defiant. "I have no idea."

Nate looked over at Nyles.

"The Archdiocese must keep records of parish assignments," Nyles said, his voice flat and emotionless.

"Of course."

"We'd like to see them."

"That will take a court order."

"It doesn't have to," Nyles said, staring fixedly at the Monsignor.

"It does if I say it does." The Monsignor returned his even gaze

"I can get one by this afternoon," Nate said, matter-of-factly. He'd been impressed by Nyles' calm, but insistent manner and he was trying to emulate it.

"Then do so." The Monsignor stood. Although he was trying to maintain his façade of formality, the expression on his face was one of profound sadness. "I believe we're done... unless you have more questions." His voice trailed off, as if his mind was already elsewhere.

"Just one," Nate said, standing.

"What?" The Monsignor asked, as if his attention had been summoned back from more important considerations.

"Why put off the inevitable?"

"The inevitable? You may never learn how mistaken you are," the Monsignor said, a sad smile on his face.

"I've got a question, too," Nyles said. He was standing but he hadn't headed for the door.

"Ask it," the Monsignor said with a sigh.

"Do you own a car?"

"A car?" The Monsignor appeared confused by the question. "What in the world has that got to do with anything?"

"Just answer the question," Nate said. He had turned back from the door and he stood next to Nyles.

The Monsignor heaved another sigh. "Of course I own a car. Just because I live on the grounds doesn't mean I don't visit the community."

"What make is it?" Nyles asked.

"It's a Mercedes – a five-year old Mercedes – are you satisfied?" There was a glint of victory in his eye and his tone was arrogant.

"Thank you," Nyles said. The Monsignor's answer wasn't what he'd expected and he was left even more confused than he had been before he'd asked the question. If it wasn't the Monsignor who had followed him the previous night, who was it?

## Chapter 40

Nate Hilton and Nyles re-entered the Monsignor's office, a copy of the court order for the record of parish priest assignments in 1982 in Nate's pocket. They were greeted by the same young secretary, eager to show off her perky smile.

"We're back," Nate announced, unable to conceal the satisfaction in his voice. "Better announce us to the Monsignor."

Her smile became uncertain. "I'm afraid he isn't in. He left the office about two hours ago and hasn't been back."

"Did he say when he'd return?" Nate asked.

"No. Did he know you were returning?"

"I'm not sure he knew it would be this soon." Nate looked at Nyles. "What do you want to do?"

"Does he normally return to his office in the afternoon?" Nyles asked the secretary.

"He usually only leaves if he has a meeting. His leaving this time was unusual. I heard him on the telephone with someone and then he left, rather abruptly in fact. He said he needed to meet someone."

"We have a court order for some Archdiocese records," Nate said, starting to sound impatient. "Who else can we see to get them?"

"We have a custodian of records. He would need to process a court order, anyway."

"Can you direct us to him?" Nate asked.

She gave them directions. The custodian of records was in the basement of the same building. She called to tell him they were coming.

The custodian of records was an overweight, young man with puffy pink cheeks and an ingratiating smile. He introduced himself as Marvin Thompson. His office desk was at one end of a large room filled with bookshelves, much like a library, and rows of file cabinets. He took the court document, then looked it over. "You're looking for the record of parish assignments for 1982, is that correct?" The young man appeared impressed by the court order and he was eager to please them.

"We're interested in the assignments to St. Aloysius church, if they're kept separately," Nate said.

The man shook his head. "They're not. Our records contain every assignment for that year." He excused himself and went to a copy machine behind his desk and made a copy of the court order, keeping the original, which he stamped with a date stamp, then handed them the copy and told them he would be right back.

Nyles and Nate each took a seat on hardback wooden chairs that were against the wall in front of the young man's desk and waited ten minutes until the clerk returned, empty-handed and with a confused look on his face.

"The records you're looking for must be checked out. I don't remember doing that and I usually remember all the transactions, but it's possible that someone borrowed the file some time ago and hasn't returned it yet. I've only been working here for six months. I'll have to check the log."

Thompson took a large journal out of a drawer in his desk and began looking through it page by page. Nyles and Nate watched him scan through several months, which amounted to twenty or more pages. "I can't find anything," the custodian of records said, without looking up while he continued to flip through the pages. After ten more minutes of looking he announced that whoever had taken the record had not checked it out in the last 18 months.

Neither Nyles nor Nate was surprised.

"Do you keep track of who comes down here to browse the records, even if they don't check anything out?" Nyles asked.

Marvin shook his head. "Anyone who I recognize can browse all they like."

"Was Monsignor Hurley here today?" Nate asked.

"About an hour and a half ago. But he didn't take anything with him when he left."

"You mean he didn't check anything out." Nate said, frowning at the young man.

"Everyone has to check an item out if they take it from the records room," Thompson said, as if Nate hadn't understood.

"Sure they do," Hilton said, the sarcasm evident in his voice. He looked at Nyles. "Let's go look for the Monsignor."

\*\*\*

The Chancery included a building in which most of the priests who worked for the Archdiocese administration had their residences. Nyles and Nate had gotten directions to Monsignor Hurley's residence from his new administrative assistant and Nate's badge got them past the security guard in the building, which was an old wooden and stone house set behind the other office buildings amidst what looked as if it was a small decorative orchard of now barren cherry trees. The Monsignor's apartment was on the first floor. When there was no answer to the knock on his door, Nate asked the security guard to open the door for them.

Monsignor Hurley was sitting on a stool in his kitchen, his head bent at an awkward angle, as if he was studying something in the sink. Both Nyles and Nate knew he was dead as soon as they saw the position of his body. If they touched him he would have toppled to the floor. His head and shoulders leaned far enough into the sink to keep him from falling backward and the sink was covered in stains of blood from a gash across his left wrist.

"I'll call it in," Nate said. He turned to the security guard, who was looking at the Monsignor's body in horror. "Call whoever is in charge of this compound – the Archbishop or whoever – and tell them to come over here."

Nyles was looking around the apartment for a note. He was always saddened when he saw the lifeless body of someone he'd known, even if he hadn't liked the person, as in the case of Monsignor Hurley. He was doubly saddened if the death was a suicide, having wrestled with the same urge, himself during the most hopeless periods of Cloris' illness, when it had looked as if she would die or live the rest of her life in a coma. He knew the depth of hopelessness the decision to end one's life represented.

What he was looking for lay on a table in the dining room. The brief note was neatly printed in ballpoint pen and signed, *Msgr. A. Hurley*. Nyles called Nate into the dining room and when the detective arrived Nyles pointed at the note, being careful not to touch it.

Nate read the note aloud. "Father O'Flannery is innocent of all the crimes of which he is accused and I take responsibility for the deaths of Tim Russell, Sister Mary Agnes and Jimmy Gleason. God forgive me, I cannot live with my unbearable secrets any longer. I am no longer worthy of the Church."

"I guess your client is off the hook." Hilton said.

# Chasing Tales

Nyles stared into the kitchen at the still body of Monsignor Hurley. He felt immense relief that Father Tom would be cleared of both the child molestation charges and the murder of Tim Russell, but he was unhappy that the Monsignor's suicide note was so enigmatic. Why hadn't he directly admitted being guilty of the crimes himself and what did he mean that he took responsibility for them? Did it mean he'd killed all the victims? Would a man burdened by such guilt be capable of killing so callously, especially when one of the people was his trusted assistant of almost ten years? Monsignor Hurley had taken more secrets to his grave than he had revealed.

"What's the matter?" Nate asked. He was in an ebullient mood – probably imagining that he would be promoted to the homicide division as soon as his superiors found out that his detective work had unearthed the real killer of Tim Russell.

"I wish he had said more," Nyles said, shaking his head as he walked into the kitchen. He looked at the Monsignor's ashen face, wondering what secrets the man had taken with him. Suddenly he was struck by a thought. "Where's the record of the priest assignments – the one he took from the records room this afternoon?"

"It's probably here someplace," Nate answered from the other room.

Nyles looked around the kitchen then walked back to the dining room where Detective Hilton was still standing over the table with the note on it. "Why steal the record if he was going to admit everything and kill himself? His secretary said he was going to meet someone. He could have given the records to someone else."

Nate narrowed his eyes and stared at Nyles. "Don't blow this, Monahan. Don't look a gift horse in the mouth. We've got our child molester and our killer. Your

206

friend will go free and I'll get assigned to fucking homicide. Let's take what we've got and call it good."

Nyles returned the Black detective's stare then walked away and began searching the tiny apartment for the stolen records.

## Chapter 41

Molly O' Flannery was embarrassed by the compliments Sean and Millie heaped upon her for the chocolate layer cake she had baked for her brother. Nyles' brother and sister-in-law were crowded into the living room of Molly's house, along with Father Tom himself, Billy Phelan and the woman named Norma, whom Billy had asked Father Tom for permission to bring along, since, he said, she knew so much about the case. Nyles had asked Mickey Ryan to come too, feeling as if the disabled young man had been the one who'd put him on the right track in identifying the true child molester. Nyles had also invited Nate Hilton, but Nate hadn't yet arrived and Nyles was doubtful that he would show up. Nyles shared the joy everyone around him was expressing, but he felt an acute sadness when he thought about the absence of Mary MacDonald.

Father Tom had been relieved when he'd been given the news that he was no longer on trial for Tim Russell's murder nor suspected of child abuse. His relief was tempered by his sadness at Monsignor Hurley's suicide. Like Nyles, he felt such an act, even by someone who might be considered his enemy, was a tragedy.

Nyles had kept his reservations about Monsignor Hurley's confession to himself, not even telling Cloris, who had similarly mixed reactions of joy that her close friend, Father Tom, had been declared innocent, and sadness that her other friend, Mary MacDonald, was forever gone.

Molly had had plenty of beer, wine, and Bushmills on hand so everyone could celebrate. Only Sean wasn't drinking. Billy Phelan was half-drunk and he was standing in a corner of the living room going on about the cases he was ready to take on. Getting the charges against Father Tom dismissed had bolstered Billy's confidence in his ability to once more defend criminal cases. His change of attitude reflected his obliviousness to the fact that it had been Nyles' and Nate Hilton's investigative work that had allowed his client to go free, and not his own courtroom abilities. Neither Father Tom nor Norma, who looked mildly uncomfortable being Billy's "date" but appeared happy to see him so confident, challenged Billy's assertions about his own role in bringing about the dismissal of the charges.

Nyles listened to Billy talk and thought that everyone was a good storyteller about himself, especially in his own mind, but much of what went on in our lives was a matter of luck. He was always amused by the famous fictional detectives, going all the way back to Sherlock Holmes, who steadfastly averred that they "didn't believe in coincidences." Coincidences and luck paid a much larger role in life than any of us imagined, he thought.

In terms of coincidences, Nyles was interested in learning what he could about Norma, the woman Billy had apparently confided in during the trial. Nyles still thought that someone had tipped Monsignor Hurley off about the investigation, although, as Billy had told him before, the Monsignor was in a good position to anticipate what records the two detectives would be looking for even without getting any help from someone who had learned about their plans. He certainly would have known about Jimmy Gleason's complaint 30 years earlier and that it would eventually have come to light.

"Billy's pretty proud of himself," Nyles said to Norma. He had noticed her glass of white wine was empty and had taken it upon himself to get her another drink, using his action as an excuse to strike up a conversation with her.

The woman, who was quite attractive, with an ample, but shapely figure and flowing red hair, thanked Nyles for the drink and looked at him warily. "Billy deserves to feel good, even if, from what he's told me, you did a lot of the work to get Father O'Flannery off."

"He told you a lot about the case?" Though his tone was casual, there was an underlying edge to his voice.

Her wariness appeared to increase and the lines around her mouth had begun to hint of a frown. "He needed to talk to someone. He was nervous."

"It was good you could be there for him."

"I thought so."

"You and Billy only met recently, after he'd gotten involved in Father Tom's case?"

She smiled nervously and nodded, raising her sharply defined eyebrows, as if she was wondering where he was going with his line of questions.

"Billy's been coming into the Hibernia Pub for years, but you two never met until now?" Nyles asked.

"I'm not a regular at the Hibernia, Mr. Monahan. I was a stay-at-home wife until I separated from my husband a few months ago. Then I started going out for a drink now and then. That's how I met Billy."

"And you live in Dorchester?"

She nodded again. "I feel as if you're interrogating me." There was a wary edge to her tone.

"Just trying to make conversation. I'm afraid I've been a detective too long. I need to learn some social skills." He was watching her calmly.

She stared him in the eyes, her questioning attitude transformed into a frank challenge. "Yes you do. If you're not just a poor socializer and you're trying to find out something about me, why not ask me up front?"

Nyles didn't appear bothered by her challenging attitude. "Do you have any connection to Monsignor Hurley or the Archdiocese?"

Her face relaxed and she looked amused. "Do you think I'm a spy for the Church?"

"Some of the information I gave to Billy may have gotten to Monsignor Hurley, which allowed him to cover up the evidence against him."

"And you think I did that?" Her tone was incredulous.

"Somebody did."

She looked around as if to see if anyone was listening. Billy was still in animated conversation with Father Tom and Sean. Millie and Molly were busy trying to get Mickey Ryan to eat more cake. "I am undercover, so to speak. So if I share my secret with you, will you keep it to yourself?"

"I'm only interested for myself. Father Tom is already free."

"I'm afraid my secret has nothing to do with Father Tom. In fact, it's the reason you don't need to be afraid that I'm working for the Church or the late Monsignor Hurley." She paused and looked around again before continuing. "I'm Jewish, Mr. Monahan. Billy doesn't know it. Nobody at the Hibernia Pub knows it. I may look Irish, but the red hair is from a bottle and I go to the Synagogue on Saturday. It's nothing to be ashamed of, and at some point I'll tell Billy, but right now I'm just rejoining the social scene after twenty-five married years and in an Irish-Catholic neighborhood, I'd like to fit in."

Nyles smiled self-consciously. "Your secret is safe with me. Do you really think it will make a difference to Billy?"

"I hope not. I like Billy a lot, except he drinks too much. I guess I'll have to find out pretty soon." Her face broke into a broad grin, the tiny lines around her mouth and eyes now revealing themselves as laugh wrinkles. "That would be something wouldn't it – a lawyer being prejudiced against a Jew?" She handed Nyles her empty glass. "Now if the interrogation is over, why don't you bring me another glass of wine and I'll go give Billy some more of my attention."

Nyles brought Norma her glass of wine, then moved across the room to talk to Mickey Ryan, who was sitting on the couch eating his third helping of Molly O'Flannery's chocolate cake, but looking a little lost in a social scene where everyone else knew each other.

"That was nice of you to invite me, Mr. Monahan," Mickey said, between bites.

"I felt as if you should be included in the celebration. It was your information that led us to Monsignor Hurley. Besides, it's a chance for you and Father Tom to get to see each other again after all these years. Did he remember you?"

Mickey smiled shyly. "He said he did, but I'd think it would be pretty hard. There were quite a few altar boys at St. Aloysius and I've changed a lot since then," his face colored as though he was embarrassed. "I feel bad about Jimmy Gleason. I read about him in the newspaper. The story said Father Hurley killed him. I feel like it's my fault for getting him involved."

Nyles felt the same way about his own role in bringing Gleason into the case. "The police already had Jimmy's name before you said anything, Mickey. Besides, his family had filed a complaint against Father Hurley 30 years ago, so the Monsignor already knew that Jimmy was a potential witness against him." He was telling Ryan the same thing he kept telling himself to relieve his own guilt.

Mickey's face showed his relief, but then his expression became clouded.

"What's the matter?" Nyles asked.

"The picture of Monsignor Hurley in the paper sure doesn't look like I remember Father Hurley."

"Really? Do you think he's just aged?"

"He has some resemblance, but I never would have picked him out as the same man unless the picture was just a bad one."

"But you said you didn't attend mass very often after Father Tom left." Nyles felt a nagging doubt that hadn't completely left him since finding the Monsignor's body.

They were interrupted by Nate Hilton entering the room. The police detective was trying his best to put on a display of friendliness, but the look in his eyes was one of near panic. He searched the room with his gaze until he spied Nyles, then came directly to him, his face reverting to his characteristic scowl.

"Did you invite me so you could prove you've got a Black friend?" Nate asked under his breath.

"Do you think that would impress this crowd?" Nyles asked, glancing around the room. "I just thought you should be here so Father Tom could thank you in person. It was your police work that got him off."

"Yeah, but there's still a problem." The detective's expression was glum. He surveyed the room suspiciously, as if he didn't want anyone to overhear what he was saying.

"Why?"

"They still haven't found those stolen records of the priests who served in '82. They were nowhere in Hurley's apartment."

"Maybe it wasn't him who took them. Anyway, his suicide note was enough to free Father O'Flannery."

Nate's scowl widened. "I'm not talking about your friend. Once the judge dismissed the charges against him he was in the clear. I'm talking about finding the real killer."

Nyles was surprised. He had thought that Detective Hilton was willing to blame the killings on Monsignor Hurley no matter what evidence was missing, just so he could get credit for solving the case. "You mean you're having doubts about the killer being Monsignor Hurley?"

"The Archbishop's office got records from Catholic University showing that Hurley was in their Canon Law School full-time in 1982 and he even lived in a dorm on campus. He couldn't have been the priest at St. Aloysius, unless he could be in two places at once."

Nyles thought about what Mickey Ryan had just told him about the picture of Monsignor Hurley in the paper not matching his recollection of the priest who had succeeded Father Tom at St. Aloysius. "So what did he mean in his note? He said he took responsibility for the murders. And there *was* a Father A. Hurley at St. Aloysius; we know that from the construction records with his signature."

Nate shook his head. "I don't know what it means. But it pisses me off. Now Spaulding's reopened Russell's case."

"You mean he's changed his mind about the Monsignor being Russell's murderer?"

"He's still the prime suspect, but none of the evidence makes sense any more."

"What about with regard to Sister Mary Agnes?"

"Leeper won't talk to me. He's still pissed that you and I interviewed Monsignor Hurley. He says we panicked him and that's why he killed himself. We took away his suspect before he had wrapped everything up."

Leeper was right. Nyles would have been angry, too if he was in the same position.

Just then Father Tom came over to thank Nate for his help. At the same time, Molly brought the detective the beer she had promised him when he'd first arrived.

Nyles left the Black detective to fend for himself with the other guests. What Hilton had told Nyles disturbed him, but he had to admit he wasn't completely surprised. Something had seemed wrong when he'd found the Monsignor's body but no stolen records. And now Mickey Ryan didn't recognize the Monsignor from his picture in the paper.

Millie handed him another beer. He sipped it and looked around the room. Everyone – with the exception of Nate Hilton – was in an exuberant mood. Why couldn't he just let it go? Father Tom was free and the identity of the real molester and killer didn't need to concern him. Except for one burning issue – whoever the killer was, he had murdered Mary MacDonald. Nyles couldn't walk away from the case, letting her killer remain free.

## Chapter 42

Detective Arnold Leeper knew that he was putting too great a burden on Roseanne Compton, but he forced himself to ask her anyway. To his surprise, she agreed to come to the morgue and view Monsignor Hurley's body, claiming that, as a nurse, she'd seen plenty of dead bodies in her lifetime and that she was as committed to determining who really killed Sister Mary Agnes as he was. Thinking about her husband and his circumstances, the young detective wondered if he would have been so civic-minded in the same situation. He frankly doubted it, which made him feel both more guilty for having asked Mrs. Compton and more grateful that she had acquiesced.

The identification was swift. Roseanne Compton took one look and was definite that, although he vaguely resembled the man on the train, he was not the person she had observed talking to Sister Mary Agnes.

"Don't look so disappointed young man," Roseanne said to the detective as he accompanied her back to her car outside the building that housed the county coroner's office and the city morgue. The old woman's suspicion had gradually disappeared over the several visits she and the young detective had had together. "The important thing is to get the right man."

"I'm disappointed that the killer is still at large and I'm back to square one." He managed a weak smile. "But I'm deeply indebted to you, Mrs. Compton. You've gone above and beyond your duty as a citizen by coming here today,"

"I'm for truth and I'm for doing one's duty," Mrs. Compton said, stopping in front of her car, which was a ten year old blue Toyota Tercel, with a dented front fender. "My mission is to teach the youngest generation how to become good people and I have to set an example myself."

"But this is your private life, not part of our job. None of those preschoolers is going to know what you did here today, and they wouldn't know if you'd refused to do it either."

"I'd know," she said, getting into her car.

\*\*\*

The afternoon shadows were lengthening and Detective Leeper debated whether to call it a day or return to his office. The disappointment Roseanne Compton had seen on his face was real. With Monsignor Hurley gone from his list of suspects, he had no one to take the priest's place. He mentally kicked himself for ignoring the Monsignor's presence in law school in Washington, DC, which should have had ruled him out as the person who'd molested and probably killed Tim Russell, because if he he'd thought about it, then without the Tim Russell connection, there was really nothing at all to tie the Monsignor to Sister Mary Agnes' murder. He had been led down a false trail by Nyles Monahan's suspicions of Monsignor Hurley. Despite his respect for the retired detective, Leeper had to conclude that Monahan's instincts had been wrong.

He sat in his car in the parking lot of the Medical Examiner's offices and methodically retraced the steps he had taken that had raised the Monsignor's profile as a likely murder suspect. When it came down to it, the most damning evidence was Monahan's assertion that he and Nate Hilton had uncovered proof that the Monsignor was concealing the fact that someone named Hurley had served as Parish Priest at St. Aloysius Church during 1982. And

# Chasing Tales

Monahan had been right about that. Nate Hilton had shown Leeper the construction invoices from St. Aloysius with Father Hurley's signature on them and the forensic report showing that the same Father Hurley's fingerprints were on the baptismal record books from 1982, suggesting that whoever Father Hurley was, he was still trying to cover up evidence of his assignment to St. Aloysius. There was also a strong suggestion that the Monsignor had taken records regarding parish assignments of priests in 1982 and hidden them somewhere. Finally, Monsignor Hurley had admitted to something, though just what it was, was unclear. His suicide note said that he was "responsible" for deaths of both Tim Russell and Sister Mary Agnes and Jimmy Gleason, although it was not clear what he had meant by his words.

The circumstantial evidence was overwhelming. But Monsignor Hurley was not the murderer – at least not of Sister Mary Agnes – nor was he the molester of Tim Russell, and Leeper sat pondering the facts of the case and trying to resolve the dilemma. Facts were facts and they were either true or false. It was in the interpretations of those facts where the error lay.

He went through the facts again. The barest of conclusions he could come to was that *someone* named Hurley had probably molested Tim Russell and tried to cover up the fact that he had been a priest at St. Aloysius. But that person wasn't the Monsignor, although the Monsignor was trying to protect him and felt responsible for what the person had done, or at least for the fact that Father O'Flannery was getting blamed for it. Those were the facts. What story, he wondered, could tie them all together? The answer was suddenly clear to him. There were two Hurleys; the Monsignor knew it, and he was protecting the other Hurley from discovery. Given their same last name, that probably meant that they were related. Monsignor Hurley must have a relative who had been a priest at St. Aloysius and that relative was both a child molester and a cold-blooded killer.

## Chapter 43

Cloris had understood why Nyles couldn't leave Boston, but it was harder to explain to Sean and Millie, although they didn't mind having him remain their guest for a while longer. He had abandoned his plan to move to a hotel as soon as he'd found the Monsignor's body and the incriminating suicide note. Sean told his brother to leave things up to the Boston Police Department. Nyles' brother was sure that the police would figure out who killed Sister Mary Agnes and Jimmy Gleason and whether Monsignor Hurley was the priest who'd molested Tim Russell and probably also killed him, or whether that person was someone else. When Nyles had told Cloris that he wanted to remain in Boston to try to find Mary's killer himself, his wife had told him she'd have been disappointed in him if he hadn't.

Nate Hilton, much to Nyles' surprise, had also seemed happy to have Nyles delay his return home. Despite his grumblings and sarcasm, Nate appeared to have begun to like working with Nyles and, although he tried to conceal it, he felt more confident having the older ex-detective helping him out. Nate's partner on the Sexual Abuse Special Task Force, Randy Colton, refused to get involved with his partner's investigation of the murders of Tim Russell and Sister Mary Agnes. In Colton's words, Nate's habit "of sticking your fucking nose where it damn well doesn't belong," would probably get the Black detective fired, or at least disciplined, rather than promoted. As far as Nate was concerned, a future in which his career was limited to investigating cases of priest sexual abuse was worse than getting fired.

The question for both Nyles and Nate was where to start. Monsignor Hurley had virtually admitted Russell's molestation and murder in his suicide note, but the records from Catholic University School of Law ruled out his service as a priest at St. Aloysius during 1982. It was also unlikely that he had killed Mary MacDonald, since Detective Leeper's prime witness had failed to identify the Monsignor as the man on the train. The Waltham police had seemed content to let the Monsignor's enigmatic confession of Jimmy Gleason's murder stand, even though a search of the cleric's apartment had not revealed the gun that had been used to kill Gleason.

Mickey Ryan's comment that Monsignor Hurley's picture in the Boston Globe didn't match his memory of Father Hurley had undermined the evidence against the Monsignor, but Nyles had already had his doubts before that. Foremost in his mind was the fact of the Monsignor's apparent theft of documents related to the identity of the parish priest at St. Aloysius less than an hour before he committed suicide. What would have been the point of taking the documents and hiding them if he was about to admit his guilt by taking his own life?

"Monsignor Hurley's behavior doesn't make sense to me," Nyles said.

"That's a hell of a big help," Nate Hilton said. He was sitting across from Nyles in his office. Randy Colton was out of the office and Nate had offered Nyles Randy's desk. They both had photocopies of various pieces of the evidence spread out in front of them.

"Our problem is we're not able to think outside of the box," Nyles said.

"What's that supposed to mean?"

"All this fits together, but not in a way we've ever thought about it."

Nate scowled at him. "How do you think of something that never occurred to you?"

"We have to stop thinking about it, then it will come to us," Nyles said, ignoring the Black detective's skepticism.

"Is that what they do in Los Angeles? Maybe we need to meditate, or get a massage or something. How about a high colonic?"

"Don't you ever walk away from a problem and then the answer jumps into your head when you're doing something else?" Nyles asked, ignoring Nate's sarcasm.

"All the time," Nate answered, a smirk on his face. "It usually happens when I go to take a piss."

"OK," Nyles said. "So go take a piss."

"Jesus Christ," Nate said, getting up from his chair. "I think I will take a leak – just to get away from this bullshit."

When Nate returned, he had grin on his face. "It worked."

"What do you mean?" Nyles asked.

"I thought outside of the box. I got an idea."

"What?"

"You've got a copy of the suicide note on your desk?"

Nyles shuffled through the papers spread out on his desk. "I've got it."

Nate sorted through his own pile of papers until he found what he was looking for. "Here it is. I've got one of the construction requisitions signed by Father Hurley. Let me see the suicide note."

Nyles handed the note to him and waited.

Nate held the two pieces of paper one over the other, so the two signatures were above and below each other. His face broke into a broad smile.

"What?" Nyles asked.

"The signatures aren't the same… not even close."

Nyles got up and moved around the desk. He stood behind Nate and looked over his shoulder. "You're right." He wondered why he hadn't thought of comparing the signatures. Hilton was a pain in the ass, but he had a good head on his shoulders.

"There are two Father Hurley's." Nate said.

"And the Monsignor was trying to protect the other Father Hurley, Nyles added, not able to keep the excitement in his voice. "Why? Are they related?"

"You mean like his brother or cousin or something?" Nate asked.

"That's exactly what I mean. Monsignor Hurley was trying to protect the other Hurley, whom he knew was the real child molester. I'm not sure which one killed Tim Russell."

"So where's the other Father Hurley? Why haven't we been aware of him?

Nyles shook his head. "Because the Monsignor didn't want us to be aware of him, for one thing, and because he's no longer a Boston Archdiocese priest, I'm willing to bet."

"You mean he was transferred to another Archdiocese?"

"Either that or he quit the priesthood. Remember, a number of priests, who were found to have molested children, were given the option of transferring or leaving the priesthood. Some of them chose to leave. And knowing the Monsignor's attitude toward such miscreant priests, he may have forced his relative to leave the Church."

"How could he have done that if he was away at law school himself?"

'I don't know, but if he was in Canon Law School, he may have been being groomed for a position in the Archdiocese hierarchy and maybe he had some influence. What we need to know is who is the second Father Hurley."

"So how do we find out?"

"There has to be a record of ordinations. I don't know who keeps them, the Archdiocese or the seminaries, but somebody has to have a record that would tell us who the other *A. Hurley* is and whether he's still a priest."

Nate smiled again, but this time it was the calculated smile that Nyles was used to, rather than the indication of pleasure he had seen a few moments ago. "So what I'm doing is continuing the investigation to find out who really molested Tim Russell. If I happen to solve a murder case or two in the process, who can blame me?"

# Chasing Tales

## Chapter 44

The weather had taken a sharp turn toward colder temperatures and the thin layer of snow that covered the cemetery lawn crunched like brittle glass beneath Nyles' feet. He wished he had taken his brother's advice and worn one of Sean's big overcoats instead of the flimsy one he had brought with him from Los Angeles. Nyles had known he'd look foolish in a coat that was several sizes too big and his vanity had won out over his good sense. He regretted his decision because he was freezing.

The priest who was officiating at Monsignor Hurley's funeral wasn't anyone known to Nyles. Archbishop O'Malley was noticeably absent from the service, due, Nyles surmised, to the Monsignor having committed suicide – a sin that robbed him of the ceremony owed someone who ranked as high as he had in the Archdiocese hierarchy. The Archbishop had presided at Mary MacDonald's funeral only a week before and Nyles reflected on the fact that this was the second funeral he, himself, had attended and both were connected to the case he was pursuing. The thought made him shiver and gather the collar of the light coat even closer around his neck.

Among those gathered at the gravesite was a handful of priests and nuns. The Monsignor hadn't many friends – or maybe, Nyles thought, it was more politically correct to stay away if you were a member of the Church. If Mary had lived she would have been here today. She didn't like the Monsignor any more than anyone else did, but she would have felt she owed it to him as her superior. Nyles scanned the faces of the few priests who had attended and wondered if there was another Father Hurley among them.

# Chasing Tales

Nyles was surprised to see Nate Hilton with his hands in his pockets, a broad scowl on his face and looking like a dark monument to anger, standing on the frozen carpet of snow at the edge of the group. He seemed to be observing what was going on, rather than participating. Nyles walked around the edge of the crowd until he was at the detective's side. "Expecting to learn something?" he asked.

Nate shrugged his massive shoulders. "We're supposed to be over at the records room in an hour anyway, so I thought I'd stop by and see who showed up. You never know when something might turn up."

"I thought the same thing myself. Other than you, though, I don't recognize anyone."

"I suppose it would be bad form to take everyone's name," Nate said.

Nyles looked at him and frowned.

The ceremony had concluded and people were drifting away from the gravesite. Nyles continued to examine the faces of each of the priests who slowly walked toward the parking lot. He decided he was becoming obsessed. He turned and headed back to his car.

"Want to get a cup of coffee?" Nate asked.

Nyles was surprised by the detective's friendliness. "Sure."

Nate told Nyles to follow him to the coffee shop and they both continued to their own cars. By this time Nyles' car was the only one in the cemetery parking lot, except Nate's. It was too cold a day for visitors unless they were attending a funeral and Monsignor Hurley's funeral was the only one scheduled for that day. From a distance, though, he could see a man in a hat and an overcoat walking parallel to the Monsignor's gravesite, but about one hundred yards away. Nyles sensed something familiar

226

about the man, but he wasn't sure it wasn't his imagination telling him so, because he'd been so intent on finding the real Father Hurley among the priests in attendance today. This man wasn't even a priest - Nyles could tell from the light brown overcoat he wore.

Nate beeped his horn and signaled that he was waiting for Nyles to get in his car and follow him. Nyles ignored him and watched the man in the cemetery, who had continued past the newly dug grave of Monsignor Hurley and was still walking, stopping occasionally at other gravesites. Nate blew his horn again. Nyles dismissed the idea that he recognized the man and got into his own car.

"Has Spaulding or Leeper found anything?" Nyles asked as he and Nate sipped coffee at a small, old-fashioned coffee shop in the middle of Brighton's business district. Even on a Saturday the shop was nearly filled with customers taking refuge from the cold behind the steamed up windows of the tiny café.

Nate snorted disdainfully. "Spaulding couldn't find his way out of a paper bag and Leeper's a smart cop, but he seems to be at a dead end."

"I think we might find something in the Church records."

"They're not going to like us trying to find another perverted priest. They're going to want it to stop with the Monsignor, just to put an end to things." Nate took another long sip. "Did you see how few people came to his funeral? It's like the Church is trying to pretend he never existed."

"That's not just because of the molestation issue. It's because he committed suicide. That's a mortal sin in Catholicism. They used to refuse someone a burial in a Catholic cemetery if he committed suicide. Now they just do a limited service and don't mention the way the person died." Nyles stopped talking and took a sip of his coffee, looking away from the other detective. He had considered suicide himself – during the time when Cloris had looked as if she wouldn't pull through. He was glad he hadn't had religious guilt to deal with. It was one more thing he could thank his father for.

"Doesn't sound like a helluva useful religion," Nate said, shaking his head.

Nate was tempted to agree. Monsignor Hurley's suicide was a result of his belief that he'd allowed the forces of evil a foothold through his own position within the Church. He'd committed suicide to protect the Church from his own weakness and the Church's response was to focus on the sinfulness of the way he had died, rather than the struggle that had led to his death. "Yeah well," Nyles said. "All you and I care about is what kind of records the Church keeps." He drained the last of his coffee. "Shall we go find out?"

# Chasing Tales

## Chapter 45

The man in charge of the records room wasn't Marvin Thompson, the Custodian of Records. Because it was Saturday, Thompson had the day off and his weekend assistant, Curtis Murphy, was an even younger man who told Nyles and Nate that he was a student at Boston College. majoring in Economics, who had taken the job as a way of earning money on the weekends. Murphy was dressed more like a student than a clerk, wearing jeans and a Boston College sweatshirt. He was unshaven and he seemed surprised to have visitors on the weekend. A thick economics textbook was open in front of him and he kept glancing back at it as if he was reluctant to leave his studying. When Nate flashed his badge, the student's manner became more professional.

Nate had a court order to examine the ordination records from the two Archdiocese Seminaries: St. John's and Blessed John's National Seminary. The young clerk had to call the Custodian of Records at home before he could give permission for the two detectives to examine the files.

There was a directory of current Archdiocesan priests but it contained no Father Hurleys. Nor were there any other Hurleys, other than the Monsignor, among the clerics who formed the Archdiocesan staff. The young records clerk informed Nyles and Nate that Blessed John's National Seminary was only for older men, above age 30, who chose to go into the priesthood, so the two detectives began with the records from St. John's, starting in 1975 and moving forward.

After less than five minutes, they found two Hurleys with first names beginning with the letter A. Andrew Hurley, who later obtained his canon law degree and became a Monsignor, was ordained in 1981, immediately before going to Washington DC to attend The School of Canon Law at Catholic University. Alfred Hurley was ordained a year later, in the spring of 1982.

"I'll bet his first assignment was St. Aloysius." Nate said.

Nyles didn't respond. He was remembering the man he had seen walking alone in the cemetery following the Monsignor's funeral. Now he knew why he looked familiar, even from such a distance. "I've seen him."

Nate put down the book with the list of names and stared at Nyles. "What do you mean, you've seen him?"

"Father O'Flannery's lawyer, Billy Phelan, has a friend named Alf."

Nate frowned. "What does that prove?"

"I saw him at the funeral."

"He was at the Monsignor's funeral today?"

"Afterward, walking in the cemetery. I thought I recognized him, but I couldn't place him. Now I remember. The name Alfred made me realize who Alf was – it was Alfred Hurley."

"So if he's a friend of Father O'Flannery's lawyer, he might have found out everything you told the lawyer about the case."

"Exactly. He and Billy Phelan drank together, probably every day, and Phelan talked a lot."

"So what's the relationship between this Alfred Hurley and the Monsignor, are they brothers?"

"We can find out. We can ask St. John's to look up their records. If they're brothers, they should have had the same parents and lived at the same address."

Nate was thinking. "Christ almighty. That means the Monsignor was covering up for his brother. It was the brother who stole the Church records, maybe even destroyed them. Did he kill Russell, too? And the Sister? And Gleason?"

Nyles shook his head. "One of them did, or maybe they both did. There's only one way to find out and that's to bring in Alfred Hurley."

"Where do we find him?"

"Let's call St. John's and be sure we're right about these two Hurleys being related, then we're going to a place you're just going to love."

Nate looked at him with suspicion. "Where?"

"An Irish Pub in Dorchester."

## Chapter 46

Nate wasn't the first African American to walk into the Hibernia Pub, but he was the only one that Saturday and he felt the stares, most of which he interpreted as unfriendly, as soon as he stepped inside the door. It felt as if a dark fog of uneasiness had settled over the room. But being on police business gave Nate a sense of confidence he would never have felt if he'd happened into the pub looking for a place to have a beer in the afternoon. After a few seconds of silence the usual pub murmur resumed and no one seemed to pay him any attention. "Is he in here?" he asked Nyles, who had been scanning all the customers, hoping to see the man he'd been told was Billy Phelan's friend, Alf.

"I don't see him. I'll ask the bartender and give Phelan a call. I thought he'd be in here himself."

The bartender, Tommy O'Donald, told Nyles that neither Alf nor Billy Phelan had been in the pub all week until today at noon, when Billy had come in, had a drink with his girlfriend, then went looking for Alf. Tommy gave Nyles Alf's address, which he kept on a piece of paper taped to the bar because, on more than one occasion, he'd had to call a cab to take the man home.

Nate joined Nyles and the bartender at the bar. He flashed his badge. "What do you know about this Alf guy?" he asked Tommy.

Tommy's expression was bland. "He done something wrong?"

"I'm just trying to get some information," Nate answered a scowl beginning to build on his face.

"He was just a customer, that's all. One of the regulars. I didn't even know his last name." Tommy's face echoed the detective's frown.

Nyles could see the impasse toward which the conversation between the two men was headed. "How long has he been a customer, Tommy?" he asked. He could see that Nate was irritated by his intrusion into his line of questioning, but he felt like, at the rate things were going, Tommy O'Donald wasn't going to provide any useful information.

"Old Alf's been a regular here for maybe ten or fifteen years. I've been here more than twenty-five. He wasn't a customer when I first started."

"He ever talk about himself?" Nyles wasn't sure exactly what he wanted to find out, so he made his questions open-ended.

"Not much. He hated the Church. He talked about that. Used to really get going against the Church when he had too many."

"What did he say?"

"He hated Cardinal Law – said he was just into power and money. Said the Bishops didn't care about the parish priests, just about being big cheeses in Boston society - in with the money boys, that sort of thing. Said everyone who worked for the Church was only concerned with gaining power. I don't remember the words so much as the tone. He was bitter, like it was personal."

Nyles knew that Nate was fuming, but he persisted in his questioning of the bartender. "Did he ever say if he'd had any personal issues with the Church or the Archbishop? Any relatives who were priests?"

Tommy shook his head. "No."

"How about what he did for a living?" Nate asked, a belligerent expression on his face, as though he felt he had to use force to get himself back into the conversation.

Tommy looked at Nate with the same bland look he'd had before, then turned back to Nyles. "He was some kind of counselor. He worked with this old psychiatrist who has an office down by Carney Hospital. He didn't work any forty hour week, but he made enough to live on, and come in here a lot."

"You didn't get to know him very well for him being a regular customer for fifteen years," Nate said. His face was drawn into a broad frown.

Tommy shrugged. "I'm just a bartender."

Nyles thanked Tommy and they left.

"Fucking asshole, didn't want to tell a Black cop anything," Nate said as they were leaving.

"There's probably some prejudice there," Nyles answered. "Your interviewing style leaves something to be desired."

"It's hard to be polite when I know someone's withholding information."

"Try it, maybe people will be more cooperative."

Nate started to say something, then thought better of it. He hated to admit it, but this old Irish ex-cop could get a lot more out of witnesses than he could. "Is that a place you used to hang out?" Nate asked, as they were leaving the bar and heading for their cars.

"Aye and me father before me," Nyles said, putting on an Irish brogue.

"I heard about you Irish drinking families. Now I know where the white cops on the force go to drink," Nate said. "Seems like an odd place for a lawyer to hang out, though."

"Phelan's more of a drinker than a lawyer.

"That's what I thought. If we don't have any luck at Hurley's apartment, we'd better talk to Phelan."

"Hurley's a suspected killer. Do you want to call for some assistance before we go to his place?" Nyles asked.

"Is that what you'd do if you were in LA?"

"Yes."

"Yeah, well we're not in LA and as far as I'm concerned, Hurley's just a suspect in a 30 year old child molestation case. If I treat him like a murder suspect, the case is Spaulding's or Leeper's."

Nyles shrugged.

"Anyway, I'm not worried," Nate said, smiling. "I've got you with me and you know how to talk to Irish priests."

## Chapter 47

Mrs. Stoneham, the overweight apartment manager, her drooping jowls quivering with worry, was dressed in a worn, flowered housedress and a pair of slippers and was anxious to help them in their search for Alf. She seemed to assume that Nyles' and Nate's investigation was out of concern for her tenant's welfare and she volunteered as much information as she could, although what she knew was meager. Neither detective told the woman that Alf was a suspect in two murders and at least as many cases of child molestation, both of them sensing that her concern for the ex-priest was working in their favor.

"See if we can find anything that might tell us where he'd go if he was trying to avoid us," Nate said in a low voice so that the worried Mrs. Stoneham didn't hear him.

"Right," Nyles answered, although he was already doing just that. He was looking through the kitchen drawers, not sure of what he was looking for, but searching through every scrap of paper for some clue as to where Alf might have gone. He found nothing.

Alf had no desk in the apartment, but there were drawers in the nightstands on either side of his bed and also in a table in the living room. Nyles looked in the drawer in the living room table and Nate searched the nightstands.

"I may have something," Nyles announced. He had found a set of photographs paperclipped together, along with a map. The photos were of a group of wooden buildings, partially overgrown with bushes, with most of the windows boarded up. On the back of one of the photos was written in ink, the name, *St. Joseph's Retreat House*.

236

Chasing Tales

The map had a red line drawn on a route leading from Dorchester down the coast on Route 3A to Scituate, a small town south of Boston on the way to Cape Cod. The red line followed a side road toward the coast and ended with an area adjacent to the side road and next to the ocean, circled.

"What do you think it is?" Nate asked. He didn't have to speak in hushed tones any longer since Mrs. Stoneham had grown exhausted, her anxiety unable to tolerate their meticulous search, and had returned to her apartment.

"It looks as if is some kind abandoned Church property. From the looks of the map and the photographs, he's visited it at least once - and recently from the amount of snow on the ground if the picture is from this year."

"Let's bring it with us. If we can't find him locally, we can always check it out," Nate said.

"When Spaulding or Leeper gets here, they're gonna find some evidence missing," Nyles answered. "We're interfering with their investigation."

"Not if they never knew this was here." Nate stepped in front of Nyles and took the photographs and map from the drawer and stuffed them in his coat pocket.

"You sure you want to do that?" Nyles asked.

"Damn right I am."

If Nyles had been on duty he wouldn't have gone along with Nate, but he wasn't on duty and the way Nate conducted himself as a policeman was his business. "I think our best bet is to talk to Billy Phelan," Nyles said. "He was looking for Hurley and maybe he found him or found out where he is."

"Do you know how to get hold of Phelan?" Nate asked.

Nyles was already dialing the lawyer on his cell phone.

Phelan was at home. He and Norma had gone for lunch and then come back to his place. He hadn't found out anything about Alf Hurley's whereabouts. "Did something happen to him?" he asked Nyles.

"Nothing happened to him that we know of, we just want to talk to him," Nyles told him. "Do you know of any place he might go?"

"The only place I've ever seen Alf is at the Hibernia Pub and he hasn't been there for a week. I tried his apartment but he wasn't home."

Nyles listened while Phelan talked to someone else in his apartment – Nyles guessed it was Norma. Then the lawyer came back on the phone. "The mystery is solved. Alf is here. I didn't even know he knew where I lived."

"Where *do* you live?" Nyles said. He knew he had to be cagey or Hurley would find out they were after him.

Billy told him his address. It was in Dorchester.

"Don't let him know I'm looking for him. Try to keep him there for at least another fifteen minutes."

"What's going on?" Phelan asked. Voices could be heard in the background.

"Just keep him there and don't tell him I'm coming," Nyles said, then hung up.

"He's with Phelan," he told Nate. "You want to call for backup?"

"No way," Nate answered. "You lead and I'll follow you in my car."

# Chasing Tales

## Chapter 48

Alf Hurley hadn't been to the Hibernia Pub, nor any other bar, for a week. He'd been doing his drinking alone in his apartment, something he disliked to do because it made him feel even more lonely than he usually felt, but, since his brother's suicide, he had been afraid to venture out into public, except on the day of the funeral – and even then only to walk in the cemetery far enough away from Andrew Hurley's gravesite to avoid arousing suspicicn – and to go to the liquor store to buy beer and whiskey. He had confessed the killings to his brother the day before the latter had died. He assumed that Andrew had already figured out that it was his brother, Alf, who had killed Russell and also his administrative assistant, Sister Mary Agnes, and maybe he'd even known about Jimmy Gleason's death, but Andrew hadn't said anything, except to shake his head in sorrow and tell his brother to leave town and that he had concealed the fact that Alf had ever been a priest and would go on concealing it. The day Andrew had killed himself, he had told Alf that Monahan and the Black cop were looking for records of priests' assignments. Andrew had gotten those records and given them to Alf. He had said nothing about planning to kill himself. Alf had no idea what his brother might have confessed in his suicide note and he'd decided to drop out of sight until he knew he wasn't being hunted by the police.

He had been almost to the door of his apartment house, with enough groceries to stay inside for another week at least, when he saw Nyles Monahan and another man, who looked like the Black cop his brother had told him about, enter the apartment house. Alf figured they must be looking for him. If the cops knew where he lived and they wanted to talk to him, then he couldn't go back home. Instead he decided to visit the only friend in the world he had - Billy Phelan.

Alf's guard went up when he found Billy on the telephone with Monahan. "What did he want?" the ex-priest asked, suspiciously.

Billy looked sheepish. "Nothing. Just telling me what a great job I did on the case."

Alf's expression turned cruel. He was still standing in the middle of Billy's living room. Norma was sitting on the couch and Billy was standing. "Don't give me that bullshit. He's looking for me and he's with a cop," Alf rasped.

"Why's he looking for you?"

"He didn't tell you?"

"No."

"Did he say anything about me?"

"He asked if I'd seen you and when I told him you were at the door, he said to keep you here until he got here."

"Shit," Alf said, then he started to cough.

"What's going on?" Billy asked.

"You're friend is in trouble with the law," Norma said, from the couch.

Alf shot her a savage look. He had walked to the window and was peering out from behind the curtain. He looked more agitated than usual. "The bitch is right," he said, turning back to Billy and Norma.

Billy took a step toward him. "I've told you to watch your language around Norma. I think you'd better leave."

"Fuck you," Alf said and he withdrew a gun from his coat pocket.

Norma gasped and Billy took a step backward. "What the hell are you doing?"

"I'm the one who killed the guy your priest got blamed for and I killed that nun and another witness too. That's why the cops are looking for me."

Billy was unbelieving. "You? What are you talking about? Why would you kill those people? You didn't even know them."

"I didn't know the nun, but I knew Russell and I knew the other guy. I used to be a priest at St. Aloysius and they were altar boys."

"You're the Father Hurley they were looking for?"

"I used to be, before I quit the Goddamned Church."

"I thought the Monsignor was the one who killed those people."

"My brother didn't kill anyone. He didn't have the guts. Just like he didn't have the guts to get me off the hook when I was charged with molesting those kids. He hid some of the records that showed I'd been a priest, but that was all he'd do for me. I'm sorry that he died, but it was those fucking cops who killed him by blaming him for what I did."

"You're brother killed himself to cover up for you, you scumbag," Norma said.

Alf waved his gun in her direction. "Don't tempt me, bitch. I'm already wanted for killing three people, one more won't matter."

Billy rubbed his hands over his face. "Jesus Christ Alf. Don't turn on us. I thought you and I were friends. You need to get out of here before the police get here."

Alf stole another look outside from behind the curtain, then turned back to the two of them. His mouth seemed to be in a perpetual sneer, but his eyes looked frightened, like a cornered animal's. "Yeah, well I don't want to hurt you, Billy... or your girlfriend, if she'll watch her mouth. You're right, I gotta get out of here. But I need some insurance and I need a better car than that jalopy of mine. I'm taking you two with me and you have to drive, Billy."

"I'm not going anywhere," Norma said, looking steadily at Alf. She folded her arms across her chest in defiance.

Alf pointed the gun at her and didn't say anything. His expression was one of panic. Norma stared back as if daring him to shoot.

"Fuck it," Alf said. He shoved the gun into Billy's chest. "You've gotta drive me, Billy. The bitch can stay here. I've got a better idea for a hostage."

"What are you talking about?" Billy asked.

"That fucking Monahan who's been dogging me. I know where he lives."

"So what?"

"So what is that he's got family. If I want him off my back then I need to grab something he values more than he values catching me."

"You're a despicable bastard," Norma said.

"Shut your mouth, bitch," Alf screamed and raised his gun and fired wildly in the direction of the couch. The bullet missed Norma but she fell over on her side in fear and began whimpering.

Alf turned back to Billy and pointed to the door. "Let's go."

# Chasing Tales

## Chapter 49

There was no answer when Nyles and Nate knocked on Billy Phelan's door. From inside drifted the thin wail of a woman's voice, sounding like the whine of a cat on a lonely night. Nate drew his gun and kicked the door open, splinters from the door jam flying in all directions.

Norma was crumpled in a ball on the couch, looking like a small, lost child. She was crying.

Nyles sat down next to her and put an arm around her. She folded herself into his body, hiding under the protection of his arm.

"What happened? Where are Billy and Alf?" Nyles said. He looked warily around the apartment. Nate stood next to him doing the same thing, but with his gun still drawn.

"Alf took Billy with him. They went in Billy's car," Norma managed, weakly.

"Are you hurt?" Nyles asked, leaning back to look at her.

She bent forward, and covered her face with her hands. "He shot at me, but missed."

"Hurley had a gun?" Nate asked. He was standing over the two of them.

She nodded. "He admitted killing three people – Tim Russell and the nun and someone else. He said he was the Monsignor's brother. I don't know why he took Billy with him."

"Did he say where he was going?" Nyles asked.

Her eyes widened in fear. "He talked about you. He said he needed a better hostage than me to make you stop chasing him. He said he knew where your family lived."

243

Nyles' felt his whole body grow cold. "My family?"

She nodded. "He and Billy went in Billy's car."

"The Goddamn bastard," Nate said.

Nyles took out his cell phone and punched in his brother's number. The line was busy. He called his brother's phone at work. Sean answered. "Who's home right now?" Nyles asked him.

"Just Katherine, I think. Millie and Kaylee are supposed to be shopping. I came in to get a little work done on the weekend. What's the matter? You sound spooked."

"Get home – now! Katherine's in danger. The man who killed all those people is coming there to get himself a hostage."

There was silence on the other end of the telephone.

"Sean?"

"I'm on my way."

"What's your brother's address?" Nate asked. He was on his own cell phone. "I've got the Milton Police on the line."

Nyles gave him Sean's address, then grabbed Nate's arm. "Let's go. We can be there in less than ten minutes."

## Chapter 50

"Where the fuck are we going?" Billy asked. The incredulity was still in his voice, but he was also angry. He was hunched over the steering wheel of his car with Alf beside him, the ex-priest's gun still pointed at Billy's side.

"Just follow my directions, Billy. I told you I don't want to hurt you. It's that prick Monahan who's going to pay for this."

Billy was headed up Adams Street into Milton. He was driving slowly along the roads, with their small rivers of melted ice and snow rushing down their gutters like tiny torrents after a storm. "Monahan? Christ, Alf you killed three people and you're a child molester. You're going to blame your troubles on Monahan?"

"Turn here," Alf directed him.

Billy turned down a side street with only a few large old houses on it.

"I wouldn't have had to kill two of those people if Monahan would have minded his own business. You never would have gotten O'Flannery off if Monahan wouldn't have dug up those church records or found out about Gleason. My brother wasn't going to turn me in. Now my brother's dead and that's Monahan's fault too." There was a petulant, whining quality to Alf's voice.

"You're an asshole, Alf. All those people are dead because of you. And what are you? Just a fucking hopeless drunk."

"Watch your fucking mouth. You and I are both drunks. I wasn't bothering anybody until Russell came forward. I live a respectable life. I've got a job, I go to the pub every day and mind my own business." He motioned for Billy to park the car at the curb.

"What are we doing?" Billy asked, a note of dread in his voice.

"We're going up to the door of this big house here."

"What for?"

"Just get out of the fucking car."

Billy clambered out of the car and stood in front of the large Victorian house. "What now?"

"We're going to knock on the front door."

"Who lives here?"

"Monahan's brother."

Billy turned to Alf. "Don't do this…"

"Shut the fuck up and knock on the door."

Billy walked up the front walk, which had been shoveled clear of snow and climbed the concrete steps onto the front porch. He could feel the presence of Alf behind him. The former priest had his gun in his coat pocket, but when Billy hesitated, Alf poked him in the back with the gun. Billy knocked on the door.

No one answered.

"Knock again – louder."

Billy knocked a second time.

The door cracked open and a small narrow face of a girl with blonde hair appeared. "Hello," Katherine said.

Billy didn't say anything. He tried to signal Katherine with his eyes to shut the door.

"Is your mother home?" Alf asked, stepping up next to Billy.

"She'll be home soon," Katherine said. Her eyes darted from one to the other of the men in front of her. A look of suspicion was starting to cloud her face. "Come back later," she said, starting to shut the door.

"We want to talk to you," Alf said, his gravelly voice containing a threat.

# Chasing Tales

Beside Katherine, the head of a large Labrador emerged, sticking its nose past the young girl and toward the two men on the porch. The dog's ears were pointed back and he let out a low, ominous growl

"I don't want to talk," Katherine said, uncertainly. "Ranger doesn't like you."

Alf reached into his pocket where he had the gun. "I'll take care of your dog…" he began.

Billy put out an arm to stop Alf. "Your uncle Nyles sent us," he said quickly. "We're friends of his."

"Shh Ranger," Katherine said, putting a hand on the dog's head. "Do you know Uncle Nyles?"

"I'm the lawyer he works for," Billy said, trying to make his voice sound as friendly as he could. He didn't want Alf to use his gun – even on the dog. "I know your grandpa Sean and grandma Millie, too. We're friends. Your uncle Nyles wants us to talk to you. Can you come outside and leave Ranger inside? I'm afraid of dogs."

Katherine seemed undecided. She looked up at Billy and he smiled his best, friendly smile. "OK," she said. She stepped outside and shut the door behind her, leaving the dog inside. Ranger began to bark.

"I'm sorry," Billy said. His face was a picture of sadness when he gazed down at the eleven year-old.

Alf reached down and grabbed the young girl by the arm, dragging her away from the door. "C'mon" he growled.

Katherine resisted, pulling backward and falling to the porch.

Alf pulled the gun out of his pocket. "Stand up."

"We're not going to hurt you," Billy said, his voice pleading with the little girl, while he looked fearfully at Alf. "Come with us and neither of us will get hurt."

# Chasing Tales

Katherine was frozen in fear. She sat on the porch staring at Alf's gun and beginning to shake.

"For God's sake put the Goddamn gun away," Billy hissed.

Reluctantly, Alf put the gun back in his pocket.

Billy put out his hand. "We have to do what this man says," he said quietly.

Katherine still didn't move.

"Pick her up," Alf said. His eyes were narrowed in anger. He swung around and looked out at the street. "We're gonna attract attention."

"She's scared," Billy answered.

"I don't give a shit. Just grab her and bring her to the car."

Billy leaned down and lifted Katherine by the shoulders until she was standing. She didn't resist but she was trembling uncontrollably and her eyes were wide with fear. Billy led her down the steps and toward the car.

When they reached the car, Alf grabbed Katherine's arm. "You drive," he told Billy and he opened the back door and threw Katherine inside, then climbed in the back seat after her. "Get the fuck out of here and head for the 405," he ordered Billy.

Billy turned on the ignition and turned the car around and headed for the freeway.

# Chasing Tales

## Chapter 51

A black and white Milton Police cruiser was sitting in the driveway with its red and blue lights flashing and Sean's pickup truck sat next to it, the driver's door hanging open. Nyles pulled into the driveway behind Sean's truck and jumped out. Nate's unmarked black Taurus screeched to a stop at the curb just as Nyles reached the first step leading up to the front door.

The front door was unlatched and Nyles could see the outlines of at least two figures, gesturing like shadow boxers, through the arched window in the top of the door. He pushed the door wide. "Is Katherine OK?" he asked, not yet knowing to whom he was directing the question.

"She's gone," Sean answered, his face ashen and his eyes wide with fear. "When I got here she was gone and Ranger was barking like a crazy dog." He was still wearing his blue, puffy parka and there were beads of sweat on his forehead. Behind him Ranger was pacing and panting heavily. Sean had tied the dog to the leg of a table using the dog's leash.

"We've got an all-points out for the girl, but we don't know who she's with or what he's driving," a tall uniformed policeman with dark wavy hair said. He looked Nyles over with curiosity.

Before he could give the cop a description of Alf and Billy's five-year old Chevrolet, Nate burst into the room.

"What's going on?" the Back detective asked, breathing heavily from having taken the front porch steps two at a time.

"Alf took my niece's daughter," Nyles said, shaking his head in disgust – the disgust he felt was directed toward himself. How could he have let his

249

innocent grandniece become a victim on account of his own actions? He cursed himself for his self-serving denial that he had been the cause of Mary MacDonald's and Jimmy Gleason's deaths and for not heeding the warning he had been given when Alf had followed him home that night. His pride in his own skill at investigating had blinded him to the danger he was causing for those around him – in this case a child he loved.

Nate stared at him, as if he could read the thoughts behind the anguished look on Nyles' face. He gave the older detective a hard nudge with his elbow. "Snap out of it. The bastard's only got a short lead on us."

"He could be going anywhere," Nyles said. He was feeling immensely weary.

"Tell us who we're looking for," the uniformed cop said, his voice insistent.

Nyles roused himself from his stupor to answer. "Two men, both about ten years younger than me – mid fifties, though they both look older. Alfred Hurley is a skinny ex-priest who wears glasses. He's the one who took my brother's granddaughter. William Phelan is a slim, average height, lawyer with glasses. He's a hostage. They're driving Billy's Impala. It's about five years old and its white. I don't know the license number but it's registered to Billy."

The policeman got on his telephone and called in the information to his headquarters.

"Sean, I'm sorry," Nyles said. He was barely able to look his brother in the eye. "Have you called Millie and Kaylee?"

His brother was more bewildered and frightened than he was angry. He shook his head in confusion. "I thought I'd wait until I understood what happened. This is related to your work for Father Tom?"

"The real murderer was the Monsignor's brother, a retired priest who hung around with Billy Phelan and learned all about the case from Billy. Now he's trying to pay me back for figuring out that he was the killer."

"What will he do to my granddaughter?" Sean's eyes were pleading.

Nyles looked his brother in the eyes. "I don't know. The man killed to save himself before, but I don't know that he'd harm a child or that he'd risk what that might bring him when he gets caught and goes to trial."

Sean turned away, as if to hide the terror his brother's words engendered.

The Milton policeman was standing on the porch, looking expectantly down the street as if he was waiting for reinforcements.

"Let's go before more Milton cops get here," Nate hissed in Nyles' ear.

"Go where?" Nyles asked. He was still too stunned to think about what to do next.

Nate reached in his pocket and pulled out the pictures and the map showing the way to St. Joseph's retreat. "Let them do their own investigating. I've got a hunch this is where Alf is taking Billy and the little girl."

Nate's words brought Nyles back to life. The reasonable thing to do would be to tell the Milton police about the pictures of the retreat and the map that he and Nate had found in Alf's apartment, but it was his brother's granddaughter who had been kidnapped and Nyles felt a desperate need to take control over the effort to get her back. He had a momentary fear that his own arrogance was going to bring on even more tragedy, but he put the thought out of his mind. "Let's go," he told Nate.

Nate gave the Milton policeman his cell number. The uniformed cop watched in disbelief when Nate and

Nyles left the house and both of them headed for Nate's car.

"Where are you going?" Sean shouted.

"Following a lead," Nyles shouted back, getting into Nate's car.

The cop started to protest, but Nate gunned the engine and swung out into the street. As he sped away from the house, he passed a black and white and an unmarked Milton police car, both with lights flashing, heading toward Sean's house.

Chasing Tales

Chapter 52

"We'll get her back," Nate said. Once he had left the small side street where Sean's house was located, he had put the red light on his dash and was going as fast as the moderately heavy Saturday afternoon traffic would allow.

"I don't trust anyone else to do it," Nyles said, almost as if he was in wonder at his own behavior. "I don't want a swat team coming in like gangbusters and pushing Alf over the edge."

"You think you can reason with him?"

"He wants to hurt me, not my niece's daughter." He looked out the window at the bleak winter landscape speeding by like a film on fast-forward. They were on the freeway and headed south toward Cape Cod and Nate was doing close to 100 miles per hour. "She must be terrified." His voice was barely audible.

Nate's cell phone rang. Without slowing the car, he pulled out his cell. It was Detective Spaulding. He'd heard about Nate's involvement over the radio and he wanted to know what was going on. Nate explained about Nyles' grandniece.

"Hurley's my suspect, not yours," Spaulding told Nate. "You said he killed Russell and the nun and the other guy in Waltham. You've got nothing to do with those cases, Hilton."

"Except I figured all that out and you didn't," Nate answered.

"You'll get a fucking award," Spaulding answered. "Now tell me where the hell you and Monahan are going."

"You're the detective in charge of the case, you figure it out."

Spaulding sputtered on the other end of the line and Nate closed the cell phone. "Asshole," he said.

"You're going to get suspended," Nyles said without emotion.

"Fuck them. We're going to get your niece back."

Nyles nodded, but his mind was engaged in trying to figure out what they would do when they got to the retreat house – assuming Alf was there. He didn't think he and Nate were far behind Alf and Billy, which meant that Alf wouldn't have time to do anything to hurt Katherine... except if he decided to kill her. Norma had said he had a gun. It wasn't clear where Billy fit into the picture, except he had been taken against his will and Alf was going to find that it was more difficult to keep track of two hostages than one. Billy might try to get away, leaving Katherine to occupy Alf, but he wouldn't be able to do that until they stopped and since St. Joseph's Retreat House was in Scituate, only about an hour down the coast, there was no reason Alf would stop before reaching his destination.

Nyles got out the map and studied it. There appeared to be two ways into the retreat: a main road that led from highway 3-A to the front entrance to the retreat and a smaller side road that took off from the main road and then wandered along the edge of the ocean before turning inward to come up behind the buildings. The smaller road may have been the original entrance to the property before the main road had been built.

"I've got a plan," Nyles announced. "Once we get there we split up. There're two entrances to the place. You let me off and I'll go in the back way on foot and you drive in the front. Keep them occupied in some way. I don't care what you do, but don't push Alf over the edge. Let him know it's just you. I don't want him thinking he's surrounded by the cavalry. I'll come in the back and try to get into whichever building he's in and get the drop on him."

Nate was still doing over 80 but they had turned off of the interstate and were on the smaller Route 3-A, heading south past occasional shopping centers and signs pointing toward the small coastal villages that dotted the south shore below Boston. They rushed past turnoffs to the seaside hamlets of Hingham and Cohasset. Scituate was the next town. "He'll wonder where you are."

"Maybe, but since you're in your car, he might not think we're together. Anyway, as long as you keep him busy, he won't be able to spend any time thinking about me."

"You sure you can go in there on foot?" Nate cast a sideways glance at him. "It might be easier for me. No offense, but I'm younger than you are."

"She's my grandniece."

Nate nodded. "There's a gun under the seat."

Nyles reached below the seat and felt the gun. He gave Nate a questioning look. Detectives were never allowed to carry more than one gun.

Nate shrugged and took the turnoff for Scituate.

# Chasing Tales

## Chapter 53

Nate slowed the car as they cruised past the driveway leading into St. Joseph's Retreat House. A rusting metal pole on which had formerly hung a sign identifying the retreat, still stood, like a lonely sentry, at the entrance to the driveway, but the sign was long gone. Both Nyles and Nate were able to recognize the distant buildings from the pictures that had been found in Alf's apartment. Neither of them could see Billy's car, but fresh tracks led through the snow on the driveway leading up to the collection of buildings, which, from a distance looked like an abandoned summer camp.

They passed the entrance and then took the next road, which headed toward the ocean. When they reached the beach, Nate followed Nyles' directions to head back north until, within half a mile, they came upon a dirt road, partially overgrown with brush and ferns, angling back toward the retreat property and away from the ocean, which crashed angrily along the beach to their left. The wind had picked up and a dense curtain of rain was moving, as if a celestial shower head had been turned on, from the ocean to the land, large sloppy flakes of snow mixing among the heavy raindrops as it moved inland.

"I'm not sure I can drive very far up that road without getting stuck," Nate said, staring into the gloomy darkness of the forest, which seemed to swallow the tiny lane after the first 200 or so feet.

"I'll walk it. You go back and get Alf's attention. Just don't provoke him into any kind of showdown with you."

"It must be almost a half-mile … if that road is straight."

"It is on the map."

# Chasing Tales

"You sure you don't want me to go on foot and you take the car?" Nate's expression showed his concern.

Nyles opened the car door without answering. He was immediately buffeted by the high wind blowing off the ocean. The rain slapped his face like a barrage of small stones. He turned his back on the pounding sea and leaned his head into the car. "I'll call your cell when I'm ready to go in." Without waiting for Nate to answer, he slammed the car door and set off down the road, fingering the .38 in his pocket for comfort. Behind him he heard Nate turning the car and heading back along the coast road.

The narrow road was rutted and there were pools of water in the center of the ruts beneath the snow, some with a thin covering of ice. Nyles would have preferred to walk along the edge of the road but the choking undergrowth was too thick to allow him any progress when he tried. He settled for walking down the center of the road, trying to avoid slipping into the deeper ruts on either side of the more solid strip of ground in the middle. By the time he'd gone 100 yards, the rain had turned entirely to fat, wet snowflakes that fell furiously onto the road in front of him making it more and more difficult to see where the center of the road ended and the ruts began. Ahead there was only the darkness of the forest and the silent fall of the snow.

Nyles legs were beginning to ache with the strain of keeping his balance on the slippery center section of the road. His breathing was becoming more ragged. Had he made a mistake? Was he too old for this kind of physical exertion? Maybe Nate had been right in offering to go on foot in his place. He pushed such thoughts from his head and slogged on. Just as he thought he could make out a dim outline of a building in the distance ahead, he lost his footing and fell hard into the deep rut beneath his right foot. He put out his hand to break his fall but the snow was as slick as if it was ice and his hand slid under him. When he landed with all of his weight on his left wrist, he felt it snap beneath him. He found himself down in the icy water and mud, cursing his age, his physical condition and the forest around him.

The sharp pain he had felt when he landed on his wrist had become a harsh ache. He felt his wrist to try to determine if it was broken but he couldn't tell. He could still move his hand, but just barely. When he stood, he tried to brush off the snow and the sticky globs of mud that clung to his clothes the way leeches attach to a wanderer in a swamp, then he peered through the curtain of snow. The cluster of buildings was visible less than 100 yards ahead.

Billy Phelan's Impala was parked in back of the largest of the buildings. There were no lights in the windows and there was no smoke coming from the chimney of the building. Nyles decided that Alf must be afraid of drawing any attention to his hideaway. Just beyond Billy's car was a door.

Nyles called Nate on his cell phone. "Have they seen you?"

"Unless they're blind, they have. I'm walking around in the Goddamn snow next to my car, freezing my ass off. How are you?"

"I'm within twenty yards of the back door. Maybe you should do something more to distract them."

"How about if I put a couple of shots into the side of the house."

"Just make them high enough not to hit anyone."

"You ready?"

"Anytime. I'm freezing, myself."

"As soon as I hear any shots from inside, I'm coming in the front door," Nate said.

"I'm counting on that."

Nyles closed his cell phone and edged closer to the house. By crouching low, he was able to move along the back of the building below the sight line from the rear windows until he was next to the back door. He reached up and turned the handle of the door a quarter inch. It wasn't locked. He waited.

There was a single shot from Nate's gun, followed after a few seconds by another. Nyles didn't wait for a third shot. By now, Alf should have his eyes glued to the detective in front of the house. Nyles turned the doorknob and cracked open the back door. There was a small hallway at the end of which was another door. He slipped inside. The second door had no lock and was a swinging door. He pushed on it with his left hand and felt a sharp stab of pain in his wrist. He heard another shot from Nate's gun and then heard Alf swearing from inside the room on the other side of the door.

Nate pushed the door open and saw Alf peering out one of the front windows. There was no furniture in the room and Billy and Katherine sat huddled together on the floor beneath one of the windows. Billy eyes snapped wide when he saw Nyles stick his head in the door.

Nyles knew he could drop Alf with a single shot before the ex-priest even turned around. But he didn't want to kill him if he didn't have to and he didn't want to have his grandniece witness a killing. On the other hand, he didn't want to put her at any more risk.

"Drop the gun, Alf," Nyles said, striding into the room.

Alf didn't turn around. He didn't drop his gun, either. "Go ahead and shoot me, Monahan," he said. "You've won every round so far, why not finish things off?"

"I don't want to kill you, Alf. There's no reason you need to die." Nyles cast a glance over at Katherine. She was sitting wide-eyed, leaning against Billy Phelan. "Billy, take Katherine out the back door. Go sit in your car."

Billy nodded. He stood up and lifted Katherine to her feet.

Nyles had taken his eyes off Alf just long enough for the ex-priest to swing part way around and aim his gun in the direction of Billy and Katherine. "I'll shoot the girl if you don't drop your gun, Monahan," Alf said, his voice slow and serious, carrying a note of sadness.

"I can kill you before you do that," Nyles said. He was pretty sure he could still drop Alf before he could get a shot off. He wasn't sure why he was hesitating.

Billy stepped between Katherine and Alf. "If your gonna kill anyone, Alf you'll have to kill me. Neither you nor I is worth the life of a little girl."

Alf's expression turned to fury. "Goddamn it Billy, I don't want to kill you. You're the only friend I've got."

"Then give Monahan your gun. I don't want to see you die either, Alf. I'm your friend, too."

Alf looked back and forth between Nyles and Billy, then he heaved a sigh and lowered his gun, letting it slip out of his hand and clatter across the floor.

Just then Nate came bursting through the front door, his gun drawn. He spun around and took aim at Alf.

Alf stood motionless, looking at Nate as if he hoped he would shoot.

"He's unarmed," Nyles shouted.

Nate kept his gun on Alf but didn't fire. He looked over at Nyles. "You do nice work for a retired cop."

Nyles put his own gun away and walked over to Katherine. The eleven year old was shaking and she was still wide-eyed. Nyles put out his arms and she rushed into them. "Everything is OK now," Nyles said.

Katherine burst into tears and buried her face in her uncle's shoulder.

Nyles held his niece tight and looked over at Billy Phelan.

Billy was looking guilty. "I'm sorry I let Alf take her, Monahan. I couldn't stop him."

Nyles shook his head. "You put your own life on the line for her. You're a good man, Billy."

They both looked over at Alf. Nate had already cuffed him and was getting out his cell phone.

"I think I'll call Spaulding first," Nate said, a triumphant look on his face.

Nyles just shook his head. He pulled out his own cell phone. "Let's call your mom and grandparents," he said to Katherine. "You tell them you're OK."

Katherine took the cell phone from her uncle and listened to it ring while she wiped the tears from her eyes. When her grandfather answered the phone, she cleared her throat and then spoke. "Hi grandpa. Uncle Nyles saved me."

## Chapter 54

Saying goodbye was hard, but Nyles had passed the point of merely missing Cloris and now his desire to get back home had become a need. Sean had brought the whole family, including Kaylee and Katherine, to the airport in his SUV. Sean had had to lift Nyles' suitcase into and out of the back of the SUV because of the splint on Nyles' left wrist. He hadn't broken his wrist, but he'd suffered a bad sprain and some torn ligaments and he wasn't able to lift anything with his left hand. Millie and Kaylee were both in tears, while Katherine's eyes glistened but she kept a stoic look on her face. When he bent down to give her a hug, the young girl kissed him on the cheek and whispered, "Thank you."

Katherine's mother was more open in her expressions of gratefulness to her uncle and she hugged Nyles and praised him for helping her in her time of need. Sean and Millie both expressed their gratitude and gave him their best wishes to carry back to Cloris.

When he took his seat on the airplane, Nyles thought about his return home. Father Tom had returned a week earlier, eager to resume his position as parish priest after having come so close to losing it. He had already reunited with Cloris and the two of them had talked to Nyles on the telephone the previous night. Nyles himself was ready to leave the cold and was surprised to find himself feeling that he was going home, despite the fact that he was leaving the area of his birth and his only remaining family.

The thought of Nate Hilton made him chuckle. The bombastic detective had not been disciplined and had been transferred into the homicide division, just as he had hoped. But, perhaps as retribution for his violation of so many department policies, he had been partnered with Detective John Spaulding, much, Nyles assumed, to their mutual consternation. Someone in the department was paying them both back for their prickly personalities.

The loss of Mary MacDonald still weighed on him. If Nyles had been younger would he have known better than to involve her? Was his judgment flawed with age? He didn't know the answer to that question and, as he laid his head back on the headrest of his chair, he decided it didn't really matter. He wasn't a cop anymore; he was going back home to be a husband. This was his last murder case.

# More from Casey Dorman

If you enjoyed *Chasing Tales,* you will love the first novel in the *Nyles Monahan series,* *I, Carlos*, originally published by Seven Locks Press.

"…an action-adventure thriller with some interesting sub-contexts, but the author is just playing with the clichés and does some interesting things with the expectations of the genre. It's an original take on a Sorcerer's Apprentice riff with enough going off in original directions to keep it from formula -- fun stuff!"

Susan R. Mathews, Philip K. Dick Award Nominee and author of *The Devil and Deep Space*

"A most unusual thriller, combing the more typical elements with a thorough knowledge of psychology and with interesting philosophical speculation. I Carlos raises important issues about machine intelligence and personal identity."

Richard Hanley, PhD, Department of Philosophy, University of Delaware, author of *The Metaphysics of Star Trek.*

To order your *first edition*, hardbound copy of *I, Carlos*, signed by the author, at a 60% discount, visit *Avignon Press* at www.avignonpress.com and look under "Fiction Titles"

## Other Avignon Press books by Casey Dorman

# Unquity Paperback: 313 pages, $14.95

When Norman Cantwell revisits the tiny New England village of Wacusset, Massachusetts after an absence of thirty-six years, he begins to reminisce about an earlier love affair. His thoughts take him back to 1975 when, as the son of one of the most powerful publishers in the country, he came to Massachusetts to take over *Unquity Press*, a small, struggling literary press in Boston. Norman settled in the small seacoast town of Wacusset where he fell in love with both the town and with one of its inhabitants, the successful and beautiful literary agent, Sandra Hallowell. The novel follows Norman's struggles to make Unquity profitable while maintaining its literary quality. He tries to maintain a relationship with Sandra, who sends him a novel written by a new author, a novel which has the potential to win literary awards as well as insure the financial success of his publishing venture. Norman must struggle with the on and off attention of the peripatetic Sandra while at the same time finding himself increasingly attracted to the young novelist. *Unquity i*s a human love story, as well as a story of a love affair with literature and a story of the Boston and South Coast area in the mid 1970's, written with grace and sensitivity, which is sure to engage every lover of good literature.

To purchase **Unquity** at a special 40% discount, visit *Avignon Press* at www.avignonpress.com

www.ingramcontent.com/pod-product-compliance
Lightning Source LLC
Chambersburg PA
CBHW061559170626
46811CB00001B/253